AFTER THE FLOOD

AFTER THE
FLOOD

P. C. JERSILD

Translated from the Swedish by
Löne Thygesen Blecher and
George Blecher

WILLIAM MORROW AND COMPANY, INC.
New York

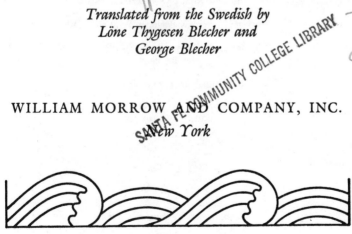

Library of Congress Cataloging in Publication Data

Jersild, P. C. (Per Christian), 1935–
After the flood.

Translation of : Efter floden.
I. Title.
PT9876.2.E7E3513   1985   839.7'374   85-278
ISBN 0-688-04902-8

Printed in the United States of America

First U.S. Edition

1 2 3 4 5 6 7 8 9 10

BOOK DESIGN BY KAROLINA HARRIS

SCENARIO I

CHAPTER 1

NOT a single gull follows the *Diana* as we leave the open sea. With the engine throttled down and the sail furled, we head in toward what looks like the mouth of a wedge-shaped bay. Now the Captain cuts the engine completely. After the chugging of the diesel, a dull silence throbs in our ears as the boat, heeling, drifts in on its own momentum. Inside the bay the water's smooth and lead-heavy; all morning the sky has been covered by an oily film of clouds.

Now that the breeze we made when we were moving has died, we all begin to sweat. The Captain leans out of the wheelhouse, his forearm pressed against his brow to shield himself from the hazy but intense gray light. Three of the five others aboard are up in the bow. One lies curled over the stubby bowsprit staring at the bottom; the other two stand ready with boathooks. The fourth is in the open engine room gasping for air in the heat, his nose just barely above decks. The Captain's ordered me to the stern to man the anchor. I'm lying bent backward like a bow, my hand on the safety rail and one foot stretched toward the dinghy to keep it from hitting the hull. This is our eleventh try at landing on this island. It's crazy to go in with the engine stripped, but it's the Captain's only choice. Only a tiny bit of oil is left in the tank. If we don't save the rest we may never get back into open water.

Without enough momentum for us to steer, the bow veers

slowly as the cutter drifts farther and farther in. The light dinghy glides by us, heading stern first toward the top of the bay. I
get up and grab the anchor by the hawser. The bay beaches
have a three-meter-wide band of seaweed around them, and
above the seaweed rise steep, barren sand hills. On top of
the one to the north, black, twisted rock formations jut out
like the fossils of some prehistoric giant lizard. On the lee side
of the rocks the wind has gouged long, sweeping hollows in
the pink sand.

— All clear! the lookout in the bow shouts.

I guess all he can see at the bottom is sand. What we're
most afraid of is shoals of glass, which can carve up the hull.
Just as cold turns water into ice, heat can burn sand to glass.

— Drop the anchor!

I heave the black, rusty lump as far as I can. Water surges
up in a jagged, gravel-gray pillar. The green-bearded hawser
stretches and bends at the waterline like a broken blade of
grass. After I tie it down, I join the others on the foredeck. As I
push past the engineer, he leers smugly and rolls his eyes up
toward the sky. The Captain orders us to eat before inspecting
the weapons and deciding who will be first to go ashore. He
takes his own portion of dried fish to the top of the wheelhouse
and stands there with his binoculars and charts; the rest of us
huddle with our backs against the railing, pulling the tough
fish skin through clenched teeth. Nobody looks up; nobody
wants to look interested, alert, smartass: That's the surest way
to get chosen the first one ashore.

— See those tall rocks? the Captain says from the roof of
the wheelhouse. Those mean that this is old coast. As usual
the chart's worthless. But let me tell you this, boys, those kinds
of rock formations weren't built in a day. Millimeter by millimeter the sea grinds the looser rocks right out of the hard skeleton of a mountain: the Baltic basin, the Yoldia sea, the
Ancylus lake, the Littornia sea . . . no tidal wave, no matter
how fucking powerful, could chisel those babies out! Believe

me, boys, this here is original coastline, and you might find just about anything: the remains of a little harbor, fishing village, or—who knows?—even the ruins of a military base! We listen to his cheery little lecture with our foreheads jammed against our thighs. What he leaves out is all the evil, all the danger lying in wait for us when we step ashore on this mine-infested garbage heap.

AS usual, he volunteers to be the first ashore. But of course we can't allow that. How would we manage without him? He knows too many of the secrets of survival. The rest of us each have just one specialty: the engine, the galley, the trawl, the sail, the pump. Only the Captain runs the whole show. But he's much more than our clever leader. Long before I ever came on board the *Diana* he'd become a symbol, a hope, of even the *possibility* of life's going on.

I know the least of anyone here. The others don't call me cabin boy; to them I'm the Little Bitch. The price I had to pay to get where I am was to become the Captain's . . . pet. That's why the others don't trust me. But as time goes on he confides in me less and less. These days I'm mostly by myself, on the outside looking in.

— We'll take a vote! the Captain says. The others just mumble in their beards.

— I nominate Edvin. He's young and strong, he says, and now the others' sour disinterest changes. They're supporting him eagerly; the engineer is even raising both hands!

Shipmates who haven't laid a hand on me for months are now slapping me on the back. Laughing and stroking the barrel like a prick, they give me one of the best weapons aboard, a Russian-made carbine with a bayonet. The Captain lends me one of his wristwatches and his felt-covered canteen, and he also tries to force on me a salted mackerel and a bag of rice. But I turn them down. Why should I take so much just for a short hour or two reconnaissance mission? The Captain stares nervously at my knees; then he goes below. But the others are only too willing to help me into the dinghy; some even lob encouraging gobs of spit into the water next to me. I have only two hours. If I don't show up by then they'll send up a flare as a reminder. Half an hour later they'll take off: Five men's safety comes before that of one cabin boy.

WITH their hands jammed down in their pockets or inside their waistbands, they stand staring at me as I row away. I don't like rowing; the past trails behind you like a long piece of string. I catch a glimpse of the Captain's sweaty face in the wheelhouse darkness. He just stands staring absently toward the beach and doesn't even lift his hand for a good-luck or a see-you-later. Don't you love me anymore? After he came he always used to whisper a soft I-love-you; the last time that happened was months ago. Lately he's been silent. Maybe he's been too drunk, his mouth too sluggish to talk? I know I've been so drunk that afterward I could blame my vomiting on the wine, not him.

Sure I like him. Not as a man—as a father. A clumsy father who doesn't know how to hold you. With a tender mouth but a rough body. Most of what's gone on between the old army blankets I want to forget: the bites, the bruises, his breath. As well as his giggles and the endless sentimental stories about his life: the injustices, all his efforts to get an education, his dead Mama, and the lies about how generous he's supposed to be. But not his talk about father and son! In my dreams he's my real father most of the time. Being the captain's son isn't the best position to be in at sea, but it's a lot better than being a lover with no blood ties. And if we were related, he'd have to teach me navigation.

It's a bad sign that the others have stopped calling me Little Bitch. A few months ago they started calling me Edvin, then more and more often Edvin the Bastard. They caught on more quickly than I did that his feelings had begun to cool. I turn my head and see that I'd better start rowing harder if I want to get the dinghy through the seaweed. I pull at the oars as hard as I can, but still I get stuck halfway through. The oar strokes rip dry gashes in the upper, rustling layers, and hundreds of flies rise from the iodine-stinking muck and swarm around me. That's another bad sign. They told us this island didn't have all the different kinds of insects that make life on the mainland unbearable in the summer, that it'd been underwater so long all the fly eggs drowned. That's obviously not true. I jump out quickly; the water doesn't reach above my boot tops. I try to keep the flies away from my mouth and eyes—I can't worry about the nostrils and ears just now. Slipping the piece over my shoulder, I head toward land with long, squooshy strides. Getting up the sandy embankment is like trying to get out of a gravel pit, but if I climb at an angle I can manage. Little avalanches go off all around me; sand pours into my boots by the bucketful. I slip the rifle off to keep from falling, get it on my shoulders and rest the stock against my neck. The barrel almost slides out of my hand; weapon grease is the only thing we have too much of on the *Diana*. Now I can't keep the flies from crawling all over my face; I need my left arm for balance.

When I finally reach the top, a hot wind out of the north hits me. Down behind me the bay lies in the lee of the wind, its surface mottled like galvanized sheet metal. I take a few more steps; where the sand ends, the ground turns into rough, barren rock. In the hollows little pools of sand are dotted with thin tufts of dry reeds. Farther to the north are gravel hills and veins of sand in crests and waves: yellow blending into gray, gray into pink. I blow the flies off my lips, turn right, and walk toward the tall rock pillars.

After emptying the sand out of my boots, I climb up on one and wave down to the boat. The only person I can make out is the Captain standing on the wheelhouse scanning the opposite shore, his smooth skull shining like a gray pearl. Up here it's blowing harder now; when the wind reaches down to the bay itself it looks like a hard rain coming down in gusts. The cutter heels; his head glistens. I shake out sand from under my watchband. Half an hour gone.

On my way down I rest against the warm stone. It doesn't smell at all. Or is there just the faintest hint of iodine, the smell of slow death? But the partially blackened surface seems uncontaminated; rings of powdery gold and silver lichen are growing all over it. The smell must come from the seaweed circling the bay. I stand up in the gusting wind; the swarms of flies scatter and head back to their seaweed bases. I rest for a while with my back against the rock, wiggle my feet in my tight boots, wipe sand off the carbine with my shirt, then head toward the top of the bay. The sand's getting firmer now, but it's still pink or the color of bleached bone, no darker areas stained by leaking oil. I could use a long pole or a thin pipe to stick into the ground. What's under my feet—just rough, rocky soil or a hidden town?

At the top of the bay I find a little stream running out from under a bare slab of rock and making its way toward the sea down a miniature sand canyon. When I get close, the sandy surface layer loosens and almost dams the flow; I have to look for another spot farther inland to approach it from. When I get to the stream, I stick my whole face in; it's lukewarm but clear, a little brackish but not oily. If this is supposed to be old coastline, then which way is the original beach, the one they drew on the chart? To the south the sand hills taper down to a hook-shaped reef where two currents meet. Since the Captain is scanning the beach to the south, I decide to take a closer look too. Here in the south there aren't any tall rocks, just a beautiful, sweeping crest of sand billowing gently in the breeze. I climb down a little farther until I'm level with *Diana* directly to my north; it completely blocks out the dinghy on the opposite shore.

Then they raise the sail! The boom clanks and they haul up the aft anchor, then the fore one! They're running back and forth on deck as if they're trying to keep the cutter from tipping over! The sail stops luffing, catches the breeze, fills. She falls off to port, heels deeply, and points her bow out to sea. I half slide, half run on my heels down the sand dune.

— Hey!!!

I wave the rifle in the air. With all its ropes clattering, the cutter heads out to sea, and now the abandoned dinghy appears in the seaweed across the water. What's happened? What danger is threatening them that I can't see? There's nothing on any of the beaches.

— Captain!!!

I'm shouting at an empty ship: Either they've gone below or they're huddled together in the wheelhouse. I sink to my knees, drive the rifle butt into the ground, and pull off a volley of shots. The weapon bucks. No response from the cutter. The wind can't be strong enough to drown out the sound of an automatic weapon! I run toward the dinghy along the dark, firm sand, the bayonet bouncing against my ass. A pile of brown seaweed rotting to red in the center blocks my way, so I head into the water, holding the weapon above my head. But the water's sudden resistance makes me stumble; I stop, turn all the way around, and watch the cutter, heeling slightly, gliding toward open water. I aim at the wheelhouse. The shots just spatter in the wake as if someone had sprinkled a handful of gravel on the waves.

WHEN I finally get to the dinghy, the north wind is so strong that if I tried to row after the *Diana* I'd get blown to the opposite shore. I can see that she's changed course to the south—heading downwind now, her stern high in the water, in the direction of the hook-shaped reef. Is the Captain so anxious to dump me that he's willing to sacrifice the dinghy just like that? Or did he leave it to show me that he'll be coming back? I pull it up onto the sand, but there's nothing to fasten it to. Then I waddle up the embankment a second time. The flies aren't sticking to my eyelashes anymore—now the blowing sand is crunching in my mouth. From the top I can see that she's come about again; now she's sailing due west. A pang of hope. Probably it was just the hard, gusting wind that made them leave their dangerous mooring place in such a hurry.

A slanting curtain of rain comes out of the sea to the west; the *Diana* disappears behind it. I start walking inland to find shelter, the yellow grass screeching in the wind. Between the sand pools the flat, rough rock lies bare, blackened in spots as though it's been burned. Shallow cracks are etched across it, most of them filled with sand as fine and hard as metal filings. In a few of the deeper ones are bunches of rust-colored lingonberry sprigs. On one of the plants hang a few of last year's berries; they rattle around in my hand like dried peppercorns till the wind tears them away. A little while later I almost fall into a ravine that I can hardly see because of the flying sand. Relieved, I crawl down inside to get out of the wind; now I can start breathing through my mouth again.

The bottom of the ravine's partly filled with large stone blocks, and the walls are terraced; a fine sand rain trickles down from the storm above. There's a smell of earth and mold, but the rock face looks uncontaminated; it's splotched with lichen. Greenblue nettles are also growing down here, stinking of old piss. I pick up a handful of pebbles and hold it to my nose. Iodine? If so, it's so faint it could be my imagination. Many people died with the smell of iodine on their breaths. I can't get a picture of Papa dying; I don't remember his face. But I do remember his hands squeezing around my head in a death grip. His hands were covering my ears so I couldn't understand any of his mumbling, but I knew he was blessing me. A memory or my imagination? The only thing I remember for sure is the stench of iodine coming out of his mouth.

At the bottom of the ravine one of the walls opens into a cave. The ground's dry, covered with sand from above. Crawling in on all fours, I slip off the carbine and lie down on my sleeping side. The last time the Captain left me isn't even a week ago. We'd anchored above a shallow underwater shelf out on the open sea. The sea was calm; they'd sent me into the water to find out why the propeller axle was vibrating. I could just stand on tiptoe and keep my nose but not my mouth above water. Then they let the cutter drift away. At first I swam after them, but I had to come back and stand on the rock with my arms outstretched and my hands waving. They were only 150 meters away; it was so quiet on the water I could hear them cursing as they argued. Finally they started the engine and came to get me. Nobody said another word about any propeller damage; weeping, the Captain took me in his arms.

A bat fluttering across my face awakens me. It's night. No more storm sounds from above. I crawl out of the cave. A round, sharpedged moon is shining straight down into the ravine. Standing with my legs apart I stare upward, my head bent back and my mouth open; it's like staring up from the bottom of a well.

I climb up. Cold and quiet in the stark moonlight, the landscape's a heap of dead embers: black, gray, ash white. I start running toward the bay, but after a while I have to slow down; my boots weigh a ton. Now I'm floundering through silvery sand toward the silhouettes of the tall rocks; they seem taller now—maybe the storm has carved away more sand. I stop as a picture from the Captain's *Famous Buildings of Antiquity* comes into my head. Those tottering pillars remind me of a jagged-edged ruin of an old temple, a half-disintegrated monument gradually wasting away.

When I get to the foot of the rocks I can't see any water below! Where the bay used to be there's only a faint indentation. To the south the reef looks the same as before, a hook digging its point into the black ocean. Not a sail in sight. I stick the weapon up in the air to shoot, but what good would it do? A little hole in the night next to the moon?

I head down toward the southern reef of the former bay, stumbling often on skull-sized rocks. The moon slides in behind violet clouds, smearing the shadows of the landscape. Am I climbing up again through sand or swimming in it up to my armpits? Then, without warning, I almost fall over the edge of a precipice—at the last moment I bend backward and fall on my knees! The moon comes out on the other side of the clouds, illuminating a crater hundreds of meters wide— and down inside it is a half-buried town! Rooftops and ruins lead in straight rows to a collapsed church steeple. The belfry's sticking out above the saltwhite sand; I can even make out two black bells lying on their sides. Closer to me, just under the edge, is a large round disk. A cistern? I pick up one of the skull-sized rocks and heave it down; it lands with a muffled, tinny thud. But I can't tell from the rumble if the cistern's empty or if it still has some oil left. If the Captain does come back, if in spite of everything they have left simply in order not to be blown into the bay, then what a coup it will be for me: an oil cistern!

Should I shoot at it to see if there's any oil? No, it's too dangerous. Instead I collect more rocks, which I start—stupidly!—throwing down. By the time I realize what I've done it's too late. Without a sound the sand starts to give, flipping me right over the edge.

*　　*　　*

WHEN I come to, I'm lying at the edge of the breakers. My left shoulder's sprained. My boots are gone. My watch too. Coughing and snorting, I pick myself up. The carbine's still strapped across my back, but my eyes are cramped shut; I can open them only one at a time. Salt water, sand, and the sun's glare sting my lips. I keep having to squat down, sometimes to cough up sand, sometimes to vomit seawater. In between retches, thirst burns my throat and sand grates in my harelip; I've lost my canteen.

I sit doubled up for a long time on the beach next to the waves lapping at small, round stones. I manage to get my right arm out of the shirt, but my left shoulder hurts so much when I try that I can't get it all the way off. With my loose shirttail, I start cleaning and polishing the piece. For hours I squat there working. Ever since I was a kid it's given me comfort to have a weapon in perfect working order close by.

Evening comes. The blue-red sun on the edge of the horizon is being squeezed between day and night. Finally I stagger back onto my feet, turn away from the cruel sun, and begin crawling on all fours up the sand dune. When I get to the top I see the rock formations right away. The reef to the south still hooks into the water. *But where is the town?* I stomp around in circles among the dunes but there's no trace of any cistern or ruins. Was it just an evil hallucination? The kind of vision desperate people see—glittering carafes of water, heaps of fried fish, tubs of sweet wine? Maybe my own longing's tricked me again. Nothing would have strengthened my position more than a cistern with oil in it.

Before it gets completely dark I find my way back to the ravine, the only safety around. The nest I made in the cave mouth is still there; in the last faint rays of sunlight I stare down into the shape of my own body in the sand. I fit myself neatly into the ready-made form. My left shoulder's throbbing and swollen. I click off the carbine's safety and lean my ear against the mouth of the barrel, shut my eyes, open my mouth, and pull the trigger. But no red fireball explodes in my head, no gas-white cloud. Only the sound of crunching sand in the carbine's dead gears.

Later that night I hear faint dripping and start to crawl around, searching for the tinkling sound. I actually find it— dripping water—and squat underneath it, swallowing like a baby bird. The water tastes cool and sweet, but it takes forever between drops. Finally thirst can't keep me upright. I tumble over onto my healthy shoulder and crawl back to my sand-nest.

A new day: I sit staring at the curtains of rain falling into the ravine. My damp, sand-covered clothes are as stiff as leather. The injured shoulder's stopped throbbing; now a steady, numbing pain makes me sit stock-still. It takes great effort just to reach out my right hand into the rain to drink. Then I see that there's greasy soot all over my palm. It must come from the cave! The numbness vanishes, and I scramble back inside. When my eyes get used to the weak light, I see a circle of blackened rocks a few meters from the entrance. There's no trace of the fire itself, as though whoever made it took the dead embers away with him. When I pull up one of the rocks, a wood louse falls off and quickly rolls itself into a little ball. How long has it been since someone made a fire here—a thousand years . . . or a week? I return to my sand-nest. The cold shakes me to sleep.

IF the *Diana* returns they'll never be able to orient themselves now. The best thing for me is to stay here in the cave. I grew up in mountain caves. In the summer they're raw and damp, but in the winter a musty heat can rise out of the mountain itself. I'd been at sea so long last summer I could hardly remember what a cave smelled like. But then they left me for two days on a big granite rock without water or food; luckily there was a shallow cave. When they finally came for me, they didn't say a word: no explanation or apology. Later I figured out it had to do with a bet. They hadn't been very far away. But now they were all red-eyed and stinking of old rice wine. In the galley I found the guts of a small shark and devoured them.

Afterward I was scared to stay aboard. The first chance I got I ran away. We were in port with two friendly boats; the skipper on one had a crush on me and invited me aboard. His boat, a former pleasure yacht with a mizzenmast, was bigger than *Diana*. She had a stainless-steel hull, but a clumsy corrugated-metal wheelhouse replaced the molded plastic superstructure, which had melted away. She had all her sails, though—even the rainbow-striped spinnaker, which the captain pulled out to let me touch. His crew was his two older brothers and a cousin. I liked it there; there was plenty of room. And the first night he didn't even ask for much; a little hugging seemed to do. But the next morning the Captain came, rifle in hand, and took me back.

Naturally I thought I'd get the shit kicked out of me—or a pistol barrel across my skull. But he just took me down to his cabin. With his hand on the back of my neck he showed me the postcard collection I'd seen so many times before—pictures of all the beaches, endless sandy beaches with thousands of people with beach umbrellas and coolers. We had a good laugh together this time too. That many people couldn't *possibly* get along together! How many people have I seen in the same place at the same time? Before Papa died, maybe fifty. And when we stormed the old bunker last fall with six other crews—there must have been more than thirty of us! But I have a very hard time imagining hundreds of people in one place. How can you tell them apart? Can nature really be so rich that it can make so many different faces—to say nothing of voices!

C H A P T E R   2

THE next morning it's foggy. It seeps into the ravine, distorting distances. Suddenly the rock face in front of me is fifty meters away. I climb the terraced walls, dragging my useless left arm behind me. It's hard to get a good grip on the arm; one minute I'm digging the claws of my right hand into the pain of the left shoulder to meet pain with pain, the next pressing the sprained arm against my body to keep it still during the climb. Every few meters I have to rest. I bring my left hand to my mouth and bite the heel of the thumb; it doesn't help the pain, but it does ease the shakes from the cold.

At the top, yellow fog billows by. I sit on my haunches, digging black boogies out of my nose while I wait for it to lift a little. My stomach's full of fetid air. I try to fart but can't; my asshole is squeezed tighter than a stingy widow around my guts. Gradually the sky grows lighter and I start a little expedition inland, careful to leave deep tracks in the sand.

Why did you abandon me? You took me aboard because you were tired of the one before me. That doesn't surprise me. He'd grown fat and lazy—and old. You didn't want a eunuch in your bed; you wanted someone on whom what was supposed to stick out stuck out, whose ribs you could count as you lay next to him while you told those long stories about your-self.

So my first task—after you tested my lovemaking—was to get rid of the eunuch just as he'd got rid of the one before him. But I haven't seen any signs of a new lover. It doesn't seem very smart to get rid of me before you've got someone new to replace me. And where are you going to find someone younger—in all my thirty-three years I've never met anyone younger than me. Anyway, I'm not like your others, always the same all the time. No, sir! Under the blankets I asked you about your dreams, your ideal: tall, active, muscular, slim? And you answered: young, younger, like a baby. So I faked it—fumbled when I knew better, acted as curious as a squirrel when inside all I felt was sadness and disgust. And it gave you a few laughs when they beat me up after I'd dumped salt in their soup or poured tacks in their boots. But real love? There's been precious little of that. I tried to get you interested again by gently blowing on your balls. But you just sat there chewing your cud—you who used to be the lowest of the low until you stumbled on a sack of allspice and bought your own boat and crew.

I have to stop and dig into my shoulder again. It's numb now, but inside the veins is a crawling sensation as though they're filled with tiny grains of sand. Suddenly I speed up and rush down a tunnel of light in the lifting fog. A silhouette of a ship shines before me—clearly visible, sharply etched—then it's gone. Waiting, I hold my breath, blood throbbing in my temples. It comes back: a motor torpedo boat with a sharp-angled profile and a long foredeck aground in a sea of sand!

I board the rusty ship from the stern. On the starboard side, ash-gray earth's drifted up into a wave breaking over the foredeck. Doors and hatches are smashed in, bulletproof glass removed from windows and portholes. Torn ropes crawl over the superstructure, and all that's left of the captain's bridge is the sheet-metal walls. Inside its round tower the antiaircraft gun points straight at the sky, its barrel plugged up with earth. Even the hull is filled with sand. I try digging down into the engine room to look for oil, but after a few seconds it gets too hot working under the sheet metal with one hand. With pursed lips I suck up a puddle of water that has formed in the socket of the portside lanterns.

When I kick one of the torpedo tubes, a dry, bone-yellow, skull-sized wasp's nest rolls out of the opening. I climb up on top of the round gun turret. To the south there's only sand, and beyond it a flat, lifeless sea. I can make out rock cliffs to the north beyond the loess terrain. Maybe there's fresh water there, and small animals: grass snakes, hedgehogs, field mice or even egg-laying birds?

AROUND dusk I reach those flat cliffs to the north and start looking for water. The plateaus are cracked and falling apart; in the hollows loose, jagged-edged boulders are scattered all around, and the higher parts are covered with pebbles. There's more earth than sand. Dead roots writhe out of the ground, but the only living things are grass, heather, and stinging nettles. No surface water to be found anywhere. I bed down behind some grass and clumps of earth.

During the night a hedgehog panting and grunting in the nettles wakes me up. I can't make it out. But I see the black plants waving against the dark-blue sky. I try flushing it out onto open ground by throwing rocks into the nettles, but it gives me the silent treatment. I climb up the cliff to make it think the danger's past. But it's just as suspicious as I am. I sit there a long time massaging my bad shoulder.

Finally I give up. Out of habit I check the different compass points. To the north a yellow-red light flickers! I climb up on a taller rock but realize that the first one was a better lookout point. The flashing light keeps coming back; I take a fix on it by laying down a line of stones so I'll be able to head straight for it tomorrow morning. Then I go back to sleep. I want to be rested when the sun comes up. I try to re-create in my head the Captain's chart of the island. But all the sea charts are alike; the land toward the interior is always white and unknown.

THE wind rattling the nettles wakes me up before the first light. I strap the automatic carbine across my back and hook the bayonet to my belt. Although I'm not carrying much, my bare feet soon start to give me trouble. At sea we always go barefoot, even in winter. Since I've been doing it since childhood, the cold doesn't particularly bother me, not even when the deck ices over. But many of the old-timers can't take it. They hobble around in boot linings, rags, or worn galoshes. I've seen more than one fall overboard.

No, the cold doesn't hurt my feet. But I am afraid of cuts. On the *Diana* we inspected the deck every watch to remove any new splinters or nailheads that had just worked themselves up. An infected cut in the sole of the foot is much more dangerous than a cut on the finger. If you're not quick on your feet, you're an easy mark in a high sea or a sudden battle. But here on land my feet feel strange to me. I always have to walk looking down; the ground's full of thorns, splinters, scrap metal, slippery rocks, hidden cracks, abandoned rabbit holes. Soon I lose my bearings. There aren't any good landmarks. Rock formations and boulders mimic each other's shapes.

At noon I come to a reed-overgrown marsh. The wind's died down again. It's hot. The marsh spreads to the east and west, but it's narrow; to the north I can see more flat rock cliffs only a few hundred meters away. I fasten the sprained arm inside my waistband so it won't jerk out in a sudden reflex; the slightest movement in the ball joint kills me. Then I put the carbine on my head, balancing it with my right hand. Between the clumps of reeds are patches of cracked white-and-red earth. I sink in up to my knees but underneath I can feel flat stones. I make my way out slowly toward the middle of the marsh to a thin, gleaming layer of open water. It's brackish and tastes musty, but not bad enough to keep me from gulping it down. But I can't catch any of the small, nearly transparent grasshoppers buzzing around in the knifelike blades of tall grass. The Captain was right after all: Compared to other places this one has hardly any bugs.

On the other side of the marsh the ground is dry limestone covered with small, round stones, knee-high bumps and black brambles creeping low to the ground like barbed wire. When I look down at my feet and pants, they're covered with brown marsh fuzz. It's getting harder and harder to walk with bare feet. I have to take long detours around the densest under-brush, and I end up losing my way completely.

In the late afternoon I come upon a sleepy lizard. I shoot it—this time the gun works! Afterward there's not much left, but I poke a little gray meat out of the bullet holes with the bayonet. In front of me a stone cliff rises a good ten meters high, but rather than climbing it, I decide to follow it to the east. I'm exhausted. With only one working arm I can hardly keep my balance.

For once in my life I'm a lucky son of a bitch. That evening I come upon a hut, a stone shelter really, leaning against the steep cliff face. It's built from piled-up rocks and has a flat roof made of irregular patches of sheet metal. There's also a brick chimney and a window in front, a porthole in a metal frame. It has no real door, just a gaping, meter-high hole in the wall next to the window. On the ground in front lies an arched aluminum door with a handle, most likely from an airplane. A rocky slope leads down to a well. On a circle of flat rocks there's a battered bucket with one end of a steel wire wound around the handle. Beyond the well stretches a forest of two-meter-high nettles. No one's around. No sound at all.

I take in all this in an instant—then dart back behind a big rock to listen. When everything stays completely quiet I move up to a better vantage point behind a pile of gravel dotted with sparse clumps of sedge; I can lie behind it and watch without being seen. The place seems inhabited or abandoned only recently: A few meters from the house—on top of a compost heap surrounded by a low wall—lie rushes and nettles, and the top ones haven't had time to yellow yet. Next to the compost heap is a small plot of sand and earth that's been plowed in short furrows; withered potato plants are sticking up. Gray-blue undershirts with knotted arms hang down from a wire stretched between the house and a pipe driven into the compost heap.

The well water is so tempting; so are the potatoes. But it's too dangerous now in the evening light. Better to wait till dawn or at least night if the moon isn't too bright. I pull back and circle the house from farther away, keeping a sharp eye out for animals who might cackle, bark, or whimper. But there's no sign of chickens or anything else. I head southwest to the limestone plains and bed down for the night.

The evening passes in absolute silence. In the west the sun's sharp edges blur. Soft as a bloodshot fish eye, it slowly flattens until it's swallowed up by the iron-blue horizon. A faint full moon, speckled as a seagull's egg, is already high in the eastern sky. Moonlight is inadequate but humane, sunlight efficient but dangerous. How many people went blind during the years after the War when the sun had grown many times stronger than before! I've heard the old-timers say that the air above us boiled away. But the moon never hurt anyone; even if you stumble in its weak light, you have only yourself to blame.

For the second night in a row, I get only a few hours' sleep. The eunuch's grinning, moon-blurred face floats before me in the dark, at one point so vividly that I jab my finger out toward one of his eyes. He'd managed to tie up his own predecessor while he was asleep and then heave him overboard. Now that it was his turn, I decided to knock him unconscious first. I didn't want to throw him in alive—the others claimed that his predecessor had gone on barking like a seal on quiet nights for years afterward. He sniveled and begged for his life. He had a terrible cold that day; snot was running out of both nostrils. That disgusted me enough to hit him. But I didn't hit him hard enough. Blood poured out of his ear and he got desperate and tried to climb the mast. The Captain took pity on him and, as a last gift of love, put a bullet in his back. It took a long time before they let me forget that I hadn't finished him off myself.

THE day's far along by the time I wake up. My shoulder's still black and blue and swollen, but I can move it a little without too much pain. On my way to the hut I stop several times to listen. Finally I hide in the sparse sedge. Everything's the same—not a detail changed. I go over to the compost heap. It stinks of piss and shit. In one corner high above the slimy mess is a kind of shit perch; dry grass for wiping is wedged in a crack in the wall. So this is how the landlubbers live; at sea we wash our asses right in the ocean. The shit perch is as thick as an arm and polished smooth and silvery with age. A rich man must live here—he sits on wood when he shits!

I click the safety off, get into firing position, and toss a stone at the roof; it comes clattering all the way down. Not a sound from inside. After a half hour I run up to the house and press against the outside wall. Then I sneak toward the door opening and crouch under the round porthole. Exactly as the Captain taught me, I jump quickly in sideways and drop to my knees. I can't see a thing in the darkness. But it smells like a human's been here recently. After a while I make out a sheet-metal table standing in the middle of the room in the path of gray light streaming in from the window. To its right is a stove; to the left the ends of two beds emerge out of the darkness. The only thing I can hear is my own heavy nasal breathing.

Gray details leap into the corners of my eyes. Next to the stove are stone shelves, on the inside cliff face hangers overloaded with clothes. Next to one of the beds a cast-iron chair. Someone's lying in the bed. I stop myself from emptying the whole magazine; if the person lying there had been armed he'd have blasted me hours ago. I go up to the bed with the weapon at eye level, then lower the barrel slowly and poke it into the motionless body. Then jab it hard. A faint thud but no human sound. I take a step toward the head of the bed. A little bald head lies on its side, its cheek pressed into a rolled-up sack. I tear the blanket away with my left hand; I'm so keyed up I hardly feel the pain. A sharp stench of piss wells up.

The person in the bed is dead. The corpse is all skin and bones but hasn't started to decompose yet. When I pick up the bent arm, it's still stiff. The corpse is dressed in a baggy sweater too big for it, but its lower parts are bare. I stare gaping at the corpse's crotch. There's no prick. Under the sparse thatch of gray-red hair it's empty. It must be a woman. It all fits with the pictures I saw on board ship, with the crew's endless stories of slits and hidden openings.

As a kid I probably saw women without knowing it. Not that everybody looked alike, but the things that might have made women look different from men weren't as obvious as other things. Everybody bundled up in whatever rags they could find. Everybody was bald, dirty, pale, full of sores—and what you noticed was that some were tall, others stooped, some bloated, others rickety and dry as sticks. I don't remember any difference between the voices of men and those who may have been women; everybody spoke harshly, hoarsely, mumbling, or in pained squeaks. Faces were the easiest way to tell them apart. If the nose was broken or straight, long or crumpled up between the eyes. Some people's eyes were close together, others out to the side like a dog's. Then there were the number and color of teeth. But mostly it seemed to have to do with the whole face, with the message you could read in it: angry, bitter, sad, hurt, rejected, abandoned, groggy, jittery, yearning, fawning, scared to death. And the color: pale pink, pale blue, pale yellow, blotchy. In the fallout shelter I could never figure out which ones were women. It didn't matter anyway. By then my own mother had been dead a long time.

When I went to sea I heard the usual stories: Women can't take the ocean, women cast spells on you, sooner or later they're struck by disgusting, contagious bleeding. Through a hole in their bodies—unclear just where—they squirted out a cup of dirty blood at regular intervals, so regular that you could use them as living calendars. The amount kept growing—two cups, a chamber pot full, half a bucket . . . but I don't believe that bullshit. If it's true, where does the bad blood in us men go? Wouldn't we have died from blood poisoning long ago?

I'VE rolled the woman up in her own blanket and dragged her outside. I tried to poke around in the crack between her legs with the handle of a knife to see what it was shaped like in there, but I couldn't find my way in. Now I'm sitting in the door opening drinking sour beer out of a metal pitcher and munching on raw potatoes. Whom does the other bed belong to? How long has it been empty—a day, a year? Most likely not very long—how could a woman this old manage here all by herself? She must be under someone's protection. Whose?

After I fill up on food and drink I tie some steel wires around the wrapped-up corpse. There's no sea here to receive the dead. Most of the ground is stone. I can't bury her in the potato field; all you have to do is stamp your foot in a furrow to feel the rock underneath. I don't want to poke around in the compost heap. So I drag the corpse a few hundred meters to a place where lots of boulders have broken loose from the cliff face, jam her into the gap between two of them, and cover the protruding feet with pebbles. My bad shoulder keeps me from loading her down with the heavy rocks she needs to keep her ghost from flying around and haunting people at night.

I take more food from the hut; I'm afraid to sleep inside. The best place is up on the cliff above. For the first time since I've been ashore I'll sleep warm and dry between stolen blankets. I take a pair of boots too. They're not big enough, so I cut holes for my heels with the bayonet.

FOR the next two nights, I sleep on top of the plateau. But then it starts raining hard, so I take a chance and move inside. Instead of lying in the bed, I manage to squeeze underneath. I'm afraid to go out for the airplane hatch and set it up in the door opening. Instead I stretch a trip wire across the threshold and put a basin and some pots in front; now nobody can sneak in without announcing himself. Because I didn't want to make a fire, I ate the potatoes raw—now they're exploding in my stomach. The beer gives me heartburn, but it also makes me happy and tipsy. At sea we had something to drink every day; one single day without booze would have led to mutiny. But no one ever knew where the Captain got all the rice wine.

THE next day I draw water from the well and wet down the potato patch. Then I check the house more carefully. There're a lot of clothes and a fair number of shoes and boots. But no weapons—which is very strange. Of course the sea and unfriendly ships are far away, but I've never met a free man before who didn't own a weapon. There's beer in a bunch of pitchers and jars but no rice wine. In addition to a sack of shriveled, blackened potatoes there's potato flour and potato bread. A small amount of gray salt too. But no dried fish. And in front of the stove hang rows of dried herbs.

I sneak around and jiggle all the protruding rocks. Behind

the first loose one is a cigarette lighter—empty of course, but with a working flint. It ought to be as valuable as a working pistol. In another niche are a needle and different types of thread—also very valuable. In a third hole I find a pair of unbroken eyeglasses wrapped in a piece of soft yellow leather, and farther along are pencil nubs and a spiral pad of yellowed paper so fragile it crumbles to the touch. But no weapons, ammunition, explosive devices of any kind.

That evening I sleep in one of the beds, the one that was empty when I came. But I still can't fall asleep; I'm more afraid of the woman than of anyone coming home and surprising me. I haven't done a thing to protect myself against ghosts. How do you do it on land? I was raised at sea; after we heaved a corpse overboard we always dropped in a couple of hand grenades to keep it in its place.

RUMBLING thunder awakens me. I get up to put the door in before the downpour starts. It's foggy outside; the storm's coming in from above. One lightning bolt merges with another, and the fog seems to catch fire everywhere at once. Even the thunder's fuzzy. It doesn't sizzle or crack, it just seems to billow out of the ground as if the earth itself is rumbling. I race out for the aluminum door. As I'm dragging it back by the handle, I feel someone behind me. An invisible someone standing looking at me. A silent someone waiting patiently for me to take my next breath. I jump into the house and jam the door in the opening.

Inside I grab the carbine, click off the safety, and stand a little way from the window—far enough so that I'm out of the light. In the next lightning flash I see her: dry as leather, bald, sun yellow. Dressed in a white dress, she stands outside stretching her hands forward, upward to me. She smiles; silver teeth flash in her wrinkled face. Her empty eyesockets beam like gilded cups.

I sink down into the bed. I don't remember my mother at all. All I know is what Papa told me: She was young and beautiful, with long blond hair and blue eyes. Papa had a photo of her in her wedding dress, just like the one the woman outside is dressed in to lure me out of the house.

If I had a few hand grenades, I'd show her who's in charge. In the darkness I work the clip out of the carbine and squeeze out all the bullets. I put two of them back. Then I kick the door open and fire. When the next lightning flash lights up the fog, she's gone.

C H A P T E R   3

I'M standing by the well, shaking my head to get the water out of my ear. Ever since the sandslide pulled me down and I woke up in the breakers, my ear's been stopped up with sand and wax. I make a loop at the end of a piece of thin wire and work it carefully into my ear. When I pull it out, a soft black lump is at the end. But I don't hear any better; it's even more stopped up. I bend forward, shake my body, straighten up quickly, and slap myself on the opposite side of my head. . . . Two men are standing on the cliff above the house!

I dive for the gun and crouch behind the only protection in sight: the dented bucket. The men wave down at me. One's unnaturally tall, maybe two meters, the other short and heavy. Both put down the sacks they're carrying. They don't look as if they're armed. As they begin to make their way down the cliff,

I can tell that the short one's old and has a slight limp. The tall one looks like he's in good shape; he can't be over sixty. I follow them with the gun. They're still too far away. I have so few bullets my only chance is a perfect shot; I can't afford to pump away at them. When they get down they separate; that makes it harder for me. I aim at the tall one. The old guy I can get with the rifle butt . . . if they're alone, that is. The fact that they're coming toward me unarmed like this makes me think that there are more of them on the cliff.

The tall one's strange in another way: His big, thick, steel-gray mane of hair makes him look like he's pulled a hedgehog skin over his scalp. I've seen hair on men before, but only thin clumps, fine down, or a ring above their ears. The rug of hair comes to a point far down on his wide forehead. His face is leather brown and smooth-shaven. He has what looks like a little knife nick under his broad, unbroken nose, but no lumpy shrapnel scars like everyone else. His eyes are small and light and set deep in his face. It looks like a mask—as if behind this face is a softer, more open one, or as if he's standing on tiptoe looking out of his own eye sockets.

He stops and nods at me while the old stooped one limps into the hut; he comes right out again and looks nervously in all directions. Then he goes over to check the compost heap. The tall one walks slowly toward me, then stops:

— Is that thing really loaded?

I nod, stand up behind the bucket, and lower the barrel. I point it at his crotch instead of his face. The old guy comes shuffling toward us but suddenly checks himself as if he just now realized that I'm armed. The tall one comes closer; he could touch the barrel if he felt like it. But he just grins, and his prow-shaped Adam's apple bobs up and down:

— But you're just a kid!

He turns and calls to the old one:

— Will you take a goddamn look at this: a harelipped kid!

I was right. The old guy looks at least seventy. And scared.

His eyes are almost hidden by heavy purple bags, and the rest of his face looks swollen too. His mouth is half open. His tongue is busily wetting his pink lips. He presses close to the tall guy: The way they're standing now I could finish them both off with one shot. Then he mumbles into the tall guy's shoulder:

— How old are you?

— Thirty-three.

The tall one roars with laughter and pokes the other with his elbow. As usual, my age cracks people up.

— Not a day older than Our Savior when He died on the cross for our sins, the old man says somberly.

The tall guy looks me up and down, squeezing one eye shut and snorting as though he can size me up by just looking at me.

— Did you come from the sea?

I nod. This he finds so amusing he doubles up and slaps his knees. But the old guy just stands with his mouth open, drooling. Before I know what's happened the gun flies out of my hands. The old one tackles me and knocks me down; then they flip me over on my back and he collapses, panting, on my stomach—he's going to crush me! The tall one grabs the carbine and pokes the barrel into my chest:

— You never did tell me if it was loaded.

WE'RE walking single file to the grave. The old man is limping in front; I'm second, my hands tied behind my back with wire; and the tall one comes last, holding the barrel of the gun against the back of my neck. When we reach the boulders, they bicker a little about whether to untie me to pull away the rocks, or do it themselves. Finally the old guy goes to work. Panting heavily, he kicks the gravel from the corpse's feet. He can't bend down to get her out of the crack; his stomach gets in the way. They switch places. Now's my chance—I can see right away that the old guy isn't familiar with automatic weapons. I throw myself to one side and butt him with my head; I can feel his teeth against my ear. I put my foot on the tall guy's ass and send him sprawling over the corpse. Then I make a mad dash for the forest of man-high nettles, dodging zigzag to avoid the bullets.

The first volley of shots whistles between my feet, the second high up in the air. The carbine is useless now. I change direction and race up to the house, stopping for a moment at the entrance. They're standing flat-footed a good hundred meters away. If I'm lucky I can get the bayonet out of the bed and make it to the limestone plains to the south; there I can take my time picking off the steel wire. I'm so at home in the hut I don't need to see. I turn around and sit on the bed; my fingers immediately find the bayonet. But the second I cross the threshold I get knocked down by a tremendous blow across my ear. My nose starts to bleed, but the pain in my bad shoulder doesn't start till I hear their eager steps in the gravel. I try to pull in my head to protect myself against the kicks they're going to give me. How did they knock me down? It felt like a rock. But how could anyone throw that accurately with a sling or an arm?

WE'RE back at the grave. The old one sticks the tip of the bayonet between my shoulder blades. I'm sobbing and throwing up, blood from my nose mixing with the puke. They've dragged out the corpse and opened the blanket. She lies on her stomach, her arms and legs slightly bent, while the tall guy examines her.

— You didn't shoot her. . . .

— What about strangulation marks? the old one asks.

The tall guy grabs the corpse under the arms and props her up against the boulder. I can't understand how this floppy doll could ever have been alive. Any more than I can understand how the two of them can be standing up moving and talking. What's in them that makes them alive?

— A beauty she never was, says the old guy. Now she's a complete mess.

Weeping, he sinks to the ground and strokes the corpse's brown-blue hand. Then he starts rocking back and forth while he sobs and grinds his teeth. The tall guy just stands poker-faced with his hands in his pockets.

After the old man calms down, they take me inside the hut and tie my hands and feet, then throw a blanket over my face before they go out. My breath pulls the blanket close and I start to panic. It's like being pushed underwater with a foot on the back of your neck. I thrash around like a madman to make some breathing space. Lint collects in my mouth, dust in my eyes, but finally I make enough of a tunnel so I can breathe. Far, far away I hear them haltingly singing a hymn.

It's been years since I heard anyone sing hymns. Not since I was galley boy on a blacktop barge. The skipper was an old man who said he'd been a priest—but that didn't make his pinches any gentler. Every time a corpse was laid out on the makeshift slab and slid into the sea, he had to make a speech and the rest of us had to sing hymns. He also wanted us to go to confession. Every Sunday we got on our knees and whispered our secrets through the skylight of his cabin—the more horrible the better. We started to compete with each other; I won because I always had dreams full of good material. But if I went too far he'd throw open the hatch and cuff my ears. He also liked to spread rumors and repeat the things we told him in confidence; it was his way of keeping us divided. Sexually he was peculiar. He didn't want to take or be taken: smacks on bare ass, that was his thing.

When we buried people at sea, seagulls always gathered in great flocks. Almost before the sick person was dead you could see them circling above. No one knows where they breed nowadays. When I was a kid you could still see occasional pairs in the outer archipelago. But lately I haven't seen one land on solid ground. You can see them bobbing up and down on the open water, packed together by the hundreds. If they follow a boat—which they almost always do—they never go farther than a few knots from land.

— SO your name is Edvin, says the tall guy as he takes another bite of his potato and paces, hunched forward, back and forth in the room.

They eat and drink while they cross-examine me. The tall one does most of the talking. The old guy—his name is Henry—doesn't say much; he just sits bent over the table, hardly touching his food. Now I know that this is his house. The old lady they just buried was named Bett.

They keep talking about my age. Of course they don't believe me; I've never met anyone who believed it right away. Over and over they ask me how old I am. It's not funny to them anymore; it's just unbelievable and almost scary. The tall guy examined me carefully. While the old guy held a lamp, he stuck the handle of a spoon in my mouth and pried it open. He also stared into my eyes. He feet my neck and balls—but not in a horny way; his fingers were curious but impersonal. Finally he had to admit that I might not be lying that much. I couldn't be more than between forty and forty-five.

— He claims his name is Edvin, he repeats as though it's news.

— What do I care what the sonofabitch calls himself?

I have to tell them all over again how they put me ashore at the southern tip of the island to look for oil and other things we could use.

— Not much fun being a pirate if you got to row or sail when the oil runs out, Henry says. His chuckle quickly turns into a sob.

The tall one asks if I want beer. He holds my head very

gently while he pours; he seems to have done this before. Then he finds some braided wire, which he fumbles with while he shapes it into a stiff noose. He ties it to the bedpost behind me and slips the noose around my neck. I jam my chin into my chest; the noose slides up above my teeth. He adjusts the loop, then stands at the foot of the bed, braces his feet against the legs, and grabs my ankles with his hands.

— Maybe he'd like to say a few last words? Henry says.

The tall one hesitates:

— You sure you want to kill him?

— He murdered Bett!

— He says he didn't. . . .

He walks over to Henry and whispers something. They go outside. When they come back the old guy says:

— You'll work for me the rest of your days!

THEY tie my hands and feet for the night and dump me on some sacks in a corner. The tall guy—his name is Petsamo—boils water and fusses with his tools and small glass bottles. Henry goes to sleep, but he wakes up again and has to be helped outside to pee.

I haven't been this happy in years. I'll be glad to work here. The old man will get to depend on me for everything. If he hits me too hard, nothing'll get done. He doesn't have to worry about me running away—where would I go? And I'm not going to hurt him: I could never make it here by myself. What I know I learned at sea. I can't plant potatoes, and the only thing I know how to dig out is glass splinters. A lot of the crew had old burns. Their faces looked like crazy quilts in ghost white, black-eye blue, punch purple, shit brown. Old scars swell and blossom like extra lips on foreheads and cheeks. Glass was the worst; almost everyone's skin was riddled with tiny glass splinters. Every once in a while their skin would push the splinters back out; they'd break through and fester.

Anybody with good eyes for close-up work and a pair of tweezers could rake in the silver and pearls. But I didn't even have those tweezers six months before they were stolen.

THE next morning Petsamo gets ready to leave. They send me out to the well while they do their business. After he trots off with his sack on his back, Henry orders me to move the furniture around. Master and slave can't sleep next to each other. I have to put my bed by the drafty outer wall. But all I am is grateful; this way I avoid the smell of piss and old man.

During the day he lets me walk around a little by myself; he wants to be left alone to read his hymn book. I wander around on the cliffs, but I never get out of earshot. If you make a good first impression, you can take it a little easier later on. Finally, in the late afternoon, he stops reading and cooks up a thick soup from potatoes and rice. We doze on our beds until nightfall; then it's time to go to sleep. While he goes out to pee, I strip and get ready; and when he comes in and stretches up to blow out the lamp, I quickly fall to my knees in front of him with my mouth open. But he doesn't understand. Instead of opening his fly he scratches his head and mutters:
— Don't ask for my blessing, boy. I'm too much of a sinner to bless anybody else.

WE get a spell of very hot weather. In the mornings Henry sits in the shade next to the house, watching me work in the potato field. The reason he dug the field here on the hillside is because it's sheltered by the cliff. He says that windstorms are the farmer's greatest worry; heavy rains come next. But at least you can do things to protect yourself against flooding. He spends the next few days showing me how to pile up rows of flat rocks around the potato field and along the furrows; we end up with five oblong basins. If the rains do come, we can't stop some of the sandy soil from washing out but the plants themselves ought to be able to hold on. He also teaches me that the easiest way to root potato plants is to put them in a nest of rotted compost on the ground and cover them with a thick layer of soggy reeds.

The afternoon heat keeps him indoors. I don't have to work either; he'd rather have company. I can tell he's sick because his feet are swollen and he doesn't have much of an appetite. I get double portions. At night he has to get up all the time. He stands sighing with the chamber pot against his thighs, but nothing comes out. I do what I can; sometimes it helps a little to put a wet cloth above his pubic bone. It's O.K. with me if he dies after a while—as soon as he's taught me everything he knows. As he sits in bed breathing heavily, his eyes bloodshot, he seems to read my thoughts:

— I used to be a prison guard. And I know the worst punishment of all: loneliness.

He won't tell me where or when he was a prison guard. As a matter of fact, he won't talk much at all. That surprises me. The older men who've been my lovers weren't the only ones who blabbered on about themselves; almost everyone I ever met wanted to confide in me. Since I don't talk much myself, people take it as an invitation to tell me all about themselves. But Henry won't even talk about his dead old lady.

— You work harder than Bett did, but she ate less. That's all he says.

He does talk about the oncoming winter whenever he can get his mind off pissing; even though we're only in August, he's obsessed with it. So after I finish work in the potato field I have to dig peat in the same swamp I passed on my way here. We put it in worn sacks and stomp the water out of it, then press it between rocks and put it on the grill-hot sheet-metal roof. There it does two things: It dries and cools down the house.

He also has what he calls a secret wood mine—a whole

grove of trees buried under sand. While he reads his black hymn book in the shade of a blanket, I dig, saw, and lug the wood away. He's always thinking about God. His greatest wish is to be able to buy a Bible. He says he knows where to get one if you have pure gold. I ask him if he has pure gold. He won't answer. But he must have something valuable; how else would we have all this rice and honey?

Sometimes I get fever attacks, and now when I get one Henry nurses me through it with honey dissolved in hot water. He also reads psalms, but I can hardly understand him through the fog in my head. Instead I see terrible scenes from my time at sea: people trying to throw me overboard when I couldn't work because of the fever, the Captain's excitement and lust when my body was furnace-hot! During the week I'm in bed, Henry seems to forget some of his own troubles. He even begins to piss again—though it comes out in weak squirts. But as soon as I feel well enough to start digging out the worm-eaten pine roots, he loses his appetite and sits around complaining about his bursting bladder.

I want us—or me—to go down to the sea and catch fish to salt and dry for the winter. I've lived on fish almost my whole life; all these potatoes give me gas. But Henry won't have anything to do with the sea; to him it stands for evil. Every August pirates came from the sea, killing and stealing everything in sight. The lucky ones got to keep just enough to survive and start next year's crop—so that the pirates could come back and take that too. The last time it happened was several years ago, but he's still scared.

Nowadays he's the only person living on the south end of the island. Bett was married to one of his neighbors, but he got shanghaied late one summer. Henry and Bett decided they'd better throw in together.

— When was that?
— Twelve, fifteen years ago. Who knows?
As long as I've got him talking, I ask him to tell me about

the big wave. *That* was the greatest evil to ever come out of the sea; it must have swamped the whole island. But he gets angry and, with a shaking fist, takes a swipe at me.

WE make traps out of steel wire and aluminum strips to catch rabbits alive. There's plenty of scrap metal but almost no tools. We can't smelt metal either. Wherever you go in the fields you run across metal: a car's universal joint, rusted farm machinery, crumpled-up sheet metal. Mostly we work with aluminum because it's soft and easy to shape. But you have to watch out: Just as in the archipelago, a lot of the metal originally had a military use. Henry knows people who've had arms and legs blown off by shells that were supposed to be dead. A small explosion is all it takes; you don't even need to be close. A couple of deep splinters and it's all over—if you don't happen to have Petsamo nearby. Henry has great faith in Petsamo's doctoring skills.

A few days later we catch a scrawny little rabbit in one of the traps. But Henry's not excited. He thinks the poor thing will eat us out of the house. We need the garbage for fertilizer, not rabbit feed. But I stick to my guns and soon we have three in a cage under my bed. It's true they eat greens but they also make pellets you can dry for fertilizer—or kindling.

ONE September day Petsamo comes back carrying a large backpack and a smaller sack tied to his belt. I'm happy to see him; Henry has had a very bad night. All night he sat at the kitchen table with his forehead against the pot, and he never even *tried* to piss. But Petsamo can help. In his backpack he has tongs, needles, ointments, bandages, alcohol, tweezers—and two curved metal catheters, which he boils on the stove. They send me outside while he takes care of Henry.

That evening the old man is raring to go. He wants to start

trading right away; he buys lamp oil, spinach, and sunflower seeds carefully wrapped in parachute silk. Then he buys a piece of amber—God knows what he wants with that. Also rice, a pair of pincers, and a box of mixed rusty nails. How is he going to pay for all this? When I ask, they tell me to mind my own business and start supper.

— Edvin makes potato pancakes, says Henry. He takes his best shovel and goes outside.

I don't know what he's after, but I volunteer to do the digging. Petsamo yells at me:

— You just stick to your stove, boy!

Henry's gone a long time. Petsamo takes out a couple of ammunition clips, which we try to put in the Russian carbine. Nothing fits. Then he takes a piece of clay and makes an impression of the slot in case he comes across others. I pour some beer and drink with him at the table; he doesn't seem to mind. Maybe to him I'm not just any slave. He even discusses Henry's health with me:

— Hasn't he said anything about moving?

— No, he hasn't; and if he had, where would he move to?

— Up-country. As long as the old lady was alive, they couldn't.

— Why not?

But he's already started talking about the rabbits. He doesn't think they can live long indoors. When he hears they've already been under the bed more than two weeks, he's surprised.

Finally Henry comes back, panting and looking grayer than usual around the eyes. He can't eat; he's got to lie down for a long time. Later that evening he takes a mug of beer and then manages to get over to the stove, where he starts washing and scrubbing things that look like pebbles. When he finally pours them into a plate, I see they're gold-filled teeth. I myself have never owned any, but people at sea use them as currency too.

I ask him why he doesn't knock the fillings out of the teeth.

— This way it's easier to tell that they're the real thing.

Then he adds without my asking:

— You'll never find out where I got them. The old lady didn't know either. What one person knows, two can't expose.

Petsamo takes out a little scale with two bowls and weighs the gold. They bicker a little back and forth about how much to take off for the teeth. But it's a friendly argument. The next morning before breakfast, Petsamo's gone.

— That's the way he is, Henry says.

ONE October night, Henry wakes me up. I jump out of bed, thinking we're under attack. He just wants to show me something. He's excited—he moves more easily than he has for a long time. I get dressed with my teeth chattering, and we head off to the marsh in the first blue light of morning. Henry stops often to check the direction of the wind. It makes no sense to me; it's hardly blowing at all this frosty morning.

We take a roundabout route, then huddle down inside a peat ditch. Henry points proudly to a little grassy island out on the new ice. In the early morning light I see four or five big, long-necked birds standing on the tiny hill.

— It's been more than thirty years since I've seen any . . . but last year they turned up!

— A little big for seagulls?

— Wild geese.

I have no idea what scares them, but suddenly they fly off in a V formation, honking. Henry thinks they're on their way south to Egypt.

CHAPTER 4

IN November we get a snowstorm out of the east that lasts three days. It's so cold we have to stay in our beds under a mountain of blankets, sacks, and clothes. Bugs thrive in our body heat: head lice, which Henry says are only on land but which I've seen at sea too; crab lice—but they hardly count because they stay in one place and are easy to pick off; and bedbugs, which are the worst. They're the ones that keep me awake; my sailor's skin is used to the head lice but not the bedbugs.

On the second day one of the rabbits dies. There's a drop of dry blood on his nose, but that's all we can find wrong. Henry wants to throw out the other two:

— They spread lice!

I heat the soup and set fire to the dead one. At first it stinks of burning hair, but soon the smell of fried meat fills the hut. Henry limps over, picks up the tongs, and throws out the charred carcass. The smell of meat doesn't mean very much to me, but in Henry it awakens uncontrollable longings. Still, he won't eat rabbit.

Even when I'm half starved, I never dream of meat; I do dream of fat herring. I could stuff myself with lightly fried, oily herring skins and wash them down with rice wine. Beer gives me terrible heartburn, and it's so weak you have to drink buckets to feel anything. Then you have to piss all the time. And it's too cold to go out. I want us to make wine out of rice: sweet, yellow, murky!

— If you only knew all the misery alcohol has caused, Henry says ominously.

I wouldn't know about that. I let it pass. Wine is a gift. I could never have managed at sea without it. If you drink too much you throw up, fall on your face, and if worse comes to worst, fall overboard. But you learn. Some of the others had a hard time controlling their drinking, but if you didn't do your job you knew you were in serious trouble. Of course, some fighting went along with the boozing, but it also made the blows less accurate. In fact most people just got sentimental and weepy—and then fell asleep. We could get real alcohol only rarely, so wine became our medicine for pain, insomnia, and fear. No one would think of going into a battle without a couple of mugs under his belt. Rice wine made life livable— and death dieable.

THE first morning after the storm the ground glistens with snow as far as the eye can see. It takes me all morning to shovel a path down to the well. I don't see the point. We could just put a little snow in a bucket and let it melt. But the very thought upsets Henry:

— Snow is just like the white ash! he says. None of the Lord's many punishments put as many in their graves as the white ash, the devil's manna from the skies!

It doesn't change his mind when I squeeze a little snow in my hand and munch on it. Thirty years later, there's no poison left in snow or rain.

— I know people who died from it only last year! he says.

I get scared, go out back and stick my fingers down my throat. The Captain told me that all the stuff about the white ash is just superstition. At first it was dangerous, but not now. Still, I feel sick. I go to bed without eating—even though Henry complains I promised to work for him all my days.

THE next day the temperature shoots up. A warm breeze comes out of the south, and a little later billowing violet fog. We hear thunder in the distance. Pouring rain follows the fog, and the countryside turns into light-brown gruel.

When I go to inspect the rabbits for the night they're both dead. Their eyes have been eaten out; so we have rats. But that doesn't worry Henry. He's happy to be rid of the rabbits, and he doesn't care about the rats since our supplies are safely behind stone and tin. In fact, they almost seem to cheer him up:

— There've always been rats in the country. A house without rats is an unlucky house.

And then the weather turns sunny and dry. Nettles sprout even though it can't be more than a few weeks till Christmas. I want us to plant some seeds to try to make use of the heat, but Henry refuses. Even though the weather is all mixed up nowadays, he thinks we're better off planting and harvesting by the calendar. He's very protective about his old calendar from the nineties. Next to his hymn book and the mysterious gold fillings, it's the most valuable thing he has. I don't get it. What's the point of keeping track of the weekdays, weekends, and holidays? The little you need to know about the seasons to navigate, you learn from experience. But for Henry the calendar's holy; he couldn't imagine life without it. Every morning he tells me the day of the week. I forget it right away.

When the ground dries out I go back to gathering fuel while Henry stays inside trying to fix an old clock. I find an almost-perfect tractor tire in the sand behind the wood grove. It still has its rim; the word Volvo is written inside an oval. After I manage to spell my way through, I feel very happy. I'm not a good reader; if the words are too long I get bored. And the small writing in Henry's hymn book doesn't make me want to practice. Henry tries to make me read aloud, but I won't. There are some things you can't ask even of a slave. He knows the hymn book almost by heart, but he wants me to practice for the day when he gets his own Bible. Then there'll be plenty of reading to do!

He lives in the world of the Bible a lot. When he can't sleep at night and can get his mind off pissing, he wakes me up and tells me Bible stories: the one about Job, about Jacob and Esau, about Cain and Abel, Lot's wife, and Daniel in the Lion's Den. The last one is O.K., but the others are a little wishy-washy for my taste. I could tell him some better stories—sea stories. But he says they're not the word of God. But if God created everything the way Henry says He did, then isn't every word the word of God? Isn't even Volvo the word of God?

Whatever he thinks, Henry's very happy about the tractor tire. He tries to help roll it home, but mostly he's in the way. Later he shows me how to cut it up and use the flat pieces for shoe soles and other repair jobs. Most of it we'll burn for fuel. Rubber doesn't smell as good as roots and stumps, but it burns more slowly and it's hard to put out. And it doesn't crackle and spit dangerous sparks like spruce or painted wood.

Sometimes I get restless. I miss the sea so much! I miss guns too. The pressure inside always lets up a little if you shoot off a few clips, either at seagulls or darting fish. But shooting at nothing is all right too. I'm not used to this safe life! All this peace and quiet scares me. I want something to happen; life can't just plod along one day after another the way it does in Henry's outdated old calendar.

At sea, life was always on the line, but there was hope. When the Captain was in the mood he liked to tell us about Trott. Trott is a man who to this day is sailing his submarine across the Seven Seas. Atomic fuel lasts almost forever, and you can take oxygen out of seawater. So Trott's only problem is food. If anyone raided the galley on a moonless night we'd know that Trott had struck again. So far no one's managed to catch even a glimpse of him. But anyone lucky enough to spot him is supposed to quickly shout out his name: The minute Trott hears it he'll stay and rule over us in perfect peace and justice.

HENRY'S worse again. He's soaked in sweat and delirious at night, and in the daytime he lies shivering under everything we can find. His piss is coming out now, but it doesn't look or smell like the ordinary kind. He's thirsty all the time, but if I let him drink as much as he wants, he throws it back up. He has to stop work on the clock. I take it over to have something to do: He doesn't want to be alone. Before long it's standing on the chair next to his bed ticking away. You can make it ring at any time of the day; the only trouble is that all times are the same to us.

After I've been sitting in the dark with him for days, I can't control myself any longer. One morning without asking permission I head for the sea. About noon I catch sight of it to the east. I find a pile of rocks in an abandoned quarry and sit shivering for hours looking at its dead, stone-gray surface. Late in the afternoon I finally pick myself up and plod disappointedly back home.

That night Henry's delirious again. He calls me Jonne and asks me to go out for the morning paper. When I protest he gets furious and threatens me with a swollen fist:

— Don't you talk back to your father!

I promise to get it. Outside, I sit for a while on the shit perch. What is a newspaper anyway? Paper with far too many tiny, hard-to-read letters . . . too valuable to burn, that's what the Captain said. I go inside to tell him that the paper hasn't come yet. Luckily he fell asleep while I was out.

*   *   *

THE weather's merciful all the way to Christmas. There's rain but no frost. Henry gets back on his feet and is pretty clear in the head; but except for things that happened a long time ago, he can't remember much. He keeps forgetting my name. He wanders away from the potato pot and lets it boil over and douse the fire. Of course, we've got the flint of the cigarette lighter and the drill, but it takes time and the rain's made the peat damp. Most of the time he walks around muttering gloomily that it's getting to be time for him to cash in his chips—but then he'll suddenly turn cheerful and sing dirty songs.

Now the whole responsibility for our lives is on me. I don't really need him any longer except as company—if you can call him company. Once I let myself get angry just to see how he'll react; he gets terrified, thinks I'm going to beat him up. I consider giving him a few smacks to show him who's boss. But I stop myself. What if his head clears and he tells Petsamo the next time he comes? Who'd believe me if I denied it?

The times he's feeling well he wants to talk. It's just as I thought; sooner or later everybody wants to tell their secrets. He starts in about his parents, about Papa who was confined to a wheelchair after a car crash and Mama who had to run the farm and drive the school bus too. I'm not interested:

— Tell me about the Flood! I insist. Tell me how you of all people managed to survive!

But of course he won't. They all seem to be guilty about it. Sullenly he asks me to tell him about *my* childhood instead. I won't. What's there to tell? That Mama died when she had me? That Papa and I lived together in mountain caves until he died when I was six? What's the point of digging up cold, darkness, hunger, damp, sickness—and that some people were eaten so that others wouldn't starve? Papa thought I never knew what he was giving me to eat.

I slept a lot those first years; sleep makes hunger and boredom easier to take. When I was four or five Papa began to worry about what he called my education. He wanted me to learn everything he'd learned in school. He was a bad teacher. What I liked most was when he talked about the things he'd done as a kid, especially the bad things. Although I didn't understand most of it, I especially didn't understand why what he thought was bad was bad. Stealing, for example. Who can survive without stealing? Or are only grown-ups allowed to steal? Papa stole. Killed too. But the strangest of all was his talk about playing. The way they played with each other when he was a kid. Who played? We kids, he answered. Were there more kids? In the caves I was the only child. I didn't even understand for a long time why the others called me a kid. I thought there was something wrong with me that made me weaker or dumber than most of the others, some kind of poison that made me only half as tall as Papa. And playing? Is that when weak people fight?

I haul home roots from the fields. Then I take a pair of shears, cut the roots into pieces and wash the pieces off. After they're flattened between rocks and left to dry, they make good fuel. One day after I arrive at the house with the usual tangle, Henry's not there. I check the compost heap and the well: not there either. Then I stop looking. Maybe he got tired of me and headed north to look for Petsamo; he talks about Petsamo and his damn catheter all the time. If he's really gone, it won't break my heart. We'd begun to get on each other's nerves. How would it have been if we'd been snowed in together all winter?

But late in the afternoon he shouts from the nettles:

— Jonne, you might as well come over here!

I walk over without bothering to correct him: I don't mind being called Jonne for a while. But when I get there, I watch where I step; I know Petsamo and Henry buried the old lady in here someplace. Besides, Henry's always talking about the elves and wood sprites who are supposed to live there. He couldn't get over how scared I was, and I couldn't hide it. But just like everyone else who's lived at sea, I've heard far too many true stories about the supernatural—and evil.

He walks in front of me down a newly trampled path. Farther in, the nettles thin out and you can see patches of bare sand. He's been digging; some holes and piles of dirt look new while others are filled with water or overgrown with grass and thistles. He steps into a long hole:

— Come here. Take a look.

In one hand he's holding an upside-down skull, in the other the pincers he bought from Petsamo. He shows how to grip the neck of the tooth and wriggle it out of the jawbone.

— Most of them are alloy and other shit. Some are steel. Just remember: Gold doesn't have to look like gold. The best way to find out is to scratch it with a knife.

What I thought were just bumpy stones turn out to be skulls. There are all kinds of other bones too, and if you kick the sand around you even find pieces of coffin planks. Henry wants me to come down there with him. I don't want to—but I do it anyway. He grabs my arm and speaks in such an excited whisper that the spit goes flying:

— There are at least a hundred left, Edvin. The day the Lord calls me home, it'll all be yours! I'm *giving* it to you! But if you tell a soul you're dead.

He starts to cry and wants me to hold him. I do it. I feel my own eyes grow hot too. But I push down the feeling, tear myself loose, and climb out of the grave. If you let yourself feel too much, you won't be tough enough to defend yourself later on.

— A graveyard is God's little acre, Henry sobs. But who can live on potatoes alone?!

CHAPTER 5

I'M dreaming about the sea. It's early morning. The sun's light blue disk has just slipped above the brass-bright water. As usual the Captain's leaning out the side window of the wheelhouse, studying us with a watchful eye. Moses the engineer straddles the bowsprit, fishing. The others are sleeping in a pile under the mainsail, which they've draped over the boom like a tent. It's already starting to get hot.

Where am I? I don't quite know. Floating around the boat like a spirit, a good demon. One moment in the weather vane on top of the mast, the next on my back in the sea with *Diana* half a knot away; then in the greenglittering water streaming with seaweed-hair, slowly swimming under the ship's blue-bearded keel. My chest heaves from lack of oxygen, my pulse is almost bursting through my ears.

Then on top of the wheelhouse with my chin between my knees. A ship glides toward us in the distance; I can hear a faint bell. As it comes closer, I see that it's painted completely white. It heaves to without a sail raised, the throb of a diesel, the glitter of oars. The rigging's covered with flowers: Flowers in all the colors of the rainbow hang in thick garlands and heavy bunches among the tiny, spring-green leaves. Now the ship lies completely still without ever dropping an anchor. A small figure in white steps down onto the water and walks daintily toward us. It's me; you can tell from the cleft lip.

Henry's shaking me. It's cold as death; the fire's gone out. Shivering, I get up with a worn old blanket around my shoulders and try to get a fire going in the pieces of tire; they still stink even though they're out. Henry needs to pee and he's too shaky to hold the pot himself. Nothing comes out. His panting turns into a quiet whimper. His hands are ice cold, with blue and pink blotches. I manage to get him into bed and prop him up with pillows. Then I drop my blanket and crawl under the covers with him, putting his icy hands between my sleep-warm thighs.

HENRY says that today's the day before Christmas. He sits at the table counting gold fillings. The last few days I've put everything else aside and concentrated on digging for skulls; we've got to use every chance before it freezes again. Gold isn't the only thing you can find. I've tried putting a whole skeleton together. Putting the thigh bones and skull in place is no problem, but the rest is one big mess. I've found three wedding rings, a pair of dentures, a pink doll—made of plastic? A silver cross and a silver chain with a pendant of a clenched fist inside a circle. In a thighbone a long, winged spike. It looks very nasty; I hope the poor bastard died at an early stage of the torture.

— You could almost call it a bumper crop! Henry says.

He treats me kindly, almost humbly, asking my permission before he sits down to look over the fillings; you'd think that I not he owned them. He's scared and impressed at the same time:

— It's no good to have so much gold around the house. . . . If pirates come, tell them it's just because the Convent left the gold with us for safekeeping.

I'm sick of all the strange things he says: what Convent? If anybody comes and overpowers us, no excuses are going to help us; we'll just give them the gold and the graveyard and beg for our lives. He takes out his everloving calendar and decides to postpone Christmas one day. Then he shows me a stack of papers on which he's tried to figure out the days of the year starting at 1994. But no matter how he does it, it always comes out different.

— Maybe Christmas was yesterday, I say.

He thinks I'm making fun of him; his eyes well up with tears.

— O.K. then, let's say that tomorrow's Christmas Eve, I finally say, and I pat him on his trembling head.

so the *next* day is Christmas Eve. Henry hangs a torn Christmas card on the lamp—a picture of a gray log cabin under a roof of blue snow. The little windows glow yellow-red, and spruce trees glitter with white snow. . . . All this whiteness makes me sick! They say that the white ash covered the whole mainland until the fall rains came and washed it away. When I was a boy white was the color of fear. Sometimes I woke up at night in a cold sweat howling, "I dreamed white!" I'd seen nothing in the dream, done nothing; there was only emptiness. The first time I saw ordinary snow I threw up.

Henry decides to cook—if I don't mind, of course—and does his best to keep himself standing on his soft, swollen feet. He takes the precious rice out of the metal canister and cooks up a huge mess of gruel; I'm pretty sure most of it will go bad before we have time to finish it. But he says we have to make enough for the Christmas elf and put it in a dish for him outside. In ours, we put honey and dowse it with beer.

— It's supposed to be milk, Henry explains.

Milk, cream, cheese . . . No one on board could describe how they tasted. Sweet, thicker than water—that's what they said about milk. Cream was supposed to be fattier, smoother, yellower—like egg yolks? Cheese was solid cream that stank of smelly feet. I'm not so sure they always ate so fucking well in the old days.

After we eat, Henry reads his hymn book for a long time. I doze off but wake up when he gets up and pulls out a rock from behind some hanging clothes; that's one hiding place I missed. He brings some bags back to the table, the biggest one full of packs of paper money, the smaller full of coins. At sea people used to drill holes in the alloy coins and wear them on a string around their necks to protect themselves from losing their teeth. From a third bag he takes a package of small wooden figures—half of them black, the other half white—wrapped in a black-and-white checkered cloth. He spreads the bills across the table:

— Three million seventy-three thousand, he announces.

I think I'm supposed to be impressed. The number means nothing to me. Of course I know it's high. I can't count that far, or even write it down. I know that a thousand has three zeros and ten thousand four zeros, but I've never had any reason to count that high. I used to count Papa's pulse because it made me feel calm. But I never got further than three thousand.

— What am I saving my fortune for? Henry asks himself. You can't write on it and you can hardly burn it.

— The Captain saved postcards, I comfort him. And books. They burn badly too.

We look at the checkered cloth with the wooden figures. It's what's called a chess game. We twist and turn the figures, line them up by size, check them underneath for marks or numbers. Then we search for a die. On the borders of the checkered cloth are A, B, C . . . and the numbers 1, 2, 3. . . .

— I used to know how to play this game, Henry complains. But I'm damned if I can remember it now.

So instead we each pick out four of the smallest pieces and

play Parcheesi as well as we can on the checkered cloth. Since we don't have a die, we mark up six other pieces, put them in a tin and draw them out.

THAT night the ghosts come out of their graves. They heave aside the tangles of blackened nettles that lie rotting in the wet snow, then line up in a row and hold their hands in front of their faces as though they're waiting to be shot. I reach for my Russian carbine in my sleep. When I try to mow them down, all that comes out of the mouth of the barrel is a pitiful little trickle of piss.

Henry wakes me up with the cane that he now takes even into bed with him. Then the usual ritual begins: I get him onto his feet, pull down the layers of pants, and put the pot against his thighs; he keeps himself from falling by grabbing my head. Nothing comes out. He starts to sway so I bring him back to bed. When I begin to pull up his pants, a little yellow pus dribbles out by itself from his prick.

I'm afraid to go back to sleep. I can still hear the ghosts outside in the warm wind; they want their gold fillings back so they can buy a place in Heaven. Are God and the Devil the same person? I've learned that you have to treat them with about the same amount of respect, maybe a little more for the Devil. There must be some system behind it all, something that keeps hedgehogs from mating with bats, grasshoppers with flies, rabbits with rats. But I'm not so sure. Last fall we spent three days near one of the outer islands because the cook insisted he'd seen three mermaids flapping around on the rocks. He said they looked like a combination of woman and seal. Nobody else saw anything, but the Captain said he heard them singing. I stayed up all three nights just to finally see a live woman.

Christmas morning Henry doesn't get out of bed. It's just as well; he's safer there. If he goes outside he might trip in spite of the cane or stand in one place and refuse to come in until the mailman arrives. But now he's too sick. He's lying flat on his back, his face as red as a brick, foam bubbling and dribbling from the corners of his mouth. I pull him up into a sitting position to make it easier for him to breathe, but his chest wheezes and rumbles so much you can hear it all the way across the room. I slide his suspenders over the crossbar. His mouth hangs open; behind his half-closed eyelids his eyeballs drift slowly back and forth as though he's reading an invisible book.

By evening he's a little better. I try to get some beer into him. But he gags on it, coughing and hiccuping—finally he collapses, not into the bed (the suspenders keep him from doing that) but as if he's drowning inside himself. His eyes bulge out. His lips gasp silently like a fish on dry land.

I have no appetite. The gruel we were going to fry dries up and turns sour. I can't stand seeing him hanging in his harness with his chest gurgling. It's raining outside. The potato field is flooded. Eyeball-sized bubbles glide over the brown surface dodging the raindrops; I count more than a hundred before the toughest one breaks. Papa said that clouds are formed by water that's been sucked out of the earth; dust and poisons follow along. But you never see the rain falling up; you only see it when it comes back down.

I want to know much more about how everything works. But nobody will tell me anything. When the Captain had just fallen in love with me, I asked him to teach me navigation. That was the first time he beat me: What right did I have to ask him to share his knowledge, his only security! For twenty-five years he'd survived because he knew how to navigate. No one was going to take his life insurance away! What is life insurance? Just a piece of paper, they tell me. There's so much I want to understand.

When the rain starts soaking through to the two layers of shirts under my coat, I go back inside. He seems much better now; he gropes for me, wants to talk. I sit on the edge of the bed and hold his hands to keep him from plucking at his bed-clothes:

— Make sure Sverker doesn't get anything. . . . He never comes to visit!

I promise to keep Sverker—I think that was his brother—away from the money. Then he wants to talk about his days as a prison guard. He keeps insisting how fair he was. He couldn't stop them from shooting up, but at least he wasn't like the other guards; he wouldn't lift a finger to help them. He liked the night shift because he could do crossword puzzles. He promises to teach me how when he gets better—it's good for the nerves.

At midnight he shouts for his Bible. He insists that I look for it in the dresser. I can't talk him out of it. I tell him the dresser's locked. So then he wants to climb out of bed and show me where in the refrigerator he usually keeps the key. I force him back down and tell him he'll get his Bible—I give him the hymn book, which he opens without looking at. He just lies there with the little black book's open pages pressed against his heart. I loosen the suspenders again; they're raising welts in his armpits.

This goes on for two more days—sometimes choking fits, sometimes calling out for relatives and lecturing them one by one. You can put your hand on his stomach and feel his hard, skull-sized bladder. When will it all end? Isn't Petsamo coming back with his tubes? Once while I'm dozing, his muffled scream wakes me. He must have had a coughing fit and got the suspenders twisted around his neck—now he's lying on the floor. My fingers are so stiff with sleep they can't undo the knots, so I cut him loose. Every time I lift him, he gets heavier. I can't understand it; even though nothing comes out, nothing goes in either.

I burrow down in my own bed to keep from hearing him. I sweat under three layers of blankets, then start to suffocate. So I get up, put far too much of our precious fuel on the fire to keep the ghosts away, and take out the big hammer. Pounding the handle into my palm, I pace back and forth exactly the way Petsamo did the time they tied me up and cross-examined me. I pray to God, the Devil, anybody, to free me from the poison that's pouring out of Henry's black lips and filling the whole hut!

When he has another vomiting fit, I run outside. He scares me more than the ghosts!

WHEN I finally make up my mind, I do exactly what the Captain taught me—wind some cloth around the hammer head so tight it can't slip off. Then I pull him gently by the feet until he's lying down in the bed. His head doesn't move but his chest's pumping hard. I can't hate him the way I hated the eunuch. I'm doing it in self-defense. No one has the right to torture someone else the way Henry's torturing me! Exactly the way the Captain taught me, I let the heavy hammer fall fairly softly between his eyebrows. His body goes limp and lifeless right away: no convulsions, not even a tremor behind the half-closed eyelids. Exactly the way the Captain taught me, I wind the belt around his neck and pull as hard as I can. Then I put on my layers of coats and wander over the cliffs above the house in the semidarkness until some green cirrus clouds in the east tell me it's morning.

I'VE tied some wire around the feet of the corpse; now I'm dragging it along behind me over the frozen ground. When I come to cracks in the earth or frozen sand hills, I have to carry or push him along. He's lighter now that he's dead. It's so cold my nostrils stick together; the marsh seems to be frozen through to the bottom already. But I'm not cold. I'm wearing a knitted ski mask and a scarf tied under my chin. I've got Henry's biggest overcoat on top of his short army fur jacket, and on my feet his heavy leather ski boots reinforced with tire-rubber soles.

The marsh reeds tinkle as I push through them. Under the bare ice you can make out layers of winding water plants and red, heart-shaped leaves. In one place a toad's frozen fast in the ice with a chain of little bubbles curling behind him. Aside from the ice, winter hasn't changed anything very much. It doesn't take long to find the little island where we saw the geese. I leave him there while I slip and slide among the peat holes to find one where he'll fit. Most are caved in or grown over, but finally I find one almost two meters long and half as wide.

I go back for the ax and spade that I tied to the corpse. It's hard work chopping through the ice—the tangles of roots give me more trouble than the ice itself. I have to rest a lot; there's nowhere to sit except on Henry's bound feet. So there I sit, turning the pages of his hymn book. Should I let him keep it? What's it worth? Who needs it more—him or me?

When I've chopped about a meter down, the marsh turns out not to be frozen through at all. Water pulses up through the ax blows, and soon I'm wet to my knees. The more I chop, the more yellow water wells up. I'm sure I can get him down into the water. But how can I keep him from floating up? I feel around under the ice with the spade to see if I can wedge him in, but roots and reeds get in the way. If I could hold him down for a couple of hours, new ice would form above him. But what'll happen when the spring sun bakes through the lens of ice and the whole bog starts to seethe and bubble? How can I stop him from haunting me? I can't. Even people who've been dumped a thousand meters down into the ocean tied to an engine block or nailed into heavy coffins and covered by two meters of dirt come back to haunt you. The only thing that would help would be a couple of hand grenades to scare the hell out of him. But I don't even have a pinch of gunpowder.

I lower him down and turn him so he'll be able to see his wild geese. Then I stand on top of him, pressing him down far enough to stick the spade like a crossbar under the ice. When I climb back up he's still lying there nice and quiet. I sweep the pieces of ice on top of him and sit on my haunches waiting for the ice to form. But then I feel my wet ski boots begin to freeze into the ice. I go home. Probably Henry wouldn't mind if I froze to death and kept him company.

CHAPTER 6

THE first night by the sea is painfully cold. I've found an old concrete bunker on a spit of land. Through the low gun slits I can see far to the north, east, and south. On the beach below, layers of dirt-gray ice floes have piled up, and twenty or thirty meters out the topmost layer slants down into the black water. The sea itself is free of ice. Everything's dead still out there; even the wind seems frozen. There aren't any clouds in the night sky, but no moon or stars either.

Because of the smoke, I can't make a fire even though I brought plenty of fuel on a makeshift wire and sheet-metal sled. Most of the way from Henry's house I pulled it across bare ground—but it was still easier than carrying everything on my back. Aside from fuel, I've got clothes, bedding, potatoes, rice, and salt. I also have the carbine, some knives, a pot, a spade, and an ax. On me I've hidden the hymn book, Henry's glasses, the cigarette lighter, a camera lens I found at the house, and the gold. And I'm so bundled up with extra clothes that my arms stick out like the penguins in the Captain's book *Animals of the World*.

Before I set fire to Henry's hut, I dragged out anything movable and smashed it up. I knocked over the flat rocks around the potato field and tore down the south wall of the compost heap with a crowbar. For two piss-cold days I chopped out more skulls and pulled out teeth. I want the house to look as if it's just been completely sacked. That's the only way I can come back if I want to: an abandoned, livable house always invites new guests.

I'm going to stay here until I see a ship! January isn't the best month for it, but at least the sea isn't frozen. After Henry died, I spent a few hard days trying to make up my mind whether to stay in the house and wait for spring, or take off right away. On what was there, I could have lived well. But not safely. Who owns me now that Henry's gone? If I'd been left alone on board a boat, anyone who wanted to (and was able to) could have claimed me and kept me for himself or sold me to someone else. If Petsamo comes back, he may think that *he* owns me now. I wouldn't mind that so much, although he's probably a harder, more demanding master than Henry. But what I was more afraid of was that people from up north would come along and think I was an outlaw—or that pirates would come from the sea, bushwhack me in the hut, and either kill me or sell me away to sea.

This is my first real chance as a grown-up to become a free man. If I have bad luck, someone will come and steal all I own; but if I'm lucky, I'll be able to buy my freedom. I can't let myself be surprised from the sea; in a situation like that I wouldn't have any bargaining power. I have to lure someone in with fire or some other trick. First I'll have to convince them I wasn't trying to ambush them. Then they'll look me over, check me out. Then, if everything goes well, we'll be able to start bargaining.

I want to buy a boat. But first I have to buy a trip to where you can buy one. The rice and the fuel should pay for the trip; the real valuables—the gold and the hymn book—I've got to hide till we get to the islands. It really is a gamble. But maybe the sailors won't rob me if I talk them into believing that I've been sent by some powerful man on this island to buy a boat and crew. I can also say that later on I'll show them the grave-yard with the gold teeth. You have to convince people that you're worth something—and worth more alive than dead.

I chopped up the gold fillings and rolled them between ax blades into small kernels not much bigger than grains of rice; now there's almost a whole handful in a purse around my neck. Before anybody gets too close, I can swallow them; I may have to do that every time I shit them out. If I make it to the archipelago before the long summertime raiding expeditions, there'll most likely be ships for sale. You can always get crews because the captains stick together. If one of them dies or disappears, the crew hardly ever takes over—it just serves under one of the other captains. If that captain doesn't want to command two ships, he'll pick the best one, hold onto the youngest crew members, and sell the rest, men and boat alike. My biggest problem is that I don't know how to navigate. I have to find a first mate—which isn't easy. Probably the simplest thing would be to buy in with an older skipper who'd teach me navigation and set me up as his heir. What I want most in the world is a little steam-driven boat in good condition. There are still a few left, with dependable old boilers you can fire with anything from cut-up tires to dried seaweed.

Raiding and trading is what I'm planning to do—not fishing and raiding like the Captain. Fishing is chancy and hard; you lose your tackle all the time, and when you finally have a decent catch it rots before you find a buyer. Dry-goods trading is better—gold, spices, salt, tools, and implements. Weapons are good too, but you have to take a lot of care of them to keep them from rusting. The best thing about arms trading is that it's the easiest of all to combine with raiding. And raiding's *always* been the most popular livelihood at sea. It pays off in both people and goods—and it's fun! All the best stories are about piracy. But during the last few years it's been going downhill; we sailors have had to raid each other more and more.

Dreams, fantasies . . . I'm just fooling myself! Any idiot can see that I don't have a chance. Ever since Henry's death I've done the one thing you can't do if you want to survive: believe in dreams.

As soon as the early morning shadows lift, I start my miserable journey back. In the course of these freezing morning hours Henry's hut begins to look like Paradise. It's going to take me two or three weeks to make it livable again. Later in the spring I can get the potato field back into shape. I'll buy ammunition and a Bible to keep the ghosts away—especially the old lady with the golden eye sockets. The farther I pull my sled inland, the more wonderful the hut seems; soon it's shining like one of the palaces in *Famous Buildings of Antiquity*. I don't understand what it is I want. How do people really function? Yesterday I was dreaming about a rich man's life at sea; that dream was so strong I destroyed the hut. Now I'm dreaming about a safe and cozy life in the same hut! And tomorrow?

The cold night in the bunker exhausted me; I can't make it home before the early winter nightfall. I find a place out of the wind and make a fire. But no matter how close I sit or how many clothes from the sled I bundle up in, the cold won't let me go. It feels as if a snowball is growing in my heart; when it gets big enough it'll fill my chest and make my breath crackle with ice. My hands won't do what I tell them to; I can't undo the knots and buckles in the luggage. I manage to melt a little snow over the smoking, fluttering fire, but when the water's

hot I can't even drink it. I just crouch down and squint at
the little blue flames until I realize that I've fallen asleep and
tipped over on my side. I dream that I'm still squatting and
working over the fire. I know that I'm dreaming but can't pull
myself out of it.

SOMEONE'S stomping on my leg. It's snowed. A man with a
fur hat pulled down to his nose is holding me down with one
foot and pointing a heavy pistol at my forehead.
  — Where are the others? he asks.
  I tell him there aren't any. He doesn't believe me; he gives
me a kick in the side:
  — Where the fuck are they?
  Groggy with sleep I try to convince him: Why would I be
lying here frozen, covered with snow, if I had friends? He can
check for himself that there's no boat on the shore, and if
there were more of us he'd see tracks in the snow. When he
sees what bad shape I'm in, he calms down a little and sits on
the sled. Now he has to make up his mind if he wants to finish
me off or take me prisoner:
  — How old are you?
  — Forty-nine, I say so he won't think I'm lying.
  He spits in the dead fire and then decides:
  — Get up, you bastard! Start pulling!
  He makes me stumble along on numb feet, pulling the
sled behind me. After a few meters he sits down on it and
mushes me along, but I can't move an inch. So then he gets
up and walks along beside me, making do with giving me a
shove every now and then. Before long we take another rest.
After untying my hands he gives me a little to drink. I'm hungry and dazed. If he expects us ever to get out of these snow-
covered hills, he's going to have to help me pull!

*   *   *

WE come to a boulder-strewn ridge. During the last hour I've fallen a lot; now we've got to rest again. He's put the gun away; I'm not going anywhere. Below the ridge lies the wide, frozen mouth of a stream. To the east are open sea and some skerries with rock pillars; in the west the bay narrows to a little stream many sizes too narrow for its wide mouth. On the opposite shore—to the north—a series of new ridges begins. About fifteen people are standing around holes they've dug in the ice; wooden scaffolding is above the holes and steel cables run down into the water. Next to some of the platforms are small sleds a lot like mine—flat-bottomed, sheet-metal contraptions. Everybody's well bundled up, and on one of the sleds burns an open fire which they come over to every once in a while to warm themselves. The other sleds are loaded down with ice-covered scrap iron—black or brown squarish lumps. At first I think they're stone blocks, but then I realize they're engines.

Before the guard shoves me back onto my feet, I have enough time to watch the men on the ice hoist up two more engines and a twisted bicycle. The guard himself stays on the sled; obviously he wants his pals to see me pulling him. And since we're on a hill sloping down to the ice, I do manage it for a moment or two. But after a few meters the sled picks up so much speed that it almost knocks me over and he has to jump off and help me slow it down. When we get to the ice, he climbs on again and points to a long stone and sheet-metal hut farther in toward the mouth of the stream.

He shoves me in. All I can see at first is the fire roaring in the stove in the middle of the room. From the crackling and the stench I can tell that they're burning seaweed. On the floor are a couple of long bundles; after a while I can make out a man with a shiny red ass crouching over one of them. The guard pushes me over and ties my feet. I turn my face to the wall so I don't have to see any more of the rape.

Men are laughing and panting. Nobody pays any attention to me. Since my hands are free, I can pull out the purse with the gold. I get the first pellet into my mouth and try to swallow; it seems impossible to do it lying down. But after it's been in my mouth for a while gnawing at my tongue, the saliva starts to flow. I swallow as many pellets as I can; they burn in my throat.

Everybody goes outside. I twist around to look at the two bundles. One of them's lying completely still, but the other is moving, sobbing and getting up on all fours. When it begins putting on clothes I can tell that it's a woman. She's licking tears from her upper lip. Her face is flat and she has high cheekbones. Her nose is flat too, but unbroken. She has clear gray eyes, and between her eyebrows is a wrinkle that seems to be a small healed scar. It makes her look surprised—or as though she's got a headache. Her skull is nice and smooth and not disgustingly shiny. I catch a glimpse of one of her breasts. It makes me feel something I've never felt before: depressed and excited at the same time. She can't be much older than I am.

— What's your name?

She jumps, pulls the torn clothes close to her and shuffles to the nearest corner. I keep my mouth shut so I won't frighten her. She watches every move I make. I nod and try to smile. Now her face is blank, as though she has no feelings. We stare at each other for a long time. Finally she lets go of my eyes, crawls over to the other bundle and shakes it. Then she looks at me again and rocks her body back and forth, sobbing quietly. I pull myself on to my elbows and tell her in a low but clear voice to lie down again, lie next to the other bundle and pretend to be unconscious. If she's moving when anyone comes in, I know they'll jump on her again. She nods but doesn't do it. I collapse again; I'm completely exhausted. It's very hot next to the stove; when I close my eyes, my eyelids glow sun red.

When I was a kid the sun terrified me! If you left the caves without shielding your eyes the sun could boil your eyeballs white. How could prehistoric man have prayed to the sun? In the Captain's picture books I saw how the Bronze Age people threw themselves on their knees before the burning sun wagon. But isn't the sun what the priest on the blacktop barge would have called the Gate of Hell? I've never seen a burning sun wagon, but I have seen burning ships. When I was fourteen and owned by the skipper of a sloop who made me wear rings on all ten fingers, we were once attacked from the sea—a burning boat loaded with explosives drifted in close to our ship. Afterward, in my nightmares, it was the sun itself that came sputtering and slithering across the water—and exploded like a hot-air balloon.

A shot goes off right outside the door. Three men, two small fat ones and one very tall one, shuffle in. The tall one walks over to the bundle on the floor.

— That one's dead.

I recognize the voice; it's Petsamo! The other two grab the dead bundle by the feet and drag it out. Petsamo bends over the girl. She just can't keep quiet; instead, she starts to whimper.

— Shut up, you idiot!

But she goes on whimpering, and when the other two come back they want to fuck her right away.

— Leave her alone, boys, Petsamo says. She can't take another round. You already killed one of them.

They start arguing. One of them apparently had his turn, so the other thinks it's unfair that he can't have one too. But he gives in when Petsamo says:

— Maybe you can explain one death. But two?

All three come over to me. One of them kicks me:

— Roll over, you Finnish asshole!

I roll over on my back and pull up my knees to protect my stomach.

— Nicke got him south of here—in the hills. The smoke gave the stupid bastard away. You understand what I'm saying? he shouts.

— Yes, yes.

— Oh, so this one wasn't on the boat.

— I guess not. Doesn't seem to speak Finnish—do you?

Petsamo bends down and peers at me. He gives me the tiniest nod. So he recognizes me. The two others untie my feet and start to undress me. They go through my clothes and of course find everything including the gold left in the purse. This cheers them up immediately; one of them even pinches my cheek gratefully. While I sit naked, they put my clothes and possessions in neat little piles. Then the younger one of the two takes out his pistol, puts the barrel at the nape of my neck and bellows:

— Out!

I jump to my feet and stumble out. The cold's as thick as water. I stand there hugging my balls. Next to the door lies a naked corpse with a bloody head. They push my face to the wall of the house. Then nothing. I stare at the stone wall in front of my nose. But I sense people milling around behind me.

— He's a young cocksucker, one voice laughs.

— He's got a harelip.

I can't hold it in; my bowels empty themselves.

— Sit down like normal people when you shit!

I sink to my haunches. Then I hear Petsamo:

— He's the one who killed Henry's old lady.

— Piss-Henry?

— So shoot the fucker!

— He's Henry's, says Petsamo.

— Well, as far as I can see Henry ain't nowhere in sight.

Someone shoves me over on my side. Laughs and giggles.

— Cute, Petsamo.

— I'll take him down to Henry, says Petsamo. Let him decide what to do.

— Why can't we just finish the fucker off now?

Petsamo pulls me to my feet and pushes me into the house again.

— Get dressed!

He ties me up and puts me in a corner. Then he sits down next to me, eating some rice that's being passed around. When no one's looking he stuffs a couple of lumps into my mouth. He gives the girl some too, but she throws it up right away—which makes everybody nervous. More men come in and stomp around to get warm. Somebody throws more seaweed on the fire. A few pull off their wet clothes. They're tattooed over almost all of their bodies; scaly snakes writhe around their muscles.

Cursing and raving, a wounded man's carried in with blood pouring out of his arm. They call Petsamo over and try to get the jacket off. The guy screams; Petsamo cuts open the sleeve instead. Then they light some lanterns while he kneels down and goes to work. The man goes on cursing and calling for his Mama.

— So why'd you have to be so damn *clumsy*! someone shouts.

THE next morning they break camp. The injured man, the girl, and I go with Petsamo. Where to? Makes no difference to me. Petsamo manages to get more clothes for me and the girl. Out on the ice they're busy checking over their sleds with the engines and other scrap metal lashed to them. We take my sled; everything on it's gone. They put the injured man (who seems more or less unconscious) on a pile of sacks and tie him down. Petsamo and I do the pulling while the girl walks along next to the sled, but she starts lagging behind. We head north across the iced-over bay. The wooden scaffolding has been taken down.

Now I notice a small boat a lot like the *Diana* frozen into the ice near the northern shore, and all around it torn clothes and the remains of a tent. When we pass it the girl breaks away, climbs over the bulwark, and wraps her arms and legs around the mast; she won't come down. Petsamo doesn't get excited; he lets her sit. When the other sleds that started after us get closer, he slaps her cheek and pulls her to her feet. He turns her head so that she has to look at the approaching men. She cries out, tears herself away, jumps down on the ice, and starts running up the embankment to the north. But halfway up she collapses and stays where she is. When we reach her she can't stand up; Petsamo ties her to the sled head to foot with the injured man.

Now we can't keep any distance between us and the others; one by one they catch up and pass us. The last ones are loaded with timber, planks, and block and tackle. On the very last sled pulled by three men sits a huge fat man with a wispy beard, brown fur coat, and high leather boots. He looks like he's on a throne. As he pulls up, he climbs off and pokes his boot into the unconscious man.

— If he pulls through, I want him back. Providing he still has two arms.

He looks closely first at the Finn, then at me:

— All women bring is trouble. . . . You sure Piss-Henry wants this one? He could work for me.

— You'd trust someone who kills old ladies?

— With pleasure, with pleasure! Never did see what Henry wanted with Bett. He could have lived with us!

That's all he says; then his men help him back onto his throne and he shouts:

— Move your asses! Too much cunt smell around here!

We wait until he pulls out of sight. Petsamo tells me his name is Roland and that all the other men take orders from him. Ten years ago his gang used to be about thirty-five men, but in the last couple of years they've begun to die off—now they're down to sixteen or seventeen even though they've taken in new members from boats they've lured ashore. Their base is only a couple of hours north of here. They still call it the Prison even though it hasn't been used for more than thirty years as what Petsamo calls a "prison for younger male offenders."

Roland completely controls this end of the island. In the old days people ran for the hills the minute he and his gang appeared. For years even Petsamo had to live with them and care for their sick. Now, however, his position has grown so strong that he's free to go wherever he wants; no one, not even Roland, wants to get on the wrong side of someone who knows medicine. And Petsamo says that Roland himself has mellowed—even he recognizes he's better off taking things a little easier.

The next time we stop for a break I tell him Henry's dead. He doesn't seem too interested. He just asks me:

— Did he suffer much?

— When his time came, it was over fast.

CHAPTER 7

I'M lying on a bed in a small underground chamber. A lantern hangs down from a black iron hook. Along the farthest wall stands a stone bench, and above it what they call a crucifix. A clay plate stands ready next to my bed, but by now I've stopped throwing up; Petsamo thinks that my body got rid of the last piece of gold yesterday. Two other sick people are down here: the Finnish girl and the guy with the crushed arm.

Petsamo comes in with another lantern. Behind him is an older woman with a light-colored cloth over her head and a wooden cross on a strap around her neck. First they check the sleeping girl, then examine the wounded man, who's running a fever and muttering, his saliva thick in his mouth. Petsamo pays no attention to me. But the woman bends down and says:

— My name is Sister Signe.

— I'm hungry.

She promises I'll get some soup as soon as they care for the wounded man. Petsamo tries to get the man's lips around the neck of a tin flask; judging from the smell it's liquor, not wine. Sister Signe goes back into the dark, brick-covered passageway—which leads where? When they carried me down here I must have been completely out. The last thing I remember is getting into a flat-bottomed rowboat and rowing across smooth, black water. By then my stomach and intestines had already begun to reject the gold.

Sister Signe returns with a small, dumpy woman dressed in the same kind of light gray cloth but without a wooden cross around her neck. The little one huffs and puffs, wiping sweat from her forehead with the back of a fat little hand. The two women hold the injured man up while Petsamo bares the man's chest and back and presses his ear against the man's tattooed skin; above his heart is a target with blue circles and a red bull's-eye. They try to get him to drink more of the liquor. He refuses. Petsamo sets the flask down on the bench, and the three of them begin to drag him out of the room. I make a dive for the flask; I haven't had a drink in ages! But Petsamo's quicker than I am:

— You stay away from that!

He pockets it and they go on pulling the man into the passageway, leaving the extra lamp behind.

I rub my black-and-blue marks. They beat the shit out of me in the hut by the stream. The ribs on my right side are the sorest, but none feels broken. I've had four broken ribs that I can remember. The first one was after Papa died. I was six years old. Axelsson, my first protector, lay down on top of me. I pleaded and begged him to let me sit on him instead, but he'd got it into his head that he wanted to be on top. Afterward he nursed me tenderly; everybody says that children's injuries heal quickly.

The next time I was thirteen. I got caught by an iron hatch as we were evacuating a shelter. My group had been warned of some trouble and took off head over heels. But others saw us and wanted to come too. I was in the rear; when someone slammed the hatch shut I got in the way. I didn't feel a thing; I was much too scared of getting left behind as we stumbled down to the raft. Afterward I got pneumonia. I was so sick they gave me up for dead. I don't know how long I lay there. I saw people and things that could never really have existed. I saw trees—at least I think they were trees if you can believe the Captain's picture books and postcards.

The third time was in a fight with a younger man—probably no older than me—who called me pussy-lips because of the slit in my upper lip. Actually, I didn't care that much about the insult; the fight was really over winning the favor of another man, the Icelander, who always talked about his distant island, which he insisted was completely untouched. A beautiful island in the North Atlantic with green grass and snowy mountains! No one could stand listening to him, but he was rich; he had an amazing way of knowing where the fish were going to be. Other boats constantly tried to follow him; that's why he'd always shove off in the middle of the darkest nights and preferably after a big drunken brawl. I was dying to sail with him, but the only way I could would be if he got rid of the lover he already had.

I began at a disadvantage. The lover was stronger. He was beautiful and well built too; for all I know, he might even have had a little hair left on his head. But worst of all was that he was such an even-tempered guy that it was almost impossible to rile him. I tried many times before he even called me pussy-lips; but that time I was so stupid I forgot to make sure that there were witnesses around. He insulted me the second time on the collapsed concrete pier that marks the borderline between the middle and outer archipelago. From what people say, none of the really terrible epidemics has hit the outer islands yet, but the middle archipelago is no man's land; it's a good idea to stay away from people who've been there. Those who've been blown even farther in—into the inner archipelago and the estuaries—and who've managed to get back out again are often shot right in their boats because of fear of contamination. But I don't know what's true: I've heard too many stories about plagues and epidemics in the nighttime gloom.

I snuck up behind him on the pier, worked my forefinger into the crack between his cheeks and whispered candy-ass into his ear. He went at me with a reinforcement bar and slammed it into my back, cracking a rib. But I twisted it out of his hands and drove it into his belly. It took him a week to die; the Icelander was beside himself with grief. He promised a working compass to anyone who captured me alive or dead. But no one even went after me. Everyone thought that he'd terrorized us long enough with his talk of green grass, clear springwater and uncontaminated mountains; he'd only got what he deserved.

The fourth time was very undramatic. *Diana* was pulling up to a dock. I was standing in the prow with a boathook ready to push off. When I put the hook into the pier the back end caught in my sweater. If the shaft hadn't snapped, I'd be a dead man now.

A lantern flickers in the passageway. They come back carrying the injured man. Now there are at least four Sisters in gray veils and baggy dresses. Petsamo makes sure the man is tied down so he'll lie still. He pushes up one of his eyelids and looks into his pupil:

— Shout if he gets restless. Even a low shout in these tunnels carries fifty meters.

Then they go out, leaving only the ceiling lantern behind. I look at the man. They've cut off his left arm right above the elbow.

IN the middle of the night—or is it the middle of the night?— I wake up when I hear the injured man tearing at his ropes. He's waving his bandaged stump, which looks like a ball of rags. Then he suddenly throws himself on the sleeping girl, and she starts hitting and kicking him. The bandages turn completely red. I hardly have time to yell before the Sisters come rushing in, pull him off, and drag him away. As the girl lies on her stomach sobbing, her naked foot peeks out from under the blankets. I can't stop looking. How do you do it? I've heard a thousand stories. They're not like the rest of us; they have more than one hole in their ass. I raise myself up on my elbows and slide closer. If I took her now, no one would know. But as I squat down trying to nudge her feet apart, a picture comes into my head: I'm bending over, looking into a rock crevice. For the first time in my life I see a flower. Triumphantly I reach out to grab it. But I can't. I just can't.

When Petsamo comes the next morning, he says that the injured man bled to death:

— If he'd survived he would have had a hell of a time with only one arm. Besides, he had pneumonia. He never would have made it.

— So why'd you cut off his arm?

— If you don't use the skills you have, you lose them.

Next time it might be someone who actually has a chance of pulling through.

PETSAMO calls the place I'm living in the Rabbit-Convent. It got its name from all the underground passages that connect the different chambers. There isn't much left of the buildings themselves except for one called the Chapel, which they say was the choir of a medieval church. Some of the passageways are very old, others newly dug; the old ones are beautifully lined with brick or sandstone while the new ones have bare dirt walls and sheet-metal ceilings held up by wooden beams. They must be rich here; they haven't burned up all their wood for fuel. At the moment eleven Sisters (that's what they call themselves) and the girl who came with us live in the Rabbit-Convent. But the Sisters themselves don't call it the Rabbit-Convent; to them it's the Sodality.

After I'd gotten all the gold out of me, I felt better for about a day. Then I got the shakes and after that a bad cough. It feels as if my lungs never really got rid of all the sand and salt water I took in last summer when I came ashore. Each night I dream less and less about the sea.

They moved the girl more than a week ago; now I have the little room to myself. Every morning after prayers, Sister Signe comes down and sits with me for a while. She's questioned me about my past; I picked out certain parts of it to tell her. She's the first person I've ever met who lives what they call a religious life. Of course, Henry believed in God too, but for him it was more like something he couldn't help. And the priest on the blacktop barge was a wolf in sheep's clothing. Sister Signe treats me very nicely, but she scares me a little too; there's an unspoken threat behind everything she says, as though something very terrible will happen if you don't follow a lot of special rules. One morning she talked about a big battle in a place called Armageddon; all the people in the world are going to fight each other there on Doomsday. I started laughing; she was very insulted:

— How can something that's already all over come to an end? I asked.

— I'm talking about the Armageddon in your heart!

The next day she came back and sat with me again. She took my pulse; I held my breath to make it go up a little. Before Petsamo took off he said I won't be able to stay here when I get well; only women are allowed to stay. So I do all I can to stay sick. The cough's been a great help, and I also pretended a couple of times to have a fit; I threw myself on the dirt floor, my arms and legs out stiffly to the sides and my face screwed up to show my teeth. A long time ago I saw one of the crew acting like that after he got hit over the head with a winch.

The other Sisters aren't as scary as Signe. One of them never says a word; she just walks around all day with her head bowed, mumbling to herself. Another is giggly; she babbles on and tells you ahead of time everything she's going to do. "Now I'm going to wash your left ear," she says, and then she does it. "Now I'm going to wash your right ear" and "Now I'm going to wash your neck." She spends twice as much time on everything as anyone else.

My lower parts I have to wash myself. At first I didn't understand that I was never supposed to let them see my crotch. Finally Sister Signe told me herself, but she didn't really explain why. Are my ass and my cock so horrible? When it was calm at sea, people shat out in the open. It's true that certain people didn't seem to want to show their cock, but I think that was because they were ashamed of its small size; they were hiding it for selfish reasons, not because they were being considerate.

One of the Sisters keeps flirting with me. Her name is Klara, and she says she's more than eighty years old. But she makes eyes at me just the way older men used to when I was a teenager. When you come down to it, men and women seem to act pretty much alike. Maybe women are a little more held back—except for Sister Klara.

— Jesus was a gorgeous man with long legs, she says while she's washing me.

On the crucifix in my room there's a skinny, emaciated Jesus. He died more than two thousand years ago for our sins. He was both a human being and a God and sometimes they called him the Son of Man. I don't think they explained about him very well—what he did and in what way it helped us. But they say he was worshiped all over the world. He was the most famous person in history.

I'm well enough to be up and around for an hour or so each day. What I like most is to take short walks around the promontory on (or rather in) which the Sodality's built. It juts out into a fairly large freshwater lake fed by underground springs; the water's warm, which means the lake never freezes over. But it smells like sulfur and there's no life in it at all.

Sister Signe wants me to spend the time I'm out of bed going to their masses or the other services they hold in the Chapel with the pointy roof. I've never seen a house with that kind of pointed roof—a real house, that is: I'm not counting the pictures the Captain showed me in *Famous Buildings*. The Chapel has a smooth stone floor, which is surprisingly warm. I go there just to get a chance to walk on it with bare feet; it gives me such a rush of pleasure my cock stands up. The services themselves are boring; I don't understand a word, but the wax candles are very beautiful—and so is the delicate bell Sister Signe rings from time to time. They have a Bible, too. She reads it aloud, but unfortunately it's usually in such bits and pieces I can't make sense of it. A lot of what goes on here is hard for an outsider to understand. They keep the Bible in a safe with a combination lock. It's the first time I've seen a safe used as a safe. On the islands in the middle archipelago I've seen thousands of safes and strongboxes—because they were hard to rebuild into anything useful, there were piles of them in the giant heaps of scrap metal. But what kind of fool would put his gold, compass, watch, wine, sea charts, needle, thread, wood, oil, eyeglasses, or cigarette lighter into a safe? What you want to keep, you either keep close to your body or bury in a safe place somewhere in the ground.

— YOU'RE looking quite well, Edvin, says Sister Signe. We'll have to show you off to Petsamo soon.

What she means is that as soon as Petsamo comes back, it's good-bye, Edvin. But it's been more than three weeks, and he hasn't come back yet. Where is he? Where does he live?

— Petsamo is one of the very few people we can trust. He has done us great services, and still continues to do so. When we pray we always first ask Jesus Christ to ease our suffering and lighten our burden. But Petsamo is a blessing too. I always keep a candle burning for him. The day he doesn't return will be the day we have no one with a knowledge of medicine. Of course Sister Anna can stop the flow of blood by her mere presence, but what good is that if we don't know where the blood is coming from, and why? In his youth Petsamo was an army medic. One day he turned up here by accident. That was almost twenty years ago—when we were led to this place by the hand of God and decided to settle here. He arrived the very day Roland's madmen fled to the east again, leaving all of us bleeding and wailing. In those days he carried many medical books with him; later, we kept some here. But the next time the men raided us they found the books and used them for fuel. The books he had with him were stolen. Nowadays, his head is the sole vessel of his knowledge—and his hands of course. Have you ever heard the expression "healing hands"?

I haven't. But I've met quite a few sailors who knew something about sickness—or at least said they did. That kind of knowledge is very useful, almost as valuable as navigation. I've seen people recover after having their blood let or getting needles stuck in their skin. But I've also seen them get well after eating an executed man's ashes or wrapping a rag with magic symbols around their foreheads. Medicine makes about as much sense to me as religion.

A dazzling spring day. A bright February sun bakes down on the black lake. On the low ridges there are still some patches of wet snow. From the ridge where I'm standing I have a view of the whole spit of land in which the Rabbit-Convent's hidden. Only the pointy roof of the Chapel is really visible; the rest of it lies concealed under moss roofing. If not for the Chapel, you wouldn't know anything at all was there.

I decide to take a look at the Convent's farmlands; they're supposed to be less than a half hour's walk north. Although there's still snow, you can tell that it's more fertile here; among other plants I recognize heather and blackthorn. In a shallow hollow I come across knee-high plants with green needles; their long, twisting trunks crawl along the ground, sending up little shoots here and there. The needles are very prickly. Some of the roots are coming out of the ground too, and you can't tell them from the trunks. In Henry's wood mine I saw pieces of many kinds of trees. This one can't be spruce. Maybe it's pine, more likely juniper. Could there still be real trees on this island? I get so excited at the thought that I run down the next ridge without looking where I'm going; I almost fall over a fence made of old bed frames. The outsides of the frames are black with rust but the thin links themselves are fairly uncorroded; they must be galvanized.

I climb over the fence. Inside, the wet ground and snow are dotted with animal tracks. These don't look like rabbit prints; they're pointier and deeper. Suddenly the animals come bounding out from behind some large boulders—five or six big dogs with skinny legs and giant bellies. I hurry back to the fence, jump over, and continue to the top of the ridge. They aren't dogs. I've seen German shepherds a few times. The owner of one of the largest boats in the archipelago had German shepherds on board. But one winter they went too—like everything else that was edible. These animals don't try to climb the fence. Their legs and heads are black, and their barrel-shaped bodies are covered with long, matted gray fur, which seems as if it's falling out in spots. Their ears are fairly small, and they stand up or lie back along their heads. When they open their mouths I can see that their teeth aren't as pointy as dogs' teeth, but their black noses look a lot like rabbits'. The strangest thing of all is the eyes: They're pretty big, and they look like they're about to pop out of their heads. The pupils aren't round the way they are on other living things; these have a slit or a crack right down the middle of the gray-yellow centers. When they lift up their heads, they look something like the llama-animals in the Captain's *Animals of the World*. But they don't have humps!

WHEN we eat, they don't let me sit on the same bench as the Sisters. But they do let me in the same room, a beautiful limestone vault. It's warm and dry here. All the ground under us is volcanic, which accounts for the pleasant temperature. The Sisters sit on a long bench with their bowls resting on their knees; the girl's at one end in regular clothes, long pants and a sweater and a knitted cap pulled down over her forehead. I'm sitting on a stool near the opposite wall, my clay bowl between my knees. Before we can start to eat, one of the Sisters says a long mealtime prayer. You're not supposed to look up—you have to stare down into your empty bowl and keep your hands folded over it. Some of the Sisters mumble or groan along with the prayer; the others just sit and stare emptily in the air.

The girl cries quietly, but when the soup comes she cheers up and shovels it in faster than anyone else.

Where's my gold? The pellets I finally shat out are probably lost, but the ones I threw up the Sisters must have noticed when they emptied the plate. I don't know how many pellets I managed to swallow; maybe there's still one lonesome filling wandering around in my body. But why should I worry about gold? All it's given me so far is trouble.

What is this in the soup? Small slices of something gray and chewy swimming around among the potatoes and turnips. Some pieces have a stem and above it a semicircular head. Could it be . . . ? I stand up, run quickly up the passageways until I get outside, then stick my fingers down my throat. It's hard to throw up when you're hungry, but it can be done. Everything in my stomach splashes onto the frozen ground. In the evening light I squat down and look carefully at the pieces. I ate so fast that most of it isn't even chewed. They tried to poison me; there were mushrooms in the soup.

Someone puts a hand on my head:

— If you stay like that, your ass is gonna freeze to the ground!

It's Petsamo; he's back! I stand up and hug him. He doesn't push me away but I can feel his body stiffen.

— What's the matter with you?

I pour out the story of the soup and the mushrooms. Why do the good Sisters want to poison me? I know they can't keep me here when I'm well—but why kill me? They could just let me go.

— They're dried champignons.

Now I remember: Champignons are a special kind of mushroom. One of the absolute rules on board was never to eat mushrooms, not even if you were starving to death on a desert island. That was the way the Captain lost half his first crew. Starving, they'd gone ashore; one of the hands had come back, shouting happily that he'd found mushrooms! They picked them and made a soup. The first one died after two days of horrible agony. Although everyone had eaten them, only half died; the others didn't even get sick. That's how unpredictable mushroom poisoning can be.

CHAPTER 8

ON my last night in the Rabbit-Convent the Savior steps down from the crucifix on the wall behind my head. He's hardly half a meter tall, and very wiry. Without the help of any tools, he frees himself from the spikes, then waits for a long time before letting go and dropping to the bench below. He cries out as though he's twisted something and sits for quite a while massaging his left ankle. He pulls off his crown of thorns, tosses it away with a sweeping gesture, then loosens his loincloth and wipes his wounds. When he stands up he fastens the cloth around his middle near his nipples; it's long enough to reach down to his knees.

He climbs off the bench and stands on the hard-packed dirt floor; I'm lying in bed with my hand under my cheek watching him. I feel like pinching or tickling him to make him say something; a person that tiny must have a very squeaky voice. But without the slightest hesitation he climbs into my bed, puts both hands against my side and, bracing himself, tries to heave me aside like a block of stone. He does it again and again; tiny drops of sweat glisten on his forehead. Finally I give in, get off the bed, let him take it over. He falls asleep right away on my pillow. His head is smaller than one of my balls.

THIS is the day I have to leave: Sister Signe herself goes with me to the storeroom to outfit me. Huge amounts of supplies are stored in the ruins and passageways and out on the open ground. First we get clothes from big, dark piles; there's an endless supply of thick, heavy clothes like coats and jackets— but not so many pants, and no shirts at all. She doesn't have to explain why; all cloth that burns easily was used up years ago. I choose a very light jacket to put on first, a warm sweater on top of that, and finally a long overcoat that's in fairly good shape except for missing padding in the shoulders. I get a pair of new boots so I won't have to keep walking around with my feet wrapped in felt. For the inside of the boots she gives me real military boot linings. I can take any mittens and hat I want.

Then we go looking for a backpack. There's a whole room full of army knapsacks, but I choose a light-blue hiking pack with a round emblem of a jumping salmon with a hook in its mouth.

— I want to pay for it.

— Anyone we care for here leaves all his possessions with us. When he departs he's given what he needs.

— And the gold?

— What gold?

I can't decide if she's lying through her teeth or if the gold just . . . disappeared somewhere along the way. In either case, we don't talk any more about it. Instead we go to another vault where hundreds of bicycles are packed tightly together. They're in all colors (even though the paint has peeled off most of them), and there are all kinds: bikes for women, men, children, even tandem bikes. And they all have one thing in common: They have no tubes or tires. Many of them don't have seats either. I don't know why they've kept them all. There are no roads on this island—in fact, there are no roads on any of the land I've ever seen. Now and then you can run across short stretches of broken asphalt in the archipelago, but most of it has been chopped up. Melted asphalt is a very good sealing material for roofs and boats. The reason we've gone to the bicycle storage room isn't for the bicycles, but to get a tent. They're all piled up in a corner of the vault. I don't get to choose my own, but I'm lucky anyway; she gives me a one-man tent with a round opening and an extra all-weather roof. Rolled up, it fits right underneath the strap of my new backpack.

It's time to say good-bye. Sister Signe holds my shoulders firmly, blesses me, and says that if they should need me, I must heed the voice of God. I nod eagerly. I'd like nothing better than for God to call me back to the Convent for the rest of my life. Except for my first years with Papa before the Great Famine, I've never been so content. The other Sisters are less solemn. Old Sister Klara can't stop giving me the eye. The girl (or the Finn as they call her) is sitting in the kitchen mashing turnips. She shakes my hand limply and smiles a little smile before bursting into tears. Maybe I'm the last link to the boat she came from, the one that was raided in the frozen stream. The Sisters strap my pack on my back and give me a few pieces of potato bread. The sun burns down; I'm sweating the moment I leave the Convent. After an hour or so I sit down on a rock to wait for Petsamo, who's also leaving today.

It takes a while before he comes, and I get a chill across my back where I've been sweating. He's not glad to see me; he doesn't stop, barely nods when he passes by with a pack that must weigh twice as much as mine. At first he ignores me. I stop when he stops, speed up on level ground when he does, slow down when he heads downhill, always keeping a distance of about thirty meters between us. Finally he stops, turns around, and calls me over to him:

— This can't go on. I have no intention of taking care of you.

— You don't have to. Just don't drive me away!

He looks at me with a mixture of sorrow and disgust, heaves his pack up on his back again, and starts walking. I wait until he's a hundred meters away before I follow. I keep that distance for the rest of the afternoon, but when he stops to put up his tent I cut it to fifty meters. At sunset he sits on his haunches outside his one-man tent, chewing on his leathery bread, his back turned to me. He crawls in and goes to sleep— so I crawl in my tent and go to sleep too. After an hour or so I crawl out again and hide behind some rocks. Sure enough: In the middle of the night he comes crawling out on all fours, stands up, listens, then quickly begins to pull down his tent. But when he sees that I'm taking mine down too, he stops. We both put them up again and sleep till dawn.

Before we start off in the morning, he calls to me:

— I can't stop you from following me . . . but we may run into people who'll consider you an outlaw—but not me!

I wave happily to him. What can I say? I'm fair game to anyone whether I tag along behind him or wander around the countryside by myself.

I let him get a couple of hundred meters ahead so that I'll be able to see if he really does run into anybody. We pass some scattered scrap-iron heaps piled with car wrecks and smashed-in concrete piping. The countryside's flat and monotonous. If I didn't have the sun to guide me I'd quickly lose my sense of direction. We're still heading due northeast.

ON the morning of the third day I wake up when someone starts shaking my tent pole. I pull out a little knife, the only weapon I have. It's only Petsamo. I crawl out into the morning chill. There's still frost on the ground; the tent lines look like frozen barbed wire. He's made a small fire on a nearby hill; I bundle up and walk over to it with him. Sleep aches in my stomach. I'm still groggy.

The sun doesn't rise in the usual way, directly out of the horizon; first it has to work its way through a layer of super-cooled thundercloud-gray fog blanketing the ocean to the east. We sit on our haunches, drink warm water, chew on our bread, and wait for the first rays of sunlight. When they break through, the whole countryside changes from ice white to gold leaf. Not a breath of wind. Complete silence. The word *holy* occurs to me, but I'm not sure what it means.

— This is the only time of day that makes me feel as if my life has any worth at all, says Petsamo. As soon as the sun is all the way up, I have to start another twenty-three hours of waiting. During the first years I was here, I had enough to do just trying to keep myself alive. That's not true anymore; now I have to keep busy to make the time pass until the sun rises again. In the mornings I want to be alone. The reason I'm sitting with you now is because I want you to hear what I have to say. I can't force you to go away—but perhaps you can understand that you should leave me alone. I don't have any-thing in particular against you; it's just that I can't stand having *anyone* near me. I can trade with people, try to heal them, eat a meal or two with them; I can even sleep a few nights in their houses if I have to. But then I have to get away. I can't explain it. But I can try to tell you how it is: From now on, I'm not going to have you tagging along!

I tell him I understand. I think that must be how most people feel. But most of us can't have it that way. It's Pet-samo's strength and knowledge that make him able to live the way he wants.

— The way I want! I don't want to live at all! But my mood is never quite black enough for me to commit suicide. I'm going to be sixty soon. When a person's as young as you are, he thinks that people's personalities change as they get older. Mature. Rid themselves of certain . . . urges. Find themselves, find—what shall we call it?—inner peace. But it's not true. Either a man works like a dog, never having time to think and therefore rarely getting depressed. Then, when sickness and death do come, they hit him like a bolt out of the blue; he hasn't prepared himself. Or else you have a life like mine: constantly brooding about my own death, the meaninglessness of life, the humiliation of being a thinking creature trapped in his own body. There's no such thing as human dignity! You've never had any education, so you don't know that people have thought this way as long as they've had spare time in which to think. But getting back to growing old: I'm not even very interested in this feeling of meaninglessness anymore. I can't get really angry, scared, happy . . . let's not even talk about love.

— I understand.

— I doubt it. But maybe you will. If you live another thirty years.

We drink and eat while the sun rises higher and the golden frost drips from the blades of grass and the rocks. I don't ask any more questions. If sunrise is the only time he feels alive, I don't want to disturb him. He breaks the silence again himself:

— When the last doctor here on the island committed suicide—that's about twenty years ago—I felt a certain joy, a challenge. I'd been his assistant for a while. He was a bad doctor. Actually he'd been trained as a radiologist . . . that means when you send X rays, radioactive beams, through the body, which give you a picture . . . I know it sounds like magic. But to make a long story short, he happened to be a radiologist. He hated people with wounds and fractures. He imagined that his patients were trying to insult him with the ailments they came to him for—and which he was so bad at curing. He collected his fees in wine; he was perpetually drunk. He didn't even have the sense to protect his medical library; I had to take care of almost everything. I was better suited for the job than he was. The real problem was that he

wasn't flexible enough to change when circumstances de-
manded it. He'd start a job with very high hopes, only to give
up halfway through when he realized that there weren't any
colleagues, any other doctors, to consult. What little that
could be done I soon learned to do better than he. He knew
the Latin names for the muscles, but I knew how to arrange
them like a cushion around the bone after a leg amputation.
Of course that threatened him, and he drank even more. He
fired me—but Roland, who already was the power around
here, made him take me back. One warm summer day he
slashed his wrists and staggered into the water. I grew better
and better at my job, more and more appreciated. And feared.
Not even Roland dared lay a hand on me. I also had the fore-
sight not to teach anyone else. I'm sure you know from your
days at sea that when anyone has a skill, he keeps it to himself.

— Why are you telling me all this? You already told me to
leave.

— Because I get the feeling that you might become like
me, that you already are a little bit. And I don't want that to
happen. Most of all for selfish reasons: I don't want the com-
petition. But also out of a certain nostalgia; a thinking man is
more unhappy than a workhorse. The thinker experiences the
misery long before it actually happens—and so he goes
through it twice. Much better to put your nose to the grind-
stone; that way you only have to die once!

I'm surprised when Petsamo reaches out his hand to touch
my arm. But he stops himself, coughs a little, and covers his
mouth with the hand instead.

— I don't think very much, I say. My imagination isn't
good enough. But I dream a lot. Mostly it's my memories that
catch up with me in dreams. I don't like it. At sea I used to
guzzle down a mug of rice wine every evening. Not only to
stand the Captain's kisses, but just as much to sleep a deep,
dreamless sleep. I think I'd rather learn how to think than be

afraid of being attacked as soon as I fall asleep. And I'd also like to read and write well. I envy you. I don't know anyone I'd rather change places with. At least not on land.

— That's exactly what I'm trying to tell you *not* to want! Thinking just causes suffering!

— I've sucked a lot of captains' cocks to survive—I'd rather think than suck. I'm pretty sure that thinking can be useful, that it can make life a little more bearable. . . .

He gets up and starts to throw pebbles in the fire. He doesn't seem so calm now. I don't think I believe that people lose their feelings as they get older. It doesn't really make sense.

— So you think there's a point to it all! he says angrily. You're just as stupid as the others. The only thing Western culture really succeeded at was blowing itself up. And they didn't even succeed at that one hundred percent. Unfortunately. Do you hear I said *unfortunately*?

— I'm not deaf.

— Human beings are programmed, designed to have children, to develop, progress, expand, whatever. We weren't meant to live in a society, if you can still call it that, that is slowly atrophying, dwindling away.

— But what if everything started over?

— What would be the point? In the course of a few hundred years the earth would be infested with people again—and then boom, all over again! The worst thing we can do is not to accept that we're through.

— And yet you still save people's lives?

— My meal ticket. Let me just tell you that when someone dies on me, you don't catch me crying. I envy them. I've killed more than a hundred out of sheer mercy. I can do it quickly, if not always painlessly. Those corpses you saw when we were at the stream with Roland? I killed them. His men torture people just to the point of death, but then they get tired and leave them there. The greatest service I can perform is *not* to cure (which I rarely do), not to lessen the pain (which I can do sometimes). My real service is murder.

He seems suddenly to realize how upset he is—just after he got through telling me he has no feelings. Disgusted with himself, he starts kicking out the fire. I'm thinking about Henry. He hasn't come back in any of my dreams to complain or haunt me; that can only mean he's content.

CHAPTER 9

THEY'VE kept me locked in this cellar for two days. Now I've got to get out to take a shit. I've had a few drinks of water but no food; I peed down the floor drain. I've got to get out. I bang on the metal-covered door with the peephole; of course no one comes. The cramps rise in waves. Finally I pull down my pants, lift up the grating, and squat over the drain. The door flies open and the same man who locked me up steps in:

— We don't shit on the floor around here!

I waddle out with my pants at half-mast. He shoves me up the narrow steps with his rifle butt, opens the door, and points vaguely out toward the level plains where the wind is sweeping the snow in long strokes over the crusted ground. I shuffle ten or twenty meters away from the low building that looks like it's been chopped off above the ground floor. Three dogs spot me and trot over with a mixture of respect and self-importance. They look like those German shepherds I saw at sea; but these have shorter legs and thicker bodies, and their tails arch upward as though to make you notice their assholes. The largest has a white patch around his neck that looks like a bib. For years a bib was the only thing left from my childhood with Papa in the shelter—then one day somebody needed it for kindling. The two smaller ones have no bibs; they're completely gray-green. When I stop, they stop too and sit down on the ground.

Behind the sawed-off house with the cellar are a few flat-topped concrete pavilions that look like they've been built fairly recently. Behind them on a hill is a stone tower—circular, maybe twenty meters high and with another section on top made of cinder blocks; now and then you can see a guard inside the walls with an automatic rifle and heavy binoculars around his neck. Built onto the foot of the tower is a small wing made of tarred planks; that's where Roland lives.

When I squat down, the dogs move up, their necks stretched forward; when I stand up, they sit down with their heads cocked to the side. I slide a few steps along the crusted ground—the dogs follow—and squat down again with my back to the icy wind. They bend their front legs, stretch their necks again, push their long snouts forward as though to lick my ass. I ignore them and do what I have to do. Before my pants are halfway up, the lead dog with the bib rushes forward and gobbles up my shit. With jerky motions, his eyes half shut with pleasure, he swallows his prize. The other two fight over the chance to lick the brown spot on the ice.

My guard's nowhere in sight. The man on the tower stands leaning over the wall, totally absorbed in looking at something out at sea with his binoculars. If I ran away neither of them would have time to react quickly enough. But I'm not going to. I can't manage out there alone. I myself asked Petsamo to take me here. Naturally they recognized me and wondered why Henry let me go. Petsamo told them that Henry'd died from a burst bladder—and that I had no master now. Right away they started calling Henry names. Everyone had something to say.

Finally they all agreed that fucking Henry was the biggest sadist
who ever walked on two feet; anyone who'd been stuck in here
for even a month knew that. Then they locked me in the cellar.

THE next morning I get a piece of smoked fish. I'm overjoyed!
I think it's mackerel, the most common fish in these waters.
The Captain wouldn't eat it because they say it eats dead
things—but of course the rest of us had no choice. But I love
it, salted as well as dried! I've hardly ever had it smoked. It's
much safer to smoke fish on land to protect your boat from
possible fires, but on our boat the first safety rule was never to
go ashore unless it was *absolutely* necessary.

I barely start to lick my piece of fish before the guard's back
in the doorway:

— Roland wants you!

I wrap it in my scarf; if I leave it here I may never see it
again. Then he leads me to the blockhouse next to what he
calls the Guard Tower.

The blockhouse seems to consist of only one room. It
doesn't have its own entrance; you have to get in through the
Guard Tower, through an opening which may once have been
a window—now there's a thick iron door in it. The doors to
the Tower are also iron and can be barred shut from the inside
with a piece of railroad track. Roland's lying in a big wooden
bed in the middle of the floor. Behind him flickers a potbellied
stove filled with tar-smelling embers. He's asleep. The guard
leaves me in front of the carved foot of the bed. The face on
the pillow is flame red, as though it's reflecting the fire. His
snoring is strong but uneven; every now and then it turns into
a series of yelps. His thick forearm covered with blue and red
tattoos is hanging out of the bed. Even the fingers are tattooed:
the forefinger with an ace of hearts, the middle finger with
clubs, the ring finger with diamonds, the pinky spades.

Clothes and weapons hang all over the walls. I've never seen so many automatic weapons in one place. Most of them are unfamiliar to me, but I can identify an M-16, an Uzi, and a Russian-made carbine just like the one the Captain gave me. Could mine have ended up here? There are also pistols, each with a detachable silencer, as well as hunting rifles, especially double-barreled shotguns. When I look at the tattooed forearm again, I notice that the hand is very close to a holster nailed to the side of the bed. A beautifully shaped mother-of-pearl pistol handle sticks out. Below the only window—not much larger than a gun-slit—orange-red reflections from the stove play over a jumbled pile of glistening bayonets.

Before I notice he's awake he starts talking:

— So you're the one they call Edvin Pussylips?

— That's right.

— And what gives you the right to take up space?

He struggles onto his elbows and glares at me with small, bulging eyes; the whites are almost as red as his cheeks.

— No fucking idea? So we might as well throw you back into the ocean, eh?

— I can work.

— How?

— Fish, hunt, grow potatoes . . . or, if you want, more . . . personal services.

The last remark amuses him immensely; he lisps in a high falsetto:

— My dear Pussylips, what I want to know is whether you can do something no one *else* can do! Just think of it like this: Finally I have the chance to talk to Roland. Roland pulls *all* the strings. What might Roland want . . . that Roland doesn't already have?

— First I have to know what you have.

— Can you read?

— Sort of.

— I don't want to listen to anyone stuttering along. It's got to be smooth and with feeling. Get it?

I don't know what to say. I shrug my shoulders and nod with my chin.

— Can you play anything? I mean musical instruments. Last Christmas we got a clarinet in a trade, but it's broken. Can you fix it?

— I'm not bad with clocks. . . .

He thinks about it for a moment, coughs, and drops a thick gob of spit into a bowl next to the bed.

— I'm too fat. Petsamo's been telling me that for years. But I'm trying to eat myself to death. And it's nobody's business but mine. Come over here!

I walk to the side of the bed. With a crooked finger he signals me to bend toward him. He tries to whisper something in my ear, but it ends up closer to my eye:

— I've stopped going outside. What's the point? But I need someone to tell me what's going on. Someone I can depend on. That person could be you, Pussylips. But why should I trust you? Give me one good reason.

— Can I think about it?

He pushes me away, sits up, and starts talking in a booming voice while his eyes drift from the window to the entryway, as though someone's standing outside listening.

— You know any jokes? *Good ones!*

— No. I told you: clocks.

— Clocks my ass. You've got to understand the gravity of the situation, Pussylips. How can I justify to my men letting you stay inside here where it's warm or even allowing you to stay alive at all if you can't *do* anything?

As he says that I spot a box sticking out from under the bed. Once I saw somebody sell one of those—it's a record player. I point to it:

— Does it work?

— How the hell should I know when there's no electricity?

— The one I saw you could crank up.

— Well, could you put in a crank?

I bend over and pull it out. It's full of dead electrical parts, but it does have a turntable and an undamaged pickup arm.

— I could try to rebuild it. If you can spare some good-sized clocks with working parts.

EVEN though I complain; they keep me locked in the cellar; since Roland hasn't told them to let me out, I have to stay where I am. The guard's emptied a whole bag of clockworks onto the floor: broken alarm clocks, a cuckoo clock, a table clock with gilded plastic angels, a car dashboard whose gauges still have numbers on them—except for the digital clock, which will never work again. I'm still waiting for the tools they promised me yesterday.

At night I dream about a pack of dogs no bigger than mice. In the daytime they sit huddled together next to the iron door, their whiskers twitching; at night they tiptoe closer and closer. While I'm in my deepest sleep, they slip into my asshole and crawl up my intestines, eating their way along. They build a lair inside me and bring up litter after litter.

I like my other dream better. I'm at sea. It's warm; a soft breeze is blowing from the stern to starboard; and a square, striped sail billows above my head. Men with long oars are ranged along the gunwales in double rows. We build up speed; the water at the prow begins to foam. Then the ship begins to rise! Immediately all the oarsmen stop rowing and hold their oars in a horizontal position as we slowly rise up and up, lifted by a veil of glittering, rainbow-colored mist. Up here it's completely silent. The horizon begins to curve. A few hours later we can't see the ocean any longer; the planet earth is turning behind us like a heavy, honey-yellow moon.

*   *   *

THEY call Roland's right-hand man Pretty Boy; he sees to it that the daily work gets done. He has an old burn scar that has curled up his left ear and left the skin on his cheek and neck gray-white and shiny. The skin across his cheekbone is taut—it glistens like polished stone—and at the front of his neck it looks like crumpled tissue paper. His mouth is thin and tight; all you can see of his eyes are slits glittering between the thick folds of his swollen eyelids. They're always tearing, and he's almost always wiping his cheeks with the backs of his hands, which are tattooed as much as Roland's. He scares me a hell of a lot more than Roland. He's all business; he has no sense of humor at all.

He tells me that I have to get up the next morning before dawn; my job is going to be earth blasting. (Nobody pays any attention to the fact that Roland told me to rebuild the record player; I can do that in my spare time.) Before I go to work, I get a mug of water, a crust of bread, and five minutes on my haunches with the dogs watching me. They get nothing to eat but shit—and whatever they can steal. Then, together with five other cold and sleepy men, I stumble after Pretty Boy into the countryside. We're pulling a sledge, and the frozen ground crunches under our boots as we approach a long, high pile of earth. Half of it's caved in and pockmarked with deep holes, but on the undamaged half two old men are sticking long probes into the ground and pumping them up and down. Apparently they're trying to find the exact location of something far beneath the ground.

This is how they do the blasting. First they dig a hole in a likely spot and take a hand grenade with a long piece of steel wire tied to the pin. With the probe they stuff the grenade as far down as possible, then pull out the probe—careful not to jerk the wire too—and put a small stick across the hole so they can pull the wire out horizontally across the ground. How much wire you get above ground depends on how deep the hole is. If you're lucky it can be ten, fifteen meters; if not, only two or three. We blasters crouch like sprinters at the starting gun, the wire wound around one finger. When Pretty Boy gives the signal, we take off, the wire tightens, and the pin is pulled out of the grenade. The average time between the moment you pull the pin and the explosion is *supposed* to be five seconds. But since the grenades are at least thirty-three years old, it can vary a lot. Some go off right away, others not at all—those are the most dangerous. You can get at them only by digging down with a spade. Or by trying to blast them with another grenade—which may not explode either.

Two of us take turns blasting; the others prepare the explosives and dig up whatever they can find—mostly old, worm-eaten electrical poles. There must have been a transformer or some other kind of power station here at one time that required a lot of poles and thick cable; the stuff around here isn't ordinary telephone cable, and it wouldn't pay to blast for telephone poles anyway, since they stand fifty meters apart. Pretty Boy would like to get the poles out in one piece so they can be used for building blockhouses. But we don't manage to do that even once while I'm doing it. Splinters and stumps are all we get—good fuel of course, but useless for building.

We blasters sit around a lot. The other's name is Klaus. He doesn't talk right; he mixes foreign words with regular ones. In a whisper he tells me that he's fifty-one and he comes from Germany. Pretty Boy has forbidden us to talk; one of the few things he's ever said is that you get more work done in silence. But Klaus can't help it; he leans up next to me, wants me to look into his eyes. But when I do look him straight in the eye, he gets nervous and his gaze wavers. His mouth is soft and yearning—I don't like it. He makes sure to tell me that he's an upstanding person who just happened to end up in the Prison more than ten years after it was used for prisoners; he sort of stumbled into Roland and his men, and they let him stay. Like me, he's got nothing to go back to; our pasts have been erased.

KLAUS shows me the tricks of the trade. The biggest danger isn't the explosion itself but the earth slides that the explosives can set off. He's been buried in several small ones, but he's been lucky and got away with only a broken wrist. If you feel that the hillside is starting to slide out from under you, says Klaus, the best thing is to try to roll down on an angle right away. Never try to run up or stay where you are. Over the years four men have been lost in blasting slides. But because there used to be more people, Pretty Boy was more careless; nowadays the ones who get killed can't be replaced as easily. I'm the first person to come along in years. I ask why they don't let stranded sailors live. Klaus says it's because most of them put up a fight. But as they've grown older Roland and Pretty Boy have also grown more suspicious. New men might upset the balance of power. However, when you come right down to it, says Klaus, the real reason is hate; the men here have an uncontrollable hatred toward anything from the sea.

— Why?

— Because the worst thing of all came from the sea. The Flood drowned fifty thousand on this island alone! And it destroyed the *City.* That's where they all came from. They were here in this institution as teenage boys, sentences of a few months, a year at most. They still long to return to the *City!*

I'M having a hard time with the record player. Nothing fits. I need a jeweler's loupe but all they give me is an old, scratched magnifying glass. So first I have to look through it, then put it down, work, then look again. I get tools only one at a time, the guard tells me how long I can keep them, and when the time's up he comes in and jerks the screwdriver out of my hand just as I'm getting something right. I've stopped complaining. Pretty Boy was down the other day glowering at me.

— You actually made Roland believe you can fix that thing?

— I said I'd try.

— But you feel we're making it hard for you?

— It could be easier.

— How?

— If I could use the workshop. And tools. And if you gave me a few more old clocks.

— Roland hasn't given any orders for you to use the workshop!

— Let me talk to him.

— *Roland* decides when he wants to talk to anybody. That's the system we've always had around here. The warden always decided when he wanted to see someone, and we've kept it that way. Don't think we don't have our traditions!

So I stay in the cellar. Every morning they bring me up for the blasting; every evening they lock me in again. I get a couple of hours with the record player before the light grows too faint. I have no lamp, but it's March now and the evenings are getting lighter. I'm wondering what Roland's going to play on my record player.

CHAPTER 10

FINALLY Roland sends for me. This time he's up on the Guard Tower's terrace. They've stretched a large hammock between the walls, and Roland lies sprawled on a mountain of pillows, his legs dangling out on either side. On a table next to him is a washbasin full of boiled meat; he uses a short, sharp knife to dig at the vertebrae and shoulder bones. He's also eating rice straight out of a pot, kneading it into little balls and stuffing it into his face; stray kernels dangle from his thin beard like white lice. As soon as I arrive he sends away the guard and the man who brought me, then tells me to make sure they really went down. Now I understand why he wanted to meet me up here: not for the view—he can't see anything from the hammock—but to make sure no one spies on us.

— I'm eating myself to death. It's an old vow I made to myself in the days of the Great Famine: When things get better I'm going to eat myself right out of this fucking life! But perhaps you, Pussylips, have a better idea?

— Not better. Just quicker.

— Don't be a wise guy. . . . Just tell me what's going on down below. I want to hear it all. Even things you think aren't important.

So I tell him about the blasting and the evenings with the record player. I suggest they let me work in the workshop. But he's not interested in the record player. He wants to know if anyone but me is locked in the cellar, who stands guard and how often they change, and if any of the old guys has seemed especially happy or unusually quiet lately. He's particularly interested in Pretty Boy:

— Has the Boy punched anyone out lately?

— Ingmar got it once. He sat down on a sled.

— Ingmar?

— The one who's always a little bent over—he says his back grew in crooked.

— Oh, Quasimodo . . . He's started calling himself Ingmar? We named him Quasimodo after the hunchback. You know, the disgusting one?

— A movie?

— Yeah, they played it on TV.

— Must have been before my time.

Roland stops chewing and glares straight at me with his bulging eyes; he must be fat inside too, so full of blubber that it makes his eyes stand out.

— Keep your eye on Quasimodo and Pretty Boy. When someone starts beating up on someone else there's always the possibility they've got something going together.

— A love affair?

— What love affair? I'm talking conspiracy! You know what a conspiracy is? It's when people gang up on you. And since I'm locked up here in this tower, how am I supposed to *know* when they're ganging up on me?

He gives me a huge wink and slaps his belly, setting off a belch that comes rumbling up from inside. But he goes right on stuffing himself with meat and rice. Klaus tells me that Roland owns all the rice on the island. Years ago he found a shipwreck with more than three hundred tons in vacuum-packed aluminum containers. A lot of it was sold off to sailors, but tons are supposed to be buried around the island. Only

Roland himself knows all the hiding places; it's been a fool-proof way of stopping anyone else from taking over. I wonder if the Captain's rice came from here.

It's cold in the Tower. Wet snow whirls out of the gray, low-hanging clouds, and you can hear the ocean better than see it.

— If I could work in the workshop I could finish the record player faster.

— Faster . . . Why *faster*? You and I should be thankful that we've got the record player to talk about. It gives us a reason for *meeting*, he whispers. So don't rush it, Pussylips. Because then we'll have to think up something else. Maybe you could come and tell jokes, or read aloud. It just so happens I have a few hundred newspapers I stopped the boys from burning up.

THE constant March rain interrupts the blasting work. As soon as we make a hole it fills with mud. So they start me chipping rust in the workshop. It's in a tall sheet-metal barn, the biggest building I've ever been in. It seems to have been built fairly recently; all the older buildings show traces of the Flood's changing water levels—wide dirty-gray or moldy-green bands. The collection of tools in there must literally be worth its weight in gold: pliers, Phillips screwdrivers, wrenches, drill bits, vernier calipers, and many others no one can make any-more. Simple chisels, hammers, axes, and knives can be ground from scrap metal. Nails can be made from wire. But not screws. Doing simple soldering or riveting isn't hard, but they can't do any welding; their gas tanks have been empty for years. Almost everything they do in the workshop barn is re-pairing, trying to patch things together. That's why half the building is filled with the biggest pile of scrap metal I've ever seen. At sea everybody agreed that in order to put together one working pump, you had to have about ten broken ones of the same model—plus material for gaskets. Here in the workshop they say they can make a pump out of only five discarded ones.

One thing I can't understand is the old men's incredible interest in motors and engines. They have a number of more or less complete ones, everything from V-8s to lawnmowers. But they'll never get them to run. For that you need gasoline, and the only stuff anyone ever comes across in barrels or tanks went bad decades ago because of the additives. I don't understand why they don't just work on diesels; with a little know-how you can make them run on anything from crude oil to vegetable oil. Once the *Diana* ran for several hours on rapeseed oil without stalling that many times; it smelled like we were frying the whole ocean! But what good are high-compression engines? Or jet engines? One of those stands gleaming in its own separate tent inside the workshop.

If they'd only use their know-how for something useful. They could set up a shipyard to repair boats; there isn't a tool shop like this one in the whole archipelago. The only shipyard I know of is over by Copper Key. What they did there was load two barges up with rocks and sink them. Now they run smaller boats into the space between and tip them over with stanchions and winches to get at the metal underplating. To have just a couple of plates replaced costs a fortune; if the Captain had brought *Diana* in there, he would have had to give them half the boat. So we did the best we could by ourselves. Either by diving, which took forever because you had to come up for air every other minute. Or by running her up on a sandbar at high tide and letting the ebb tip her over. The old-timers claim that in the past there was hardly any tide in the Baltic. Not that what's there now is anything to brag about.

I have to chip rust from engine parts and pipes. The castings crack a lot no matter how careful I am. The Butcher says that the metal gets tired after a number of years on the bottom of the ocean, and once that happens it's dead and you can never use it again even if it's melted down and recast. I don't believe it; I think the failures are more likely due to bad casting techniques. I've never seen anyone manage to get a high enough and even enough temperature no matter how many bellows and how much good charcoal they have.

When I'm not chipping rust I help in the kitchen. I've never seen so much food. Unopened aluminum rice containers stand in high stacks; when they're empty they're used for salting down fish. There are potatoes too, but they've been stored badly and allowed to shrivel up and sprout. And turnips and some long green things called corn. No farming is done here at the Prison; the Convent supplies almost everything, even the potatoes and rapeseed oil. If there's any meat around, Roland's the only one who gets it. The strangest thing is that they don't make any beer or rice wine. And I've noticed that the old men never smell of alcohol or act drunk. According to Roland, there are two great threats to male friendship: broads and booze.

SUDDENLY it's spring. A warm, rosy haze covers the countryside. The ocean stinks of last year's seaweed. Now all eyes are turned to the sea. Even Klaus and I haul seaweed—because of the flies it's spread out to dry a good kilometer south of the Guard Tower. When we're let out to shit in the mornings, the dogs aren't interested in us anymore; they're more interested in the seaweed.

Klaus and I also go on beachcombing patrol. We're supposed to get as far as we can either north or south, then turn around and report back to the guard in the Tower before dark. The beachcombing is always done in pairs so that one person can run home and get the others if they're needed.

We set out before dawn, jogging north, our eyes glued to the ground so that we won't twist our ankles. After a while, as the light starts to rise in the east, we slow down and comb carefully through big piles of stones; a guard in the Tower can still see us through high-powered binoculars. Soon we arrive at a small promontory with the usual square concrete bunker. Klaus slides down against the bunker's north side:

— Come, friend. No one can see us now.

I fall to my knees next to him, breathing heavily.

— No, *sit!*

He pats a large flat rock. I lean back against the wall. The rock under my ass feels warm and smooth. Klaus takes my hand; I let him. We sit like that for a while, half an hour maybe, squeezing each other's hands and breathing in the thin, salty breeze that the mounting light drives in from the sea. Then we start off again, carrying our boots. I try to pretend that Klaus isn't really fifty, that we're both kids—finally I've got a playmate! Laughing, we leap over blocks of bone-smooth stone. We're each carrying a backpack for the things we find; no one's been on the beach since Christmas, so they expect it to be littered with treasures. It isn't. Klaus has been combing this beach for years, and he says that there's less and less to be found. But we know that if we come back empty-handed, we'll have to pay the consequences—as Pretty Boy puts it. Klaus knows just what to do: He's brought along stuff from the Prison, which he lines up on the sand:

— An electric light socket, a bottle neck, some corks, half a shoe and so . . . a spark plug!

He lets me hold it. I used to collect plugs. The enamel on this one's chipped but you can still make out the brand name: Bosch. The plug is the very life of an engine, the spark that sets everything in motion, producing hundreds, even thousands of kilowatts of energy. Do people and animals have something like spark plugs inside them too? Is *that* what makes us alive?

— We share, says Klaus.

— Will it be enough?

— No problem, he says, pushing down the back of my

neck so that my forehead hits the sand. What do you want most? The spark plug?

— I'd never be able to give it in.

— Then take the corks too. Give back those.

When we get farther north, the usual red sea mist lifts. Now the sun itself is visible; as always, it makes me a little nervous. But I forget about it when Klaus shows me something he's found: a piece of board that fire has scorched to look as if it's been run over by a tire. We jump for joy. It's an exciting find! They'll study it for hours in the Prison. Was there a fire at sea? Or did currents take it here all the way from the Continent? Maybe they'll think it's so important that we'll get to show it to Roland ourselves.

When the small, fierce sun is hovering directly above us, a black dot whirling in the heavens, we lie down out of the wind, eat dried fish and cold potatoes, and wash it all down with warm water. Below us a small lagoon has been formed behind a line of almost completely worn-down rock pillars; water from the ocean comes in when the clucking little waves spill over the sandbar. The lagoon is maybe ten meters wide, almost half as long, and at the most half a meter deep. Klaus wants us to go swimming. I don't know; all winter I haven't washed anything but my hands and face. If I go in now, it'll make me notice my own smell; I'll know how soaked through with dirt and sweat my skin and clothes really are. To make me do it Klaus throws in the burned piece of wood. But I don't go in, so he pulls off his pants and wades in himself.

— It's warm!

I don't believe him; his gray ass has goosebumps, his half-erect cock shrinks to the size of a pinky.

— Come in, friend!

I roll up my pants legs and hesitantly step in above my ankles. A chill runs up my calves.

— Don't get your pants wet, idiot!

But I'm not taking them off; I don't want to have another
lover boss me around. I toss the piece of wood onto shore and
get out too. He shuffles behind me in a sulk. Then he suggests
that I dry him off and I do it because I don't want to get him
any more annoyed. As soon as his prick revives from the cold,
though, I stop. He grabs his pants angrily and walks off to put
them on. I'm relieved . . . and disappointed. I can feel how
swollen my prick's gotten—it's been so long since I've been
close to someone.

— I tell you something if you promise not to tell. His
voice is friendlier now.

I don't say a word. It's up to him if he wants to trust me.

— A small boat wouldn't be hard to hide . . . and the
easiest way to get food is to kill a dog.

— If it's so easy why haven't you done it?

— I don't know how to sail. But you . . .

I shrug my shoulders. He can interpret it any way he
wants.

— And you know navigating too? You've been so many
years to sea.

— Only by landmarks.

— That's good enough.

— Where to?

— Ah, where . . .

Then we just sit there, our noses to our knees. He begins
to cry, and I take his hand, then put his head on my knee. I
wish I could say what I'm thinking: Of course we'll run away.
But not by sea. Out there the only things waiting for us are
death and destruction, storms, hidden shoals, barren coastlines
. . . and pirates. But on land we could go to Henry's place, dig
up gold in the graveyard, and then maybe head north, past the
Prison, and try our luck at the north end of the island. Or we
could go to the Convent, buy a good tent and other things we
need and keep moving along the cliffs till Roland's men get

tired of searching for us. They're all getting old now, and they don't feel much like traipsing around the countryside. But to tell him all this now would be too risky. It's still too soon.

IN the middle of the night I hear a volley of shots; in the morning the ground's covered with snow. Instead of chipping rust they want me to dig a grave—they take me to a spot east of the workshop and give me a spade and an ax to chop through roots. When I've dug about a meter down they bring the corpse sewn into two sacks and drop it next to the grave, leaving without another word. Who is he? Why were they shooting? Was it an execution, a duel, an accident, a suicide? The deeper I dig, the more convinced I am that it's Klaus. They discovered our escape plans, shot him, and now they're making me bury him to put the fear of God in me. I've always been scared of corpses, especially if they're covered up or in boxes. They seem more dangerous when you can't see their hands or faces; you don't know what they might do.

After I've dropped the sack into the grave, I decide I have to take a look; I cut open a seam with the ax. It's not Klaus but Ingmar—Quasimodo—staring straight up with his jaw tied shut and two coins pushed into his eye sockets. One of the coins slides out and slips under the jaw binding.

That evening a few of the boys go out after dinner and fire some warning shots over the grave.

A couple of days later Roland sends for me again. Klaus has heard rumors that he might be sick; the only thing they're sending up from the kitchen to the Guard Tower is watery, mushed-up rice. When they push me across the threshold Roland's sitting in his enormous bed, his forehead pale yellow and his eyes staring wearily in front of him. Petsamo sits on a stool next to him.

— And here comes ol' Pussy-Puss.

Petsamo barely looks up; he's busy digging something out of his knapsack.

— Petsamo says I have to stop eating. I've got gallstones.

— Not stop. Just take it easy, says Petsamo.

— As far as I know, no one's ever managed to eat himself to death on mashed rice!

He tries to laugh but it turns into a pained grimace. Petsamo picks up his knapsack and ties it shut.

— Don't act like I'm contagious, you fucking baseball star! Pussylips, don't suppose you've ever heard of baseball?

— No.

— American ball game? Never heard Petsamo talk about it? Or seen him throw a ball? He can hit a bird in the fucking air . . . if there were any birds around. Everyone thinks they named him Petsamo after some goddamn Russian harbor. Wrong . . . Petsamo, Missouri! Hasn't told you about that, has he, kid? All right now, here's the point: Petsamo wants you to sail him up to the radio station. I assume you *can* sail?

— If the boat isn't too big.

— An aluminum skiff; you ought to be able to handle that. But tell me: What other man on this whole damn island would have the nerve to march in here and expect to walk away with one of my men?

— I'll have him back in a week, says Petsamo.

So it's decided that I sail with Petsamo the next day. But we don't. At dawn the alarm sounds; the Tower's spotted a ship. All lanterns and fires are put out. Everyone gathers behind a long sand dune on the beach. They decide to use the skiff I was supposed to sail for Petsamo to lure in the unknown ship—Klaus and I are ordered to man the boat, and we row out about fifty meters. Men with automatic weapons and mortars position themselves behind the sand dune. A couple of the old guys get in a canoe and hide among the boulders along the beach. Then the Tower reports that the ship has changed course to the north. They tell us to head farther out to sea. We paddle and row with our sails slack to the wind. Ever since I told Klaus that I'm going away with Petsamo, he's been upset. One minute he wants us to take off right now in the skiff, the next he realizes it's impossible and swears he'll kill himself if I leave him. We get farther and farther from land until he finally pulls himself together and yells out for us to stop; he's seen others go out too far and get captured because the people on land couldn't get to them in time.

We just paddle around for a couple of hours before we decide on our own to go back. The mood is at an all-time low. For once Roland has had himself carried down from the Tower to the beach, and now Petsamo's standing next to him, his bushy white head visible above all the other shiny ones. If he hadn't been there, Klaus and I could have been in big trouble.

CHAPTER 11

ALL it takes is a day and a night to reach the lake with the black water. Petsamo's in a good mood; he always is, he says, when he's just gotten Roland's smell out of his nose. Or rather, Roland's pals'. Roland himself has been in bed so long now that Petsamo thinks he's losing control of things. If he dies or gets deposed, a whole new power structure might develop here; none of the old rules would apply. For instance: They let the Convent grow things only because Roland wants potatoes and rapeseed oil; the one who takes over may have other plans.

— With the exception of the five last years before the end of the century—when everything was total chaos—it's taken us nearly twenty years to create what little stability we have now. What that means is that it's been bearable for about eight years.

— And before that?

— Everyone was fair game. Especially the women. Some of Roland's boys got the idea that they wanted to be married. It didn't work. They'd spent almost all of their youth in prisons and institutions; they didn't know how to live in couples. What they really wanted to do was live in the gang—with men. When the tension grew too much for them, they'd go on raids, plundering and raping. The women who survived gravitated to Signe. And God knows living with her as leader is no bed of roses!

We push the flat-bottomed aluminum boat along the last stretch to the black lake. It's worked well as a sled too; we've dragged or poled our way over sand and swamp across the island from east to west. The stretch between Roland's Tower and the Rabbit-Convent is the narrowest part of the island. Tomorrow we can paddle our way downstream from the Convent's lake to the ocean on the west side. From there we'll set a course north toward the radio station, which they also call Castle Rock. We're taking somewhere between one hundred and two hundred kilos of cargo; we'd have needed at least four or five men to carry it by land to Castle Rock.

In the late afternoon we beach the boat below the Convent. It's April now, and a patchwork of tilled fields is in flower among the low ridges; hay and leaves glitter gold, green, violet, rose. But the lake is still black and lifeless—except for the giant bubbles belching up in a regular stream from the depths.

Signe greets Petsamo warmly; I get a nod and some stern looks. I'm not supposed to be here. Maybe she's afraid I'm coming back to try to stay. She sort of snaps an apology that I have to sleep in the boat while they invite Petsamo in. But it's all the same to me. Obviously one of us has to guard the cargo. I don't even bother to put up the tent; I just spread the sail over everything and crawl in under the gray-white roof. In the evening sexy Sister Klara comes down with a bowl of porridge. I tell her to come aboard; giggling, she lifts her skirts and lets me help her over the gunwale. Then she sits down and swallows me with her eyes while I eat.

— You're so young and handsome, she says, patting me on top of my head.

I ask her to tell me the story of her life.

— You probably won't believe it if I tell you I was born a princess.

— Was your old man a king?

— The King of Norway's cousin. They called me the Snow Princess because I moved in the winter sports crowd. From February to April it was all slalom, after that some state visit or other, then in the summer sailing of course, in the fall hunting, and later on the Ball Season. I was married twice. Once to a Hessian prince, once to a well-known architect. Don't get the idea I've *always* lived like this!

— How many times have you been raped?

She's terribly insulted, as though I made a shameful suggestion; she picks up the bowl and spoon and tries to climb over the gunwale. But she isn't the first person to tell me she's royalty; at night on the foredeck many sailors told me how highborn they were.

When I put my arms around her waist, she changes; she sighs and falls into my arms. When I try to set her down on the thwart she clings to me.

— Kiss me!

I don't want to. But I also don't want her hanging around

my neck. Finally I twist her arm up behind her back until she screams. Then she lets me set her down.

— I love it when you hurt me!

— I'm not trying to hurt you. Can't you just tell me what it's like to live in the Convent? I don't get much of a picture.

— Only if you hit me again.

I promise; I'm dying of curiosity. Then she begins to talk. At first she's very vague. It's as though nothing really happens here—nothing's really good, nothing exactly bad; everything just runs together into a big blob. So I have to start to ask questions, not general ones—details:

— When did you get up this morning?

— Aren't you silly! I don't get up in the mornings and go to bed at night. I'm in charge of the altar candles. I'm up for three hours, then sleep for two, work for three and sleep for two . . .

— How long have you been doing that?

— A long time. Fifteen years . . . maybe twenty?

I begin to get a picture of how they live. Everyone has a particular job; one is the cook, another does the cleaning, and Klara's in charge of the wash as well as the candles. They never change. It's the same at sea; one person is the engineer, another makes the soup in the galley—they'd never think of switching places. One of every three waking hours has to be devoted to what she calls religious practice.

— Like what, for instance?

— Praying.

She shows me a worn, greasy, shiny rosary, which she uses as a sort of abacus to keep track of her prayers.

— When I notice my mind wandering, I pray backwards—but you mustn't tell a soul!

I guess it's a sin to pray backward, but sometimes if she doesn't make herself say the words backward to keep out the memories, she can't concentrate.

— Which memories?

— Men, of course!

When she's not praying she shuffles on her knees around the altar or bows six times sixty before it. She says the bowing's especially good because she's stiff in the hip joints and it hurts when she does it.

— Is it better if it hurts?

— Of course!

— Why?

— Because Our Savior suffered; my insignificant pain brings me closer to His great suffering.

— So what if you thought up some kind of really terrible suffering, like stabbing yourself in the stomach?

— That would be presumptuous! No suffering can compare to the Savior's!

— Is being hung up on a cross really supposed to be the worst possible suffering? I'm sure I could . . .

— No!!

She throws her arms around my knees, repeating over and over that no suffering can compare to the Savior's. I agree with her just to calm her down. After she's been lying for a while with her head in my lap, she wants me to hit her. But I won't do it. Not because I hate the idea—I've whipped plenty of asses for the fun of it—but because she seems so fragile. I don't quite know how and where to smack her for it not to do any damage.

— Then give me a kiss!

I lift her out of the boat and give her a dry, tight-lipped kiss. She sobs a little from disappointment—but then the next minute wants to make another date and tell me about the Alps. I get out of it by saying we have to shove off in the morning.

After she leaves, I undress and take a long swim in the still water before pulling my stinking clothes on again and curling up under the blankets. I dream about America where Petsamo lived when he was young. Yesterday evening in the tent I asked him to describe it. All he said was that in America there were lots of people, lots of children—and everybody believed the best was yet to come, not already behind. I picture a big island so full of people that everyone has to crouch or stand. People are all shapes, all sizes, and hundreds of speedboats with roaring motors race along the beaches. Everybody's laughing; they're beside themselves with joy. Since they're all standing or sitting close together, their bursts of laughter make the sea of people move in long, billowing waves while the air above them trembles with body heat. When the speedboats veer on a turn, they send towering white wings of cool water over the crowds of laughing people.

STEPS on the beach gravel awaken me. I reach for the submachine gun on top of the supplies. There's just a half-moon, but it's enough to light the gray, stark landscape and the glittering black-and-white lake. Someone dressed in the Sisters' baggy sackdress and white veil is running along the beach. She stops, looks up toward the Convent, then sits on her heels with her face pressed into the palms of her hands as though she's praying.

I put the weapon back and step out of the boat so I can hide behind the hull. The woman's standing up again. She lifts her veil; the moon shines on her wooly head and broad face. She tucks up the long dress and fastens the hem into the rope she's wearing around her waist like a belt. It's the Finn. She's much fuller now; her calves are wide and firm, her thighs spool-shaped and luminous. She walks into the water with her hands clasped across her stomach. The cold makes her hesitate; she pauses with one foot tucked behind the other, massaging the hollow of the knee. Huddled up, knees bent, she takes a few more steps out into the water. Then she turns around, stands hugging herself, and glares up at the Convent. Just then I notice a lantern near the Chapel. She turns again, takes some firm steps forward and flounders ahead, raising her elbows higher and higher.

Suddenly I get scared. I run a few steps toward the water. Someone shouts in a high voice from up on the hill. Out in the lake the Finn turns again. She stands with her head tilted back and her hands stretched toward the sky. Then she drops her arms, squeezes her nostrils shut with both hands—and throws herself backward into the water. She disappears. I splash into the lake and swim toward the center of the ripples. A couple of times I have to stand up and raise myself out of the water to figure out which way to head. She hasn't come up. I begin to dive systematically as I've done many times when we lost something overboard or the Captain threw someone in to give the others a laugh. When I finally do find her, she's lying motionless on the bottom on her back, her hands clutched tightly around her nose and mouth. Even when I grab her under the armpits, pick her up, and drag her toward the beach, she never lets go of her face.

When we get to shallow water I lift her by the waist with her face downward so the water will run out of her. But even now she doesn't let go; stubbornly she holds in the water that's already inside her. By now people with lanterns are gathering on the beach. I lay her across my knee and pound her back. She has a coughing fit and then retches without getting anything up. I bend over her and stick my finger into her mouth to pull out whatever junk might still be stopping her up. She lunges up and bites my chin—hard, resolutely. I stagger backward and we both end up in the water. On all fours I watch as the others bring a cloth stretcher and carry her to shore. Blood's dripping from my chin.

THE chill hits me only when I'm back under the sail. As I lie there, my teeth chatter so hard they make one of the aluminum cases rattle. It's not the usual chill after a nighttime swim. At first I don't want to admit it to myself, but these are the same shakes I usually get. The Captain said I had malaria. I asked Petsamo and he said it was doubtful—malaria is more predictable, and the attacks come closer together. My shakes don't seem to follow any pattern. Sometimes they're over in a few hours; sometimes they last as long as a week. But maybe it's malaria anyway. According to Petsamo all of creation—including the human body—is like a complicated clock that was dropped on the floor thirty-three years ago—and now is being badly put together by an amateur.

I get back into the cool, black, sulfur-smelling water. My speeding pulse and brain calm down a little. Along with the shakes come nightmares, scary pictures racing through my head the way you flip through a pack of cards: blotches of color, two-headed monsters. I pull my feet up toward me and sink below the surface. That calms me down even more. Once upon a time I lay in black water inside my mother's womb. As a child I thought that sounded ridiculous and disgusting—now it seems like the greatest happiness.

I sit on the bottom for a while, then float on my back watching the moon's sharp edges blur as the sky itself turns a cloudy gray-white, like sperm. I fall asleep for a moment and of course wake up when I get water in my nose and throat. Then, bent double and snorting, I walk back and curl up in the boat. The shakes are gone. I sleep deeply until I wake up bathed in sweat.

THE sun is baking through the sailcloth. My chin is a little sore, but otherwise I feel O.K. I pull on those pieces of clothing that have had time to dry. A faint bell's ringing up at the Convent, and farther away a sheep bleats. Those were the animals that looked like llamas. I'm hungry but don't want to use anything in the boat, so I walk up the sandy slope toward the ruin where there's an entry to the kitchen. But as I grab the iron ring to open the hatch, I notice something glittering near the Chapel. An outdoor service? Good—then no one's in the kitchen. I sneak down the tunnel and grope my way to the room with the big baking oven. A kettle simmers on the embers, potato breads hang on a pole fastened to the ceiling. Sitting down at the cast-iron table, I wolf down one of the breads and drink warm water—which immediately gets my bowels rumbling. With half the bread still uneaten, I hustle back outside. But when I get out in the open I stop. Up at the Chapel, someone is screaming and sobbing. I'll have to shit some other time. Making a wide arc I sneak in that direction.

Man-high stone walls are all that are left of the nave and tower. Probably the stone walls are actually a good deal higher, but sand and dirt have blown in and collected around them. About ten people are in the ruins of the nave—eight of them Sisters in long veils—and three are holding a naked woman down on a table. They've spread her legs and bent them at the knees. One of the Sisters is bending over the woman's crotch with a mirror, trying to catch the light. A beam of sunlight flutters over the crowd, shyly seeking the woman's crotch. Petsamo's sitting on a box next to her, a shiny instrument in his hand. I crawl closer, trying to make out details in the hot, shimmering light. He's holding the metal catheter like a pen between his thumb and forefinger, the same catheter he used on Henry.

The person they're holding down on the table is howling. It must be the Finn; my chin's still throbbing from the bite she gave me. The inside of her thigh is smooth and gold-colored. Between her legs I can see a slit topped by a small tuft of hair. Now she manages to free her head and bend forward with her chin on her chest.

Two Sisters bear down on her, pushing her head back. Her body arches, then goes slack. The Sister with the mirror—I think it's Anna—guides the trembling sunbeam to the slit. Petsamo pulls the box up under him so that he's sitting be-

tween the Finn's legs. He presses his cheek against her thigh as
though to brace himself. Then he puts the catheter in. Someone helps him attach a thin hose to it, fastened at the other
end to an upside-down bottle. He stands up, holds the bottle
in outstretched arms over his rumpled head of hair. Sister
Signe massages the Finn's stomach. Someone else brings a
net attached to a long handle. Petsamo puts the bottle in the
net so he doesn't have to hold it above his head, and they
stand taking turns holding the net by the handle high in
the air.

I hear the Finn vomiting. They have to raise her a little to
keep her from choking. They raise her higher and higher until
her chin almost touches her stomach. She's panting and snorting. Petsamo twists the catheter and a moment later pulls it
out. Black blood gushes out of the slit. They put a tin platter
under her and Sister Signe kneads, no, plows down on her
belly. Then they pass around the plate with the blood and
Petsamo pokes at it with the catheter. I leave my hiding place
and walk down toward the boat, crushing the remaining piece
of potato bread under my heel.

An hour later Petsamo comes down. He's got the plate and
catheter with him.

— I want to show you something you've never seen before.

He holds the plate out: dried blood, some lumps of hard-
ened blood and mucus bubbles. In the middle something small
and bluish pink that looks like a naked baby bird embedded in a
jellyfish. Once with Papa I went looking for birds' nests above
the mountain cave where we lived. At that time there were still
some seagulls who nested on land. An old man who slept in the
same corner as we came along. When we found a bird's nest
with a chick and two eggs, he stood on one leg and whooped
with joy. The chick tried to crawl away. It had pink, humanlike
skin, and it tried to row and paddle over the rock with its wing
stumps. The old man grabbed its neck and pried its head off
with a bottle opener he was very proud of.

— One of Roland's men is the father of this thing, Petsamo says.

— That's why she tried to drown herself?

— She didn't want us to take the fetus.

— But you had to?

He looks at me in a disapproving way that isn't really like him. I've never seen him amazed or surprised about anything before. But then his face smooths out:

— I forgot you grew up at sea. . . . The few times someone's got pregnant here on the island we've always aborted it. But the last time was so long ago I was actually a little worried that I wouldn't be able to do it.

— Why?

— You mean you think that we need children? That's the *last* thing we need! Why should we turn the whole meat grinder on again? Besides, they're all deformed monsters. You can keep them alive for a year or two if you spend twenty-four hours a day on them. But every one ends up dying on you anyway.

He puts the plate on the ground and places the catheter across it:

— Wash this out while I go and say good-bye.

I take the plate up the slope, dig a deep hole with my bare hands, and shake the lumps into the hole. I guess we all looked like baby birds at one time or another.

CHAPTER 12

I'M back at sea! The wind's blowing from the usual direction—
west southwest—which means that for long stretches at a time
we'll be sailing free to the north half a knot offshore. As long
as the wind direction holds, we can also quickly tack to starboard and scoot in behind the ribbon of boulders that juts out
from the very shallow coastline. It's not like the southern tip
with its sandbars; here rocks and ocean are all that nature gives
us. We've run aground a few times but all we have to do is
step into the shallow water, push the boat off, and hop back in;
the shoals are as smooth as seals' backs.

Petsamo has his mane of hair, but I have to wind a rag
around my head so the sun won't burn the skin to a crisp. My
chin's infected from the Finn's bite. They say bites are the
most dangerous wounds; heated-up bacteria can go straight
from one person's mouth to another person's body.

— What exactly is a bacteria?

— A kind of animal that lives on other animals. So small
you'll never see one.

— How do you know they exist?

— You can see them in a microscope.

— Is it like a magnifying glass?

— A tube with a system of lenses that enlarges things hundreds of times.

— Have you ever seen one?

— The doctor I worked for bought one. But someone who needed a pair of glasses stole it. He knocked out the lenses, wired them together, and put them on his nose.

— Did he see bacteria?

— Nothing but fog, the stupid ass!

Lenses are valuable. In addition to the one I found at Henry's, I've owned two—and then lost them. The first I got out of a camera, a black box with a bellows in front that you could pull out and fold in. I got it from my first protector, the one who also gave me my first broken rib. The camera was in perfect condition; there was even film in it. Film's good for kindling. Originally they used it to catch pictures the way you catch flies on a sticky strip. In my six-year-old loneliness I used to think a lot about how it might have worked. How can you get a picture without anyone's drawing it? The old-timer who gave me the camera said you could make an imprint of nature itself. But then how can nature still be there, just as before, undamaged? Of course the film in the camera was ruined. Just like any other film, it'd been exposed during the moment none of the grown-ups would talk about, and which I therefore didn't want to believe in. I held the film at one end and let it unroll itself (it really did look like flypaper) and managed to unscrew the lens from the camera without damaging it. Then I sat down next to the wheelhouse and let the sun shine through the rainbow-shimmering lens onto the film—which immediately began smoking and smoldering. Naturally I got spanked; I could have set fire to the boat.

A few hours before sunset the wind dies down. We head into shore, but not all the way in. If pirates are a danger on the open sea, on land there's also the danger of someone waiting for you with an automatic weapon. We take down the mast and sail and row—or rather pole—ourselves in among the offshore stone reefs. We find a clump of tall boulders forming a good windbreak where we can moor the boat. Then we take blankets, supplies, and the automatic rifle and jump from shoal to shoal to another group of rocks a few hundred meters away. We set up camp for the night. There's no question of lighting a fire; we just eat potato crusts softened in the evening dew and wash them down with warm water.

Petsamo takes the first watch. He sits in a crouch, pointing the rifle toward the boat. Even though my body's aching all over from all the work with the boat, I can't sleep. My chin throbs; my mouth itches.

— Where do all the big rocks come from? Who rolled them into the sea?

— They were pushed out by the ice.

— How can that be? Every fall I've seen the sea freeze along the shore . . . but I've never seen any rocks roll out onto the ice by themselves.

— Ten thousand years ago all the land was covered by glaciers several hundred meters thick. The glaciers pressed the landmasses underwater, smoothed down the rocks and pushed earth and stones ahead of them like enormous plows.

— And the people? Did they live on top of the ice?

— No one lived here then. People came from the south, from the warm places, only after the ice began to melt and break up.

— From Africa?

— I don't know if there was an Africa at the time.

— Is there an Africa now?

THE next morning the sea is calm. We row out as soon as it's light enough to tell the prow from the rocks. Of course now and then we scrape against the rocks; the aluminum clinks and thuds. Petsamo gets annoyed; we were supposed to slip out unnoticed in case anyone was lying on the beach waiting for just enough light to take a shot at us. He doesn't know this stretch of the coastline particularly well. It's a long stone plateau that the army used to use as a training ground in the old days. From time to time pirates winter here, so every spring Roland's gang—even though as they grow older they don't like to do it—scour the place looking for contraband and stragglers. I even used to hear them laughing and calling each other "policemen."

— When there really were police . . . did they just take whatever they needed from anybody?

— They were paid by the Government.

— What did the Government look like?

He thinks it's a funny question. Every once in a while the old-timers talk about the Government: The Government kept order, the Government made sure the sick were taken care of, the Government paid for this and that. But nobody can describe it! I guess it's the same with God. They say that God is a thought, something so big that you can't understand it, something much more than a smart old man on a cloud surrounded by golden sunbeams. Was the Government even bigger than God?

We row the whole second day—in the morning because there's no wind, in the afternoon because we have a head wind and we can't tack. We don't have a jib, the boat has no keel, so at the end of each tack we run the risk of either drifting out to sea or running up onto the rocks. Neither of us has done much rowing. You couldn't row the boats I've been on before. When I rowed at all it was in rubber rafts or dinghys, short trips between ships or in landing parties. I think a lot about great longboats rowed by many men, several at each oar. That kind of boat wouldn't need wind or oil. It would need hardly any draft either—and if you ran aground all you'd have to do is climb out and pull it free.

After a while we have to wrap rags around the blisters on our hands; the kinds of callouses we have aren't the right ones for rowing. A few hours before sunset we give up and look for a place to anchor. It's deeper here, so we have to go closer to the steep cliffs. Then, to the north, Petsamo sees something white a little way out to sea. We quickly ship the oars to hide the glitter and huddle down behind the gunwales. Was it just a whitecap—or a sail? We let ourselves drift for a few minutes, then realize that this isn't any safer; we'll either drift back south or be pulled in toward the coast. Petsamo puts up the mast and boom and climbs up to look out, and I start rowing again. My hands are numb; my chin throbs—the bite's begun to fester.

— It's a little skerry!

We aim ourselves, then ride the prow right up against the rocky little island. It makes quite a crash; the whole hull shivers. But nothing's damaged and we drag the boat all the way up. In a place like this no one'll ever get at us from shore without letting us know he's coming!

At night we're both too tired to keep watch. We sleep behind the hull like dead men, our hands wrapped in wet rags. Since my chin began to fester it's stopped aching.

ALL morning of the third day a warm haze covers the ocean, and we row by following the sound of the breakers against the steep coast. In the noon heat the haze finally lifts; Castle Rock towers before us. It's on a spit of land connected to the mainland by a narrow reef so low in the water that some waves wash all the way over its stone-littered spine. The Rock itself is high and flat-topped, maybe one hundred meters high, a mighty stone slab resting on a foundation of other rocks like a huge, blue-gray piece of glacier. Here and there big stone boulders have come loose and tumbled down the cliff, stopping either at the beach or rolling farther out so that the Rock is protected on the ocean side by a jagged palisade of underwater rocks. On top, two radio masts glisten like spiderwebs in the lifting haze.

Before we head into the narrow reef, Petsamo fires a volley of shots. We sit drifting for about ten minutes until three shots answer us from the top. Petsamo tells me that island natives say that remnants of the earliest inhabitants have been found here; they were seal hunters who lived seven thousand years ago at the edge of the receding glacier. We row in and pull the boat into the crease between the reef and the Rock; the cliff's been split and cracked in so many places that there are plenty of footholds for climbing. We unload and tip the light boat on its side between two rocks. Then we start climbing, carrying only our most valuable things; the rest we'll have to come back for later.

If Petsamo didn't know the way, I could never make it up here by myself. It's a maze of stairways where what you think is the most direct way turns out to lead only to a rocky spit over a narrow crevice so deep the sunlight can't touch bottom. Rocks have been placed all around, just about to tip over, and there are hidden trip wires too. Halfway up we take a break. We have a wonderful view of the broad, flat main island spreading before us: lichen-gray expanses of stone merging into dirty-yellow sand lakes broken by patches of marshland overgrown with year-old light-gray reeds. The only man-made structure to be seen is the ruins of a wall cutting across the steep path that zigzags down from the island plateau to the reef. During the Middle Ages the wall was Castle Rock's first line of defense against attacks from land. Before we start again, Petsamo fires a single shot. As soon as we get an answer—this time almost right away—we climb on.

A few meters farther, there's a sudden change in the plant life. Below us all we see are the usual nettles and thistles, but up here there are green bushes and all kinds of shrubbery: Petsamo points out sloe, hawthorn, Swedish whitebeam, wild roses, lilacs. Big yellow flowers grow on grass and moss-covered rock terracing. I've never seen so many beautiful plants before! I'm so awed I have to sit down. How is all this possible?

— When the Flood came and the ocean rose, the salt water came up exactly to here. They say there are other oases farther north, but this is the only one I've seen with my own eyes.

The upper part of the path is made partly of steps chopped into the rock. Now I'm walking ahead of Petsamo; he's more winded than I am. Suddenly I feel so free I start running up the winding stairs.

— For Christ's sake, stop!

Puffing, upset, he rushes up to me and points at the moss-covered steps:

— I don't see anything.

— Land mines!

Some of the steps have been mined in a cunning way: not every second or third, but in what Petsamo calls a random series. If you don't know the series by heart, you'll never know what hit you.

Up on top, the Rock's landscape is a miniature of the main island's—only greener, lusher: mosses, lichen, heather, and last year's grasses, now dry and shuddering in the wind. Between the two tall, apparently undamaged radio masts held up by cables is a hollow about thirty meters wide. Here the plants are astounding: huge lilac bushes several meters high billowing out of the green grass, and right in their midst a white stone house whose metal roof still shows traces of red paint. In front of the door is an intricately carved wooden structure painted a gray-blue color that reminds me of a ship's bridge. A few wide stone steps lead down to a well-tended gravel path with flowers growing along either side—at least ten different kinds in all colors and sizes. In the middle of the path stands a grinning man; he's short and round and has a red-brown face. He's wearing a gray hat with a black sweatband and holding an automatic rifle so polished it's blinding!

— Petsamo! Back from the dead!

Lanky Petsamo drops his pack and runs up to the little fat man. They hug each other. It looks funny, partly because two men are hugging each other in what looks like sheer friendship, partly because the fat man's so short his cheek presses into Petsamo's belly. Chuckling out loud, they slap each other's shoulders; now the stiff, reserved Petsamo has completely disappeared. He calls me over to shake hands, a form of greeting you see only rarely at sea.

— This is my sidekick Edvin! My friend Halvar!

He takes his hat off to me. Right above his eyebrows is a sharp border, and above it his bald head is gray-white, like an ass cheek. His eyes are blue with clear whites; his tanned face has no scars of any kind, and he even seems to have all his teeth. A little hesitantly I stretch out my hand.

— Give me your whole hand, boy, not just three limp fingers! Feels like shaking a codfish tail. . . . You can't help having a harelip—but saying hello, shaking hands, anyone can learn to do. Well, we'll take care of that later. Tell me now: How high is Niagara?

I look at Petsamo, but he just grins. Is Niagara a tower?

— One hundred meters, I blurt out.

— Wrong. How wide is it? And I'm talking about the part they call Horseshoe Falls.

— Fifty meters?

— And how many gallons of water go over the entire falls per minute?

— Save the quiz show till later, Petsamo says.

Laughing, Halvar buzzes around us. He waves the rifle with one hand, shakes Petsamo's arm, then punches me in the stomach—in a friendly way, but so hard I double over.

— Come in, come in!

He pushes us up the steps and through the narrow double doors, which still have all their glass panes. As far as I can see, there isn't a broken windowpane in the whole house, and they're not the usual mixture of cemented-in portholes or old car windows either. The house has a room for cooking on the right, another room on the left, and between the two, narrow steps leading up to a second floor, which also has two rooms:

Halvar's bedroom and another room full of junk. There are a number of wooden tables and chairs. Even the floor is wood—and it has striped, rectangular pieces of cloth lying all over it that are longer but not as wide as blankets. There are flowers inside the house too—stuck in clay pots in the windows. The walls are covered with patterned paper, and glass-sealed pictures are hanging all over. Mostly they're faded photographs, but there's a piece of fabric with the alphabet sewn into it and above the stove a picture of the house itself. One wall is lined with low wooden boxes into which he's stuck rows of books.

— Nothing's changed—that's all Petsamo says.

I feel uncomfortable. So Papa was right; this must be how people lived before, when they could choose how they wanted to live. I don't particularly like it—there's too much furniture, too many *things*. It makes me nervous; I feel stupid and ignorant not knowing what everything's for.

While Halvar goes into the kitchen, we take a closer look at the pictures. One photograph is of a square tower with an enormous four-bladed propeller that looks like it's made of nets.

— A wind-power generator?

— A windmill, Petsamo says.

— For electricity?

— A mill is a mechanical, wind-driven power source that was used to turn large stones to grind grain into flour. I don't suppose you've ever even seen flour? Mills were invented during the Middle Ages; when they first came along, people down in Europe burned them to the ground because they took away jobs.

Petsamo spots a book:

— Can you beat that! Here I am standing right next to literature's best-known story about fighting windmills—*Don Quixote*.

— What's literature?

— It's about a tall knight and his fat little squire. They

fight the Saracens, but it turns out that their real fame comes
from fighting windmills!

Halvar calls from the other room; we go in. In the kitchen
two big iron pots are sitting on the black stove. He kneels,
opens a door with a hook and pokes at something that looks
like moldy potato bread.

— Guano . . . birdshit! Millions of seabirds used to nest
here. Above the flood line you can pick up a bucketful in five
minutes. Burns fantastically well, but stinks like cod-liver oil.
But tell me now, Edvin: What's the energy content of one
gram of dried guano expressed in watts?

— How's he supposed to know that? He's only thirty-three.
He never went to school like you and me.

— Thirty-three?!!

He cackles like a maniac! I leave it to Petsamo to tell him a
little about my life; while he talks, Halvar stares at me, nods at
Petsamo, and tries to control the giggling fits that keep bursting
out of him. Then he wants to cross-examine me himself, but
Petsamo won't let him.

We all sit down at the kitchen table. It's pure wood too,
supported by a wooden frame that can be moved around with
hinges; I almost kick the table over before they tell me to look
out—it's what they call a "gateleg" table. Then he takes out
some glasses and, while the water is being heated up, we have
"drinks"—fuller, not so sour and cloudy as Henry's potato
beer; the sweet taste of alcohol cuts through, and I want more.
But he doesn't offer any; the water's already boiling.

— I ran in and put the kettle on the minute I heard the
first shot, Halvar grins. But it boiled dry twice in the meantime!

In the larger pot he's boiling nettles; later he'll pour the
water over all the plants and vegetables to keep the bugs and
animals away. In the smaller, cylinder-shaped pot he's warming water for ear flushing. Every time Petsamo comes, he
flushes out Halvar's ears. First, Halvar takes off his shirt and

sits on a chair in the middle of the kitchen. Then Petsamo
puts a rag across Halvar's shoulders while I hold a deep plate
pressed against his neck. Petsamo sucks warm water up into a
rubber ball with a spout, spurts a little on his forearm to check
the temperature, then holds Halvar's ear and tells him to keep
quiet for at least thirty seconds. Then he works the spout into
his ear and squeezes. The water splashes right out again.

— Plug's stuck in there like a bullet wedged in a rusty
pipe, says Petsamo. Halvar laughs so hard I have to take the
plate away so he won't spill all over us.

We try again. This time Halvar won't sit still; water pours
out over his chest and down into his pants. He gets up and
shakes his pants leg, but not a drop runs out.

— If you've got a piece of thin wire we can soften it up a
little.

But Halvar doesn't *want* it to be softened. Flushing is what
he wants—even if he has to start another Flood to do it. His
joke makes him laugh till tears run out of his eyes—then
he launches into a lecture about every flower in the garden.
He ends by throwing a question at me:

— Edvin, what's the Latin name for bluebell?

— Just for once, Halvar, will you please shut up?

He's not insulted; he just settles down and tilts his head a
little for the next round of ear flushing. Before long, brown
flakes and a black lump wash down into my plate. He shouts
with pleasure:

— Now I can use the telegraph without earphones!

AT the other end of the garden is a little gray-green metal shed:
Halvar's workplace. Steel wires run from the roof up to the two
masts on either side of the garden. Halvar's in a hurry. First he
has to read the water level in a little glass container—which is
empty since it hasn't rained. Then he checks the thermometer
and another instrument called a barometer, both housed in a

little white wooden cabinet standing on long legs. He takes us into the sheet-metal shed filled with lots of metal boxes with knobs, buttons, and gauges; there are quite a few weapons around too. I've seen setups like this in shipwrecks, but never one that worked. On one of the masts is a wind propeller to make electricity. The Captain tried to put together a thing like that once but couldn't get it to work.

Halvar puts on a pair of earphones and flips a switch. Bulbs light up. He fiddles with the knobs, picks up a small ball covered with metal mesh and talks into it:

— Castle Rock: clearing fog, nineteen degrees Celsius, "one-oh-one-five" millibars, wind northnortheast three meters per second . . .

— Why does he do it? I ask Petsamo while we wait outside for him to finish with the knobs and switches.

— It's what he's always done. It's . . . his job.

I wish I had a job like it. It seems better than Petsamo's. He has to travel all around healing people; it's a risky business. But Halvar just sits up here on his Rock. At sea there were two rules we'd never break: Never raid a church; never destroy a radio station.

THE meal we have that night is unlike anything I've ever had before. While Halvar putters around in the kitchen, Petsamo shows me how to spear frogs in the flowerbeds. They live in small holes, and if you peer down carefully you can see their shining eyes and flapping chins. Halvar gives us some strong pieces of steel wire bent and sharpened at one end like a fish hook. You jam the spear quickly into the hole and pull up the skewered frog. But you can't pull too hard or you'll rip up the flowerbed.

Then we feast on fried frogs' legs; smoked and dried fish; some of Roland's boiled rice; fried potatoes; sunflower seeds;

some kind of long, brick-red, potatolike fruit they call carrots; and bread made from flour—all of it washed down with Halvar's "drinks." I get drunk and sleepy almost right away; I can't eat as much as I'd like to. But Halvar's in great spirits— throwing questions right and left, telling jokes and trying to squeeze some gossip out of the quiet Petsamo. Then, in the middle of everything, he sits down on the floor, puts his arms around his knees and bumps along on his ass. We almost fall off our chairs laughing. When we're on our way to bed, he throws me one last question:

— Edvin, kindly tell me the speed of light expressed in kilometers per second.

— Three hundred thousand, I answer loud and clear— just the way Papa taught me.

CHAPTER 13

LARGE areas of jagged rock pillars seem to stretch endlessly along the coastline north of Castle Rock. It's as if hundreds of pillars are fleeing from the rocky shore into the sea. Most of them are still up on land; others have stopped a little way into the water; still others are farther out, crouching right at the edge of the breakers. It's impossible to sail here; we have to row between the pillars. Petsamo thinks they look like mammoths, a kind of prehistoric elephant, whose bodies and heads have been chopped off; only their thick legs are left, sometimes connected to each other to form portals and arches. Where underwater rocks make it too shallow for rowing, we get out and tow the boat with a cable.

As I row hour after hour, the same thoughts keep going through my brain. With every pull of the oar Klaus appears before me, then fades away. Do I love him? I know—at least I think—there's something that you can call love. It's more than friendship; it's a wish to melt into another person. When I was seventeen, I think I fell in love with a dowser. Everybody wanted him. He could do wonders with his copper-thread divining rod, his hammer, and the tuning fork he pressed into the rock crevices. But it wasn't his work I was interested in; I only cared about his eyes, his way of looking at me. That look wasn't horny or amused. I can only describe it with one word: direct. I looked for all kinds of excuses to be near him. As he squatted next to his tuning fork, I wished I could just touch his forehead. He could have asked me for anything. But he didn't—and then they came and brought me back to the barge and whipped me for laziness.

Is it like that with Klaus? Could we really live together? Could I live with someone like him who always wants to give in to me? It would make me be the leader—and I'm the one who's always been led.

— Look out, goddamnit!

I hadn't seen Petsamo waving from the stern, and now we crash into a rock; the metal mast, resting in the boat with its point over the prow like a bowsprit, buckles against it. As we get out, I'm crying inside; wrecking a boat isn't just an ordinary mistake. A boat isn't a common thing like a house, a hammer, even a person. It's a *being*—how else could it float on water?

— Clumsy, Pussylips. But we can still use it even if we can't raise the sail all the way.

Since we've stopped anyway, we decide to take a break.

We eat some smoked mackerel and use the skins to grease the insides of our hands. The old blisters have just about healed and we don't want any new ones. Far to the south we can still make out the flat-topped cliffs of Castle Rock floating above the waterline like a violet hull.

— I can understand no one wanting to hurt Halvar. Someone has to listen for messages. But how come no one else settled there? It could feed at least a dozen people.

— Ah, because right from the very beginning Halvar's known how to keep people away. In the early days large lifeboats used to gather in groups and try to land. It was harder to keep them away then; the Flood hadn't completely receded. If anyone managed to throw a rope around a jutting rock in spite of the high seas, Halvar shot at them. I don't know how many he actually hit before they got the idea he meant business. If the station was to go on operating, it couldn't become a gypsy camp.

— A gypsy camp?

But he acts as if he hasn't heard the question. He leans forward and greases even the soles of his feet with the fatty mackerel skin. We get sores under our feet from pushing against the bottom of the boat; it's too hot to row with our boots on.

— For Halvar and me it isn't just a matter of killing . . . the way you keep monsters at bay. We were brought up to think there was no worse crime than to kill another human being. It's different with you. How did you kill Henry? I don't suppose you let him suffer to the bitter end.

— The way I was taught: with a hammer blow to his forehead.

— I can understand if you couldn't stand all his yammering. But don't tell me you've got a guilty conscience!

— A guilty conscience?

— Don't tell me it hurt you deep down inside!

— It did. When I think about it, it still does.

— You'd kill me without blinking for these two catheters under my shirt. If only you knew how to use them!

He leaps to his feet, starts slinging our supplies into the boat, and pushes it off the rock. I've never seen him so angry. I don't know what I've done. Why isn't it supposed to hurt inside me? Why can he have a guilty conscience and I can't?

— We're shoving off!

— First I want to know . . .

— Get in, you scum!

But I stay on the rock. Petsamo pushes off, grabs an oar, and poles his way out toward more open water. Then he stops, pulls the oar in, and sits with his forehead tucked in the crook of his arm, letting the boat drift. I splash through the shallow water, but when the bottom suddenly disappears I pitch forward, swim out, and grab hold of the cable trailing behind. I pull myself around and climb over the gunwale in the stern.

— What's the matter with you? I say.

— There's a difference between just killing and feeling remorseful about it!

— Why can't I feel . . . remorseful?

— You've never lived in a civilization. No one ever taught you anything except to take what you need and kill anyone who gets in the way.

— You won't believe that I can feel remorseful if no one taught me to?

— Exactly. Primitive man's a barbarian, a predatory . . . it was a temporary anomaly in the history of the world that a few generations lived in a civilization that seduced us into thinking that we were something more than barbarians.

I don't understand half of what he's saying. Maybe I understand how he's thinking, but he's using words I've never heard before. At Roland's I learned what an "institution" was—a house where they lock people up. But what's a "civilization"?

*   *   *

NOW we're in the Coke Desert. The ground is covered with gray-black, potato-sized rocks that look like coke, burned pit coal; if you pick them up, your hand gets sooty. Normally Petsamo loves to throw rocks. Whenever he finds one that feels just right in his hand, he stands legs apart, bending the top half of his body back so that the hand with the stone almost brushes the ground—and then lets it fly with a hard whiplash. In America he didn't play more than three seasons of baseball before they deported him. But he doesn't like to throw the pieces of coke. They're so light the wind blows them off course.

There's a hot, dry north wind. We hid the boat in a cove where the coke reaches all the way down to the sea, making the surface of the water oily and shiny. Now we're heading due east toward the center of the island across wide, gray fields of cinders that crunch under our feet. Not a trace of water or plant life anywhere. By evening the coke ends and we get to the sandy ground with the long, sweeping dunes that I know so well. The first thing we do is pull off our boots and walk barefoot in the pleasantly warm sand. It's late spring now, and the evenings are long; we hike a good five kilometers more before pitching camp for the night. We're on our way inland to look for a library Halvar's heard rumors about.

Petsamo starts a fire from roots that he digs out of the sand with his hands. I'm surprised:

— You want somebody to attack us?

— No one would come here at night. Not even Roland. It's called the Land of the Lepers.

— Lepers?!

— They're just poor dregs of humanity who live about a day's hike inland. People *call* them lepers. About twenty-five years ago, before things settled into the positions they're in now, those of us from the southern end of the island met up with some people who'd settled here. We took a couple of prisoners—one of them with a nose missing, another a couple of fingers. Immediately people decided they were lepers and drove them off.

— But they're not?

— Hardly. I've seen several—never one without a nose, only one missing an ear. Most likely it got ripped off by a dog. But it doesn't really make any difference; leprosy's one of the least contagious diseases. Halvar and I are the only ones who'll have anything to do with them. And don't tell Sister Signe or Roland that we've been here! They might kick you out like a dog with the mange!

— And these . . . poor dregs have found a what . . . a library?

— Collection of books.

— Books don't burn that well.

— Well enough for us to hurry.

PETSAMO falls asleep right after we've crawled into the tent. But I can't. The night wind beats at the tent cloth, and I imagine that I can hear crunching noises as the lepers sneak in a crouch toward us from far off in the Coke Desert. They're small and skinny and dressed in old sacks pulled over their heads like pointed hoods. From the waist down they're naked. The skin on their swollen bellies looks like last year's potatoes; their thighs are brown and thin; dirt-gray bags dangle to their knees. I've seen all this (even the coke!) once before. I was only nine. We'd discovered an island made almost completely of fused-together coke. My protector at the time had me standing guard over prisoners digging the coke; at night we lived on the boat, but they were kept on the island day and night. We thought they were Russians; whatever they were, no one understood one word of their language. At night we gave them water and some fish heads and guts. As long as there was the least bit of light they spaded the coke apart and carried it down to the makeshift harbor. It only lasted two or three weeks. Many died of exhaustion. A few jumped into the sea. I shot five myself.

They'd given me a submachine gun to guard them with. If anyone made a move off the trampled path, I was to first shoot a warning shot, then shoot to kill. It was my first piece; I was incredibly proud. But it wasn't easy to handle; I knew that if you don't hold an automatic weapon down, it can start bucking. One of the prisoners who'd loaded up too heavily stumbled and fell over. The skipper was standing nearby. I got so scared all I could do was fire a warning blast. The first shots spattered into the coke, but the rest hit the prisoners who had stopped. Three died on the spot, two the next night. To punish me for slowing down the work, they took my gun away. At that point I didn't feel remorseful about killing them; I'd seen too many die. But I cried my heart out over my lost submachine gun.

NEXT day we reach the marshes, some still salty from the days of the Flood, others filled with fresh water. In one of the salt-water marshes we scrape a little sun-dried salt from a rock. Our boat would have come in handy here; as it is, we have to jump from hummock to hummock, always worrying about spraining our ankles. So far we haven't seen any lepers, but in one of the freshwater areas there was a half-rotten, hollowed-out log; we cut some chips for fuel. That night we spend in the reeds, not inside the tent but on top of it, sitting up and sleeping back to back on our tent raft; there's no way to put up the poles or fasten down tent lines. In the old days you couldn't even spend a night in a swamp without being eaten alive by insects; now there's only an occasional dragonfly.

Again I see the lepers carrying heavy sacks of coke; long lines of them step out of the crotch of the Finn in the Convent. Petsamo and I sit on the wall by the nave of the old church throwing stones at them until they drop. Not one tries to run away.

BY the time we reach limestone plains dotted with low shrubs and heather, we still haven't seen a single person. But late one morning—even though I can't figure out how Petsamo can get his bearings here—we find a little gravel pit dug out below a ridge and the partially exposed ruins of a lightweight concrete house. It's the library, exactly where Halvar said it would be— next to the Coke Desert's southernmost arm. A few primitive shovels are leaning against a wall. But no people, no ashes, no dried shit or other garbage. The top floor of the house is completely caved in, and there we find some large books with faint numbers on their bindings. The first floor is underground. Someone's ripped a hole in the floor of the second story; when we look down we see piles of gravel and sand that have poured in through the shattered windows. Books are everywhere, some in drifts, others packed tightly in untouched rows of shallow shelves. Suddenly I get very uneasy:

— You think it could be a trap?

— It's no trap. The lepers would never touch Halvar or me. We're their only connections to the outside world.

EVEN though we have only enough food and water for a week, we stay in the library eleven days. A sandstorm comes up, and we have to raise the tent inside on the lower floor to protect ourselves from the sand whirling through the opening in the roof. Petsamo goes through every book, shelf by shelf, stack by stack, pile by pile. He has trouble reading down here in the unchanging twilight, so I have to help him even though I can hardly read. I spell and sound out while he snorts impatiently over my shoulder.

— You'll never learn to read letter by letter. You have to recognize whole words!

— How many words are there?

— Tens of thousands. Most of them are dead and found only in books. On this island they use maybe a thousand at the most.

— But you can't learn to recognize ten thousand words!

— You can learn the most common ones. Think of a face. When you meet someone you know, you don't take his face apart bit by bit: an ear plus a nose plus a forehead. You recognize the face as a whole. It's the same with words.

I'd rather look at picture books with animals, cars, ships, cities, airplanes, submarines. Can all of it really have worked? How can something heavier than air stay up? How does an automobile know which way to go? How do you steer a streetcar? Wouldn't a submarine crash deep down in the ocean without the sun or the moon to see by? A compass can't work underwater, can it?

The Captain used to talk about something he called intuition, an invisible compass certain people carry around inside them. And once I knew an Estonian wine merchant who never used instruments; they said he could find his way no matter what the weather was like. *He* said it was because he'd nailed the skull of a master pilot to the base of the bowsprit; and the Captain, who'd been belowdecks, actually did see a skull shining in the darkness. But I think the real reason was that the Estonian stayed mostly in one place or only moved between established ports of trade; if he'd ever gone into rough seas, all his bottles would have shattered.

Petsamo tosses all the picture books aside. He's looking for manuals about ddseases and their treatment, and books with pictures of the insides of human bodies. At one point I make an incredible find: COM-PLETE CA-TA-LO-GUE OF DRUGS, I spell out. I present it to him as though I'd written the book myself. But he leafs through the thick volume quickly, then

chucks it on the pile of books he's already examined and discarded.

— You're not thinking, Edvin. The only one of all these
drugs we can make is low-grade alcohol.

Later he himself finds a book about herbs. He decides to
keep it even though out of the thousand or more plants the
book mentions, we could find only ten at the most on this
island.

I ask him what books he'd really like to find.

— A book on how to ease pain without opium, how to
heal open leg fractures, how to speed up death for the dying.

— Not one about how to cut out fetuses?

— You don't cut out a fetus. You irritate the uterus until it
expels the fetus by itself. But I know how to do that already.
Besides, I hope I've done my last one. Aside perhaps from
hand amputations, they disgust me the most.

I'd like to find a navigation manual. And something about
operating a telegraph. And a little later I actually do find one
about how to navigate large ships with the aid of lighthouses; it
tells you to always approach the light from the side that shines
green, not red.

— If you find something about telegraphs, I say, don't
throw it away.

— Those are reserved for Halvar! And everything about
medicine is mine!

I'd like to go back to Halvar on the Rock. If I read all the
books in this library, maybe I could answer at least half his
silly questions. I'd sit at his feet and tell him all about Niagara
until he couldn't do without me. In return I'd make him teach
me how to operate the telegraph. And if anyone else tried to
get up there, me and my new father, Halvar, would do the
same thing that he did in the nineties: We'd shoot at anyone
trying to climb up on the Rock and drop hand grenades on the
boats below. But Halvar'd never let me live on Castle Rock;
not even Petsamo can.

One evening when it's almost impossible to read (you have to feel the bindings with your fingertips), I find a book: THE LIT-TLE SUR-GEON. But I don't tell Petsamo. I hide it in the gravel under one of the caved-in windows.

THE sandstorm keeps us down in the hole. When the wind finally dies down enough so that we think we'd be able to stand upright outside, I wind rags around my whole head except for one eye. Petsamo gives me a boost, and I climb out into the lashing wind. He's told me to follow the ridge to see where it ends; there might be a marsh or spring nearby. We have only one day's worth of water left. But the second I get up above, I stumble over a large clay jar driven into the ground next to the hole. It wasn't there the last time we were up. Terrified, I slide back down. But Petsamo's unruffled. He climbs up and comes back with it under one arm. The bottom tapers to a point so that it can't stand in the usual way—it's made to be driven into sand or leaned against a wall. Covered with a lid of dried clay, it's filled with fresh water.

So the lepers do exist; I forgot we were in a place where other people have been living for years. That evening we find some raw potatoes wrapped in cloth.

— Why are they giving us food and water?

— They're asking for our forgiveness.

— For what?

— They've got the idea that they're the source of all the evil in the world. I don't really know how it happened; I don't understand much of what they say. But they've assumed the guilt for everything. They're forever asking the rest of us for forgiveness. But no one even lets them close. Only Halvar and I know they're harmless.

— But the War's not their fault.

— I think they want to find an explanation for their own suffering. Of all the people I've seen or heard about here on the island, the lepers look like they've suffered most. Someone who's endured terrible torture can make his suffering a little easier if he gives it meaning—or if he can assume the burden of guilt for it himself.

WHILE Petsamo is still asleep in our tent the next morning, I crawl quietly out to look at my hidden treasure, *The Little Surgeon*. It tells how to sew up wounds, drain bladders, how to tell the difference between serious and mild heart attacks, what you can see if you look into an ear, how to remove particles from an eye . . .

— What have you got there?

Naturally he noticed that I'm doing something unusual! Maybe he heard me mumbling as I read; it's easier to put the words together if I say them out loud.

— Why did you hide it?

What can I say? I deceived him, fooled him, tried to steal the thing he needs most of all.

— You numbskull, what did you expect to *do* with this!

I squat down, stare between my feet. Then I close my eyes, waiting for him to hit me. But he grabs the back of my neck and shakes me hard:

— I'll *teach* you! If you swear on everything that's holy to you that you'll use what I teach you the way I tell you to . . . and never use it *against* me! If you promise that, I'll teach you!

He lets go and turns his attention to the book. I try in vain to find what he asked me for—everything that's holy to me. Then I take a long walk out on the quiet, sandy plains. No one's ever given me such a gift; I'm going to know how to *do* something. But what will he ask for in return? Maybe one day in the fall or next year, he'll suddenly remind me that I haven't paid him. And what will he want from me then? He's not interested in physical love—or gold or weapons. I'm getting more and more nervous. What will I have to pay—and how? Does he want to influence me, mold me, take out of me what's me—then fill up the hole with himself so he'll be able to live on in a younger body?

And he hasn't said one thing about how he can work it out in practical terms: Roland is the one who owns me.

THE next day we leave the Land of the Lepers. Sand and red dust have almost completely covered the ruin. After we gather up our equipment and about sixty books, we cover over the entry hole. I ask if we should leave the lepers a thank-you gift so they'll let us come back, but Petsamo says no. A gift would only confuse them. They don't want anything but for their guilt to be acknowledged.

It's drizzling, but in spite of our heavier packs Petsamo is in great spirits.

— There's something called the Hippocratic Oath. It's a list of rules about how a doctor should and should not behave. You know what it says? A doctor should never expose his gums when he's talking or laughing. Pussylips, you've got your work cut out for you!

CHAPTER 14

SINCE the storm kept us in the Land of the Lepers longer than we intended, every day there's more and more chance of running into pirates if we go south by sea. So we leave the boat and hike southeast through the Coke Desert. The dampness in the air makes the coke so slippery we have to spend the night there. We can't fasten the tent poles down again; the tent sags, but luckily there's not much wind. The ground is lumpy and uncomfortable; it's like being thrown naked into a hold full of potatoes.

Everybody at sea is full of stories. But everyone I've met on land seems more secretive. Especially Petsamo. When we take breaks, I study the medical books and he asks me questions. But he doesn't tell me anything about himself or what happened here.

— Tell me what happened on the island before I came.

— Hunger, cold, sickness, darkness, hate, death . . . The same as at sea I imagine.

— But there must be stories. . . .

— You tell one.

So I tell him what the engineer on the trawler *Sea Urchin* told me. After the first great wave, the one that smashed up even the large vessels and sank them on the rebound, the engineer found himself stranded on an island. He huddled under a tree that had lost all its leaves even though it was the middle of summer. His vomit and shit were full of blood, and when he got up in the mornings great handfuls of his hair stayed on the ground behind him. Even if there'd been anything to eat, he wouldn't have been able to eat it. The gulls had eaten their own eggs; some mysterious instinct had told them to avoid the heaps of dead fish that were piling up on the island's windward side.

When he'd given up all hope of being rescued, he heard a ship heading into the cove below him. It was a gray minesweeper towing a barge filled with large, dull pieces of glass, some no bigger than a crouching man, others as big as lifeboats. They had a crane on the barge, and the crew started unloading the glass onto the section of the pier that hadn't been swept out to sea or heaved up into the dead forest. They lowered the glass blocks extremely carefully; their surfaces were a dirty, fuzzy green, but if you scraped at them a little with a knife they sparkled with all the colors of the rainbow. The last piece was as big as a dinghy, and as they were about to lower it onto land, the barge—which now had no ballast—listed suddenly, and the lump of glass careened onto the concrete and cracked. Of course it made an awful lot of noise but the strange thing was that sound kept coming from the broken glass for minutes afterward. It screamed and whimpered, water gushed and fire crackled, windows slammed and walls split open. It went on and on. At first it was so loud that the crew ran for cover, then it grew fainter and fainter until it finally faded away in a helpless little trickle of children's voices.

The lieutenant gave orders to crack open one of the other glass blocks; five men went at it with spikes and sledgehammers. And the same thing happened again—a flash of light and a sharp clanging sound just as the glass cracked, then a chorus of voices and screams. The engineer had never heard anything so terrible in his whole life. He asked where they'd picked up the glass and they told him they'd got it in the inner archipelago where the sea meets the large inland lakes—in the place where a million people are supposed to have lived in the old days.

They cracked open a third block, and out of it poured a hymn, a desperate choir that seemed to be trying to drown out the screams and cries for help in the background. By then the lieutenant had had enough; they dumped the rest of the glass in the cove, blew up the barge, and headed out to sea after putting up one of the many large signs they had on hand: "Warning! Danger!"

— You shouldn't tell other people's stories, Petsamo says.

— But isn't it amazing how all those sounds and cries and screams were locked into the glass?

— Sailors' bullshit!

— But why? If you can get a whole orchestra into the grooves of a record, why shouldn't you be able to store screams in a ton of glass?

WE leave the Coke Desert and come to bare limestone plains. It's easier to walk now but also more dangerous. If you made a false step in the Coke Desert, the worst that could happen was that you stumbled and dislocated something. But here the land's crisscrossed with deep cracks, and you can easily fall thirty meters down into darkness. Yet there's plenty of fresh water and patches of juicy grass. Baby rabbits crawl all over on long, wiry legs, bellies close to the ground. They're not at all scared; you can pick them up the way you'd pick up a potato. They seem to be used to having no natural enemies, no gulls, predatory birds, no foxes or badgers—Petsamo says that badgers were a sort of big, smooth-haired hedgehog. And though we do see an occasional hedgehog, we prefer the sweeter meat of the rabbit. There isn't a single human being anywhere around; we're too close to the lepers.

We take our time, walk only a few miles a day and rest whenever we see an inviting spot—there are many. If the wind's up, we have no problem finding shelter; if the sun's too hot, there's always a shady rock around. If it rains we have our trusty little tent. But it doesn't rain: The sun is shining like a small, bright candle very high in the blue sky as though it's September or October, not the middle of May. It doesn't bother me. But Petsamo is like Henry: He grew up on the old, fixed calendar, and now he has trouble accepting that even the seasons are out of kilter.

One night while we're resting after we've eaten, I tell him about the Icelander who was once one of the richest captains in the Baltic before he lost everything.

It happened in Berga when you could still use the underground harbor. Of course the giant stone cave had been completely gutted, and there was no trace of the old naval base except some crumpled-up iron railings hanging like twisted train tracks here and there. But it was still a pretty good anchorage. In the winter—and in the height of the summer when the sun was too intense—many boats took shelter there.

The Icelander held court in his big trawler, which had even crossed the Atlantic. Toward people he liked he could be extremely generous; but to others he could be so cruel he'd drive them to suicide. The other master in Berga grotto was an ex-naval officer who commanded a coast guard cutter. He insisted he was the only remaining legal representative of the Authorities; I think he meant that he was the only one around who had been appointed by the Government. But whatever he meant, he wanted to be the boss over all the other ships. He was trying to take on a kind of power he couldn't really back up, not in terms of crew, weapons, or wealth.

The Icelander and the officer never openly showed how much they hated each other. On the contrary. They treated each other very, very politely. But we all held our breaths; we knew they'd have to face off sooner or later—we just didn't know when or how.

The fight began over a gift. The officer gave the Icelander a little flag from his collection of signal flags; the pattern was supposed to be the same as the Icelandic flag. The Icelander accepted it and ordered the flag to be raised. In return he gave the officer a box of multicolored light bulbs to hang in the rigging on special occasions. But it didn't stop there. The officer came back with a lifeboat, which was an ambiguous gift since you could take it to be saying that the Atlantic trawler wasn't seaworthy. The Icelander countered by giving the officer his navigator, an almost outright insult. And in return he got all the reserve provisions the coast guard cutter had on board.

Before long, they were both trapped in a murky tangle of presents and return presents. The crews got all mixed together and paddled back and forth in rubber rafts between the two ships, only to find out that the ship they thought they belonged to had just given them back to the one they'd left. It was even crazier with the equipment: One day the trawler was loaded down with heavy weapons but no ammunition; a few hours later it might be just the opposite. The end was tragic. The Icelander had given away all his fuel oil and gotten airplane fuel in return. One evening the coast guard cutter went out to sea to shoot off some fireworks in honor of Iceland. When the trawler tried to follow, it blew up, not from a cherry bomb or Roman candle but simply because double, turbocharged diesel engines aren't designed to use airplane oil. The Icelander had allowed it all to happen with his eyes wide open.

— I don't want to hear any more bullshit, Petsamo says.

— Do you want to hear what really happened?

— Not that either. I've heard enough about starving men trying to get through the winter up to their necks in garbage and lice while they huddle under tarpaulins frozen stiff as boards.

So there won't be any more stories about the sea *or* the land. Instead I study and he asks me questions. He has an amazing memory. He can recite which ailments he treated week by week since last summer: rheumatism, asthma, ileus, bone fractures, burns, gallstones, urinary blockage, coronary thrombosis, pneumonia, cataracts, etc. When he says "treated," he means that he answered questions, gave advice, held hands—and every once in a while put a bone in place or cleaned a wound. Even though most people here lost their teeth years ago, sometimes someone needs a piece of a root taken out or an abcess drained.

When we sit by the fire at night, he acts out different

symptoms for me. He ies there whimpering, pushing his fist into his stomach or pretending to be paralyzed; then I'm supposed to guess what's wrong just by asking questions. He loves to moan and twist to make my work harder, and he's always telling me that the only experience that counts is doing it for real. Almost angrily he says:

— Book learning won't do you a damn bit of good, because when you actually have to *do* something, you forget it all!

WE turn west and head straight for the Convent. Three days north we come to a deserted farm, which Petsamo hasn't visited since last winter. The moss and sheet-metal shed's empty. A few steps away we find two graves with sheet-metal crosses. Three old brothers used to live here, one of them paralyzed for years from the waist down. The other two had a harder and harder time each year supporting all of them. Their specialty was getting salt out of the saltwater marshes next to the farm through a complicated system of canals and shallow ponds. They'd sell the salt to the Convent and give it to Roland as "protection tax." At first Petsamo thinks that they were murdered because they didn't pay the protection tax—but the metal crosses suggest otherwise. More likely the work got too hard for them—the digging and the back-breaking job of hauling water buckets from the lower marsh up to the shallow ponds on the cliffs. Heavy rains may also have changed the salt content of the marsh itself. Only last fall the sick one asked Petsamo to "help him over the edge"; he'd known for a long time that two couldn't work enough to feed three. But the other brothers kept such a close eye on them that there was never a chance for Petsamo to do what he was asked. Probably the invalid and one of the others starved to death during the winter. But what about the third? While Petsamo looks for—

and doesn't find—the body, I wait a little way off. I don't want to meet up with one of those unburied souls even if it is the middle of the day.

THREE days later—according to Petsamo's 1992 pocket calendar it's May 20—we reach the Convent. From the north ridges we have a clear view of the golden promontory hooking out into the black lake. Here on the heights the rapeseed plants and potatoes are turning green while down in the shade of the slopes thousands of pink dandelions are still in blossom. I pick a few to smell them; to my surprise the white sap turns my hands black.

After the Sisters welcome us, Petsamo goes to check on his patient the Finn. She's feeling fine but is still mute; she can hum but not speak. Maybe she doesn't want to. Since the abortion she's already had what Petsamo calls her first "period." In *The Anatomy of the Human Female* he shows me how the tiny egg leaves the potato-shaped ovary, travels down through the Fallopian tube, and into the uterus. On the way it meets the most energetic of millions of sperm cells. I can't even count the times I've been down on all fours spitting out other men's sperm! But this makes me realize that the white slime isn't just disgusting—it's something precious, the slime of life. Both of us are very tired. We wash our blisters in warm salt water and curl up in the same underground room where I lay sick many months ago.

The next morning I wake up before dawn and walk down to the lake for a swim. Ever since I've become a landlubber, I swim so little I'm afraid I'm forgetting how. Papa was very careful to teach me to swim. There were two rules he drummed into me: Practice your swimming, and never eat or drink anything that you're not 100 percent sure is not contaminated, no matter how tempting it looks. He couldn't stick to the second rule himself.

After I swim a few hundred meters and start to head back toward the beach, I see the Finn sitting with a lantern a little way up the sandy slope; there's still so little light the lantern glitters faintly. I stop swimming and let my feet sink to the black bottom. What's she thinking of doing? Is she going to drown herself again? But she stays there, hugging the lantern as if to protect it from something. I start feeling cold; I decide to get out of the water.

— Morning! I shout, waving just in case she hasn't seen me already.

She raises the lantern in reply but stays where she is. I run up onto the beach and begin to jump from one leg to the other to shake the water off. Then I hear her laughing. But I don't pay any attention—I just keep jumping and knocking the water out of my ears, turning my back toward her. When I've pulled my clothes on and turned to face her, I see that she's up near the Chapel; the first rays of sunlight are bouncing off her lantern. I guess her job is to clean up before morning prayers.

I run after her. By the time I get there she's already inside, changing the drooping dandelions in the vase on the altar for newly picked ones.

— These things make your fingers black. . . .

She puts her fingers to her lips; I forgot you're not supposed to talk about worldly things in here. I wait. She changes some wax candles and shakes out the altar cloth. I try to catch her eye to get her to come outside with me so we can talk. First she pretends not to see me, then I catch a glimpse of her face—she's having a hard time holding back a laugh.

— What's your name?

She walks past me out the door. At the threshold she stops for a moment as though trying to say her name. But her lips move totally silently. I follow her out. She's facing me now; tears are welling up in her eyes even though she's still smiling. It's probably because of the memories I bring back to her, memories of the raid on the boat in the frozen stream. I haven't felt like this since Papa died. I don't know if I'm happy or sad. I want to run away and at the same time I want to be close to her, as if all the terrible pictures would go away if I could just grab her arm. But when I make a move toward her, she immediately turns away and runs over to a hatch leading down to the tunnels below. I race after her but she's too quick and she slams the hatch shut on the knuckles of my right hand.

I go back into the Chapel and kneel the way I've seen the Sisters do. I feel like I can't breathe. Every time I try to take a breath, my chest seems to expand as though the air I take in won't go out. It's not just my chest; my whole body feels as if it's expanding. After a few minutes I think I'm going to explode. Blood's pulsing behind my eyes. I turn my face up toward the whitewashed cross vault. That calms me down; it's like looking into a soft, fine drizzle. What is it about women that makes me feel so strange?

HEDVIG, one of the older Sisters, has such bad eyesight that she can't do any chores and can barely take care of herself. I hold the mirror while Petsamo examines her eyes in the sunshine. Both her pupils, especially the left one, are cloudy white; they look like they've been boiled.

— Cataracts, says Petsamo. I'm afraid I may be getting them myself.

I ask to look at his eyes while a Sister holds a mirror. But his eyes are as clear and black as the lake below, sometimes turning slightly greenish, like a distant reflection of seaweed and algae.

We go back to Sister Hedvig. If we took away the cloudy white button on the lens of her worst eye she'd be able to see again. Maybe we could also make a pair of cataract glasses out of old camera lenses. We thumb through *Common Diseases of the Eye*. Thousands of years ago they were already performing lens extractions; the diseased lens would be pushed away from the center of the pupil so that light could flow directly into the eye. In the book are pictures of how you can do a lens extraction with a few simple cuts and procedures. We have no real tools, but it's easy enough to grind a regular table knife down to a scalpel and make a probe out of steel wire. The old lady gropes for Petsamo's hands, trying to kiss them; he pushes her angrily away.

Then he walks down to the lake. I follow behind.

— Leave me alone. I'm thinking!

He starts scudding flat stones over the surface; they whirl and skip at least a dozen times. I'd love to see him in his full baseball uniform! He's told me about the small cap with the long brim, the red shirt with glittering silver letters, the arm guards, leg guards, spiked shoes, and shiny jacket that he slipped over his shoulders when he was resting. . . . How beautiful he must have looked with his steel-gray hair! But maybe his hair had a different color then; I've heard that hair changes color with age just as grass changes with the seasons, but I've never been able to check if it's true. The world is full of old wives' tales.

— Shall we cut her or shall we not?

I'm confused that he's asking my advice.

— If it'll make her well.

— Well? Of course it won't make her *well*! The most we can hope for is that she'll be able to manage another couple of years. Assuming of course that we actually do make a pair of glasses to replace the lens. Otherwise she'll only be able to tell light from dark.

— Then leave it up to her.

— Her? She's already got it into her head that I'm the Savior Himself who's walked across the lake on a path of sunlight to remove all burdens from her frail shoulders. She wants miracles, not temporary improvements!

— Then don't do it.

— Besides, the eye'll probably get infected. With a little bad luck an abcess could spread . . .

— Don't do it.

— But we might learn something! And next time we work on an eye, maybe we can actually accomplish something!

— We?

— You.

— Me?

He picks up a little stone and draws something on a big, flat rock:

— We'll cool down the eye with ice. Then you'll cut— look here—a curved incision . . . three, four millimeters. Then all you have to do is pick the lens off, maybe cut it loose first, we'll see . . .

— And if I chicken out?

— You won't. Take the book. Study it. I'll be standing right next to you. You can have a drink first. I learned that from marksmen.

I sit cross-legged in our little room, reading under the ceiling lamp. I close my eyes and try to see the diagram of the eye in my mind. It's not hard. Everything seems so simple. Too simple. I don't trust pictures of the body and its organs. Once I saw a man's eye get knocked out by a snapped cable. He became hysterical and wanted us to put it back. With the bloody blob in his hand he begged and pleaded and threw himself at our feet. We turned away. You couldn't tell that it had ever been an eye.

The Finn comes in so quietly that I smell her before I hear her. Everyone has a smell, but hers is different. Maybe because she's young—or because she's a woman? She sits next to me, takes my book and opens it. I want to touch her but I'm afraid of scaring her away. I don't feel at all the same way now as I did last winter when she was lying in here on the floor and her thigh made my prick stiffen and I could taste salt in my mouth and I felt such a strong urge to force her, to dominate her. Now I feel so soft inside: I just want to collapse and rest my head against her knee the way Klaus did that day on the beach. I try to catch her eye. But she's leafing through the book. Doesn't she notice anything? Can't she tell that my thoughts are so strong they're flickering in the lantern light? . . . I lick my lips to see if they taste the way they tasted last winter. Suddenly she gets up, pulls from under her shirt a chain with a little figure on it, kisses the figure and puts the chain in my hands. But I fumble with it, and it slips onto my knee. I pick it up with thumb and forefinger. It's a miniature crucifix with a Jesus no bigger than a crucified flying ant.

THAT night I lie awake. I can't decide whether or not to do the lens extraction. Why do I have to start with something so small and difficult? Why not a simple wound, an infected glass splinter, maybe a broken bone? But of course the sick people aren't going to come in the order I'd like—easy ones now, harder ones in a few months. If Petsamo thinks his eyesight isn't good enough to do *this* cataract operation, he won't do it next time either. My eyesight is good. But my courage isn't. Why do you have to have courage to cut open another person? I won't feel any pain at all. It isn't me who may get an abcess, not me who may die. She's the one taking all the risks. It feels almost as though I've been asked to kill her!

Around dawn I must have dozed off for a while, for when I wake up Petsamo's gone. The little crucifix I was holding in my right fist slipped out during the night; I find it digging into my cheek. I get up and kiss it the way I've seen the Finn do, then hang it around my neck. It gives me enough courage to decide to say no. Charms have always helped me through tight spots. When I had to dive under the trawler to do repair work, I wore a burnt-out digital watch on a wire around my neck.

The others held me under water with a boathook wrapped in rags so I wouldn't come up too soon; without my magic watch, I'd never have let them do that. Later, of course, it was stolen. But no one's going to get my crucifix.

Petsamo sits in the kitchen eating. He raises his spoon as a greeting:

— She's dead.

— Sister Hedvig?

— They found her in bed. She was holding her hands in front of her eyes as though she'd just beheld a Heavenly Light . . . at least that's Sister Signe's interpretation.

We've got to get out in a hurry. I manage to wolf down some food but don't have enough time to say good-bye to the girl. They want us out so the funeral preparations can begin; the corpse has to be buried by sundown. At the funeral itself the Sisters will perform a holy dance that no man has ever been allowed to see. But Petsamo knows about it anyway. They dance in the Chapel for hours—until their clothes get too heavy, and then they fling them off and dance till they collapse, one after the other. One of the exhausted women will go into a trance when an alien spirit—usually an evil one—gets inside her and takes her over. Usually the spirit leaves the woman sometime after she falls asleep. But if it doesn't, it will have to be driven out of her.

CHAPTER 15

JUST before the narrow creek empties into the ocean, it forms a pond in the reeds below the Prison. A pier has been built out of driftwood. Klaus and two others are helping Roland out of his wooden bed. They pull off his nightshirt; then Klaus walks backward into the water leading Roland by his left hand. Petsamo's sitting at the end of the pier. I'm standing by the reedy beach.

By now Roland isn't just very fat; he's swollen too. He can hardly look out over his lower eyelids, which are as thick as lips. The left corner of his mouth hangs slack, and when he gives orders to the helpers the cheek flaps loosely. His skin's grayish white, like soggy paper. Yellow, red, white, and black scratches range over his shoulders, chest, stomach and thighs.

— O.K., you damn lice, better learn to swim now . . . he says thickly, leaning backward until he hits the water.

Klaus and the two others stay out of his way while he floats out onto the pond, lazily splashing at the water now and then; he seems more dangerous now that he's moving under his own steam. Petsamo sits on his haunches, looking intently at his face, watching to see what he's going to say:

— What happened to my boat?

— We had to leave it. A sandstorm stopped us from getting out to the west coast in time.

— In time for what?

— For avoiding the peak of the piracy season.

Laughing, Roland starts to swallow water. Immediately his lips and eyelids turn bluish purple, but when he starts to cough he regains his mottled gray-white-pink color.

— Your boat's in the cove just north of the big area with all the stone pillars. You know, where the Norwegian ran aground with a hold full of grenades?

Petsamo's trying to cheer him up with pleasant memories, but I'm not sure that Roland—whose ears are underwater—hears him at all.

— You didn't bring the boat back.

— We'll get it next time.

— I suggest you buy it off me. In its present state. And location.

He paddles toward shore and stands up on the bottom; his helpers move closer to him. Klaus has a blue bottle in his hands, and at a signal from Roland all three start rubbing his torso with white gook from the bottle.

— Rub harder, you assholes! bellows Roland, slapping the water so that everyone including Petsamo gets soaked.

Then he puts both hands against the edge of the pier and sidles in toward the beach while they keep smearing his back, his suprisingly small, sagging ass, and his spindly legs. They take buckets of water, pour them all over him, scrape him down with pumice; he groans with pleasure and tosses his head. Klaus tries to take a tick from his belly button, but he gets only the body, not the head.

— Hey, watch it! Shit, I can't see a thing without glasses. . . . And just in case you fucked up, says Roland, dropping a gob of spit right on Klaus' forehead.

They put clean sheets on Roland's bed, dry him with towels made of sackcloth that's been washed until it's smooth, dress him in a clean nightshirt, and put him into bed. He waves me over.

— And what does Pussylips have to say for himself?

— We delivered the stuff to Halvar. And found a library with quite a bit of fuel.

— And where *is* that fuel? Still there with those noseless, sack-covered spooks?

Petsamo comes down from the pier and stands next to me.

— I couldn't have managed without Edvin.

— How's Halvar doing?

— Chipper as always, Petsamo says.

— Did he pick up the Top Twenty on his radio yet?

Roland barely has time to laugh at his own joke before he's seized by another coughing fit and his face turns violet, the same shade as the blotches on a cadaver. The coughs make his loose left cheek flap like a foresail, and his piercing eyes fight madly not to sink behind his eyelids for good. To stop his coughing they help him into a sitting position.

— Edvin's become something of an assistant to me.

— Ass-is-tant!?

The word seems to infuriate him. He slumps down and glares sideways at his helpers. Then he chews on his gums, swallows, and gazes off into the air.

— I'm trying to teach him a little bit about medicine. Who knows how long I'll be around?

— You'll be around as long as I'm around. Can't worry about what happens after we're gone. Just feel sorry for the poor bastards who'll still be here.

— Don't worry. I'll take care of you. But Edvin could do a lot of the other work. That way I'd have more time.

— How much will you give me for him?

— He can't be worth too much . . . he's been just a prisoner here; you never let him carry a gun.

— But now he has *medical training*, might even start going around calling himself a *doctor*. . . .

— How much do you want?

— And I've got to get paid for the boat too—which you just bought.

— How much? And what kind of currency?

— Opium.

— Hasn't been any around for fifteen years—as you know perfectly well.

— Lucky for you. If it got out that you'd had a stash somewhere . . .

— Instead of opium?

— Anything special we need, boys?

They mention ammunition for automatic weapons, gasoline, shoes, lead for soldering, needles, thread, pepper, honey, thermos bottles.

Petsamo has none of them.

— Gold, I suggest. Petsamo's eyes widen in surprise.

— There's gold and gold, Roland says. So many different qualities. You have gold, Petsamo?

— I know where he can get some.

— In that case he'd better have an escort . . . just so he doesn't lose any nuggets along the way.

They decide that Petsamo will buy me and the abandoned boat for four hundred grams of pure gold. In the meantime I'll stay here and work for Roland—hard labor, not doctoring.

The evening is the first chance I get to give Petsamo the details about Henry's gold mine. He's going to go south as soon as he can, but there's a lot to do first. It's not only peak season for pirates but also for luring in ships—and Petsamo also has to go back to the Convent for an exorcism.

— What's that?

— When a woman commits a mortal sin, often sexual in nature—or if a demon gets into her in the dance I told you about—she has to go before the altar and confess that she's been possessed. Then the demon's driven out of her. It's an old Christian tradition. And it must be done by a man.

— But you're not a priest.
— I'm a man.

THIS time they don't lock me in the cellar. I'm allowed to live with some of the others in the Pavilion, the low building that used to be divided into cells but now, at our end, has only two rooms: the dormitory and the latrine. Eight men live in the thirty-square-meter dormitory; the latrine's just a bench with two holes. The building itself is on the side of a hill, so when you're in the latrine you sit with your back facing the slope. They've cut an oblong opening into the lower part of the wall. At dawn the dogs gather outside: Following their own clear order of rank, they tiptoe forward to breakfast.

Chuck, the Chief of the Pavilion, answers directly to Roland, but unlike Pretty Boy, he lives with us. His most noticeable characteristic is that he's got only one good eye; the other's overgrown with gray-white cartilage. Usually blind eyes turn inward and hide behind half-closed eyelids—but Chuck's bulges out, swelling like an egg, twitching and moving inside the pale lump as if someone's trying to chop his way out. He owns eighteen harmonicas but can't play a single one; the first question he asks me is if I can play a mouth organ. But I can't play any instrument at all. When I was ten they made me stand and beat a drum from dawn till dusk. I've hated instruments ever since.

Klaus lives in the Pavilion too. He's got the right to tell me what to do because his number is seven and mine is eight; Chuck is number one. The whole system here at the Prison is based on the principle of everyone knowing his exact place. While they kept me prisoner in the cellar, I didn't have a number; I didn't even know the system existed. But I did notice that there were hardly any fights. At sea the ordinary seamen fought all the time, but here the pecking order is just as strict as among the dogs. Being even the lowest on the scale gives you a certain feeling of security; power struggles become unnecessary.

They also have a voting system based on the pecking order, but reversed. Number one, Chuck, has eight votes; number two, Hans, has seven; and so on down to Klaus who has two and I one. But they hardly ever take votes; more than anything, the system seems to be a holdover from the old days when the place was a "prison for younger men." Aside from the way everyone is ranked, the most important rules are that there's absolutely no booze, everyone has to work, and you're allowed to keep 10 percent of anything you get either by plundering or by just stumbling across it. This means that the old guys (or " the boys," as they like to call themselves) do a lot of trading among themselves. Aside from things like gold and jewelry, which you hardly ever see, they mostly trade shoes, unbroken glass bottles, calendars, pictures of naked people and fucking, and souvenirs from the past without practical value— pocket calculators, paper money, advertising labels. If there's a disagreement about something's value, Chuck has to decide— or, if he doesn't want to get on anyone's bad side, they'll take a vote. There also seem to be a lot of unwritten rules I'd better learn soon if I don't want to get into trouble. One is that all jewelry or precious metals should always end up in the hands of high-ranking people. If someone finds a ring, for instance, they make sure it's slipped discreetly into Chuck's pocket— although not so discreetly that Chuck doesn't know who put it there. I lie at night clutching my little crucifix. To be on the safe side, should I slip it under Chuck's pillow? Or is a steel crucifix considered a souvenir from the past without practical value?

ON the other side of the sand embankment on the beach, automatic weapons are coughing out two or three shots at a time.

The four highest-ranking people are having target practice. The rest of us (the ones who aren't allowed to carry weapons except in emergencies) haul seaweed from the beach up to the drying area. To pass the time we try to guess from the sound which weapon's being used: Kaskolnikov, Steen, M-16, Virapuru, Husqvarna, RR, or Uzi.

Since Klaus and I are numbers seven and eight, we're always paired up. With pitchforks we load the red seaweed into an old net and gather up the corners of both ends so we can carry it on our backs. While we're laboring over the embankment, Klaus stops:

— I love you.

He lets his end of the net drop, takes my head in his hands and starts kissing my lips and teeth. I don't kiss him back but I don't push him away either. I like him but that's where I want it to stay. Maybe I loved him a tiny bit that day when we were combing the beach. But not now. He doesn't make me feel soft inside; I feel more like laughing. Men who try too hard to make you like them start to seem ridiculous.

— Let's move it before anyone sees us.

— Don't forget our escape plans, he whispers. I thought so much about it.

He lets go of me but not fast enough to avoid a few nasty remarks from Arno and The Boot who're on their way down toward us:

— Hey, lovebirds, don't just stand there with your tails in the air!

After we empty the net and pick out the seaweed stuck in it, we squat on our haunches and take our five-minute break. I'm listening to the shots, but Klaus wants to kiss again. Then we hear a scream from the other side of the embankment. The shots stop. Chuck comes running to the top shouting:

— Roffe's in the marker ditch!

We hustle up the slope. Under the cans held in the air by sticks—those are the targets—runs a shallow ditch in which a

marker can scurry back and forth without getting in the line of
fire. Two men are trying to get Roffe out of the ditch; Chuck's
standing around barking advice. We climb down and just
stand there without knowing exactly what to do; actually
there's no room for us to do anything. The two guys get Roffe
on his feet. All three are groaning and cursing. They lean him
against the dirt wall. He's hurt his shoulder—his right arm is
dangling down.

   — Why the fuck isn't Petsamo here when you need him!

   — Edvin has been taking lessons from Petsamo, Klaus says
as if he's trying to impress them.

   — Pussylips?

I keep my mouth shut; I don't want to be dragged into this.
But Chuck comes down, glares at me with his cartilage eye,
and grabs my shirt:

   — What are you, some kind of doctor's apprentice?

He shoves me toward Roffe, who's sitting and howling and
holding his arm. Tears run down his dusty cheeks. He looks
up at me pleadingly:

   — Can you fix it? I'll give you my hand pinball game!

   — Can you fix his arm?! roars Chuck.

I tell them to pick him up. When I compare right and left
shoulders, I can see that the right one's narrower, as though
the upper arm has slipped out a peg. There's a picture just like
that in *The Little Surgeon*. If I'm right, it means that the
shoulder's dislocated. But it can also mean something is broken. I close my eyes and try to think clearly, try to see the
picture in the book. It says that you have to do an X ray to
make sure there's no fracture. What would Petsamo do?
Would he take a chance and pull the shoulder back into
place? Or would he just wait and see? But if you're going to try
it, you have to do it before the muscles stiffen with pain. Or
would Petsamo think to himself that if Number Four's right
arm is busted, he won't grow much older around here. And
maybe then I'd move up a peg.

— I'll switch numbers with you, Roffe begs me.

— Nobody's switching any numbers, says Chuck. Can you fix the arm, Pussylips?

I tell Roffe to lie on the ground. Two men have to hold him down. I brace my bare foot against his armpit, get a good grip around his elbow—and pull. Nothing happens, except that he howls like hell. I let him rest a few minutes before I try again. Again nothing happens. But this time he passes out.

— Hey, motherfucker, you trying to yank his arm off?

I start feeling sick myself; cold sweat runs down the back of my neck. The only thing I can do is try a third time. This time my sweaty hands make me lose my grip, and I stumble backward. I wipe my hands off and yank again. I can feel the suction when the ball of the joint slides across the threshold into the socket.

ROFFE spends the next several days in the Pavilion. He lies with his bad right shoulder facing up; the whole upper arm down to the elbow is swollen and blue. Is it broken? At this point (it's the fifth day), Chuck won't even let me look at him. He just says:

— You know, it could cost you to break somebody's arm around here!

It's too soon. I know that. There's still a chance it was only dislocated. I work and wait. Only Klaus and I are on the seaweed detail; the rest are standing guard at the Tower and up on the ridges, or combing the beaches. Sooner or later a ship has to turn up. On the sixth and seventh days, Roffe still isn't better. Chuck says nothing; he just thoughtfully, almost gently, drops a gob of spit on my feet as he walks by. That night I try to get over to Roffe to look at his shoulder. But the others shove me back to my place by the door. How will they punish me if they decide his useless right arm is my fault? If Roland thinks he can do without me, they'll use the old, old principle of an eye for an eye, a tooth for a tooth; we do the same thing at sea. But if they break my shoulder they'll lose two workers. They'd only do that if they expect to get people from the outside. So at night I rub my crucifix and mumble the way the Sisters taught me: Dear God, please don't let a ship come!

If a ship doesn't bring new men, maybe they'll be satisfied with some sort of "disciplinary action." That's something the Pavilion Chief, not Roland, decides. It's another holdover from the old days, but this one the prisoners themselves took care of. The lightest punishment was for everyone to spit in the guilty man's food and drink. Another—which they could do only on weekends in the old days when the guards wouldn't check—was to tie the man to a chair. In the winter he'd be put in the latrine, in the summer outside with the dogs. There he'd have to sit for two or three days. The others would feed him but he couldn't leave the chair—he'd have to shit and piss where he sat. Then he'd just sit in his own muck. They say that in the winter the worst part was the lice. In the summer it was the flies, plus the constant circle of slobbering dogs.

THE next morning there's a general alarm. They've finally sighted a ship! We put out all the fires. No one can say a word or move around in any way that might be seen from the water. We all get weapons; Klaus and I each get a double-barreled shotgun. Then, where the stream meets the ocean, we set up mortars and get some small boats ready. Ever since the last unsuccessful try at luring a ship ashore, they've been working on a better plan. They've outfitted a big herring boat with extra tall masts with silver-glittering foil flags fluttering on top. But we wait all day, and we still can't see anything from land; only the lookout on the Tower has the ship in his sights. We spend the night at our battle stations. I lie awake and rub my crucifix and take just short naps. Once I dream of the Finn hanging on a big cross above the altar in the Chapel. When I get near her and kneel before her, she laughs wildly. The sound flies into the vault and bounces back and forth with a clattering echo.

Just before sunup, we can make out the ship in the distance. At first it looks like a huge blue pillar floating above the fog belt to the east. Then, when the sun actually comes out, we see a terrifying, mysterious object bearing down on us: not a pillar but three giant columns connected at the top by some sort of platform, like a three-legged stool. Backlit by the sun, the stool looks blue. It comes closer and closer, towering higher and higher above the horizon. It's taller than Castle Rock, taller than anything I've ever seen. Now it's close enough for us to see that the pillars are resting on enormous half globes floating on the water. As the sun moves directly overhead, the monster's legs look rust pink; the top part has rusted to a charred black.

Someone shouts for Roland—where is he? Why isn't he down here on the beach with his men? A rumor starts flying around that he's dead, but before long someone catches a glimpse of him in the Tower. Two men start whispering that we ought to get out of here; whatever it is, it's big enough to be carrying a thousand men. But no one sounds the retreat. The three rusty columns revolve slowly so that one pillar is hidden behind another. Now it looks like a giant so tall his body disappears above the puffy cumulus clouds—a giant like that could cross the island from east to west in two strides. It makes no sound: no engines, no clattering cables, no shouts of command from the platform. When it gets into shallow water it's bound to tip over; and if it does, it'll crush the Tower easily.

We get the order to open fire. We unload everything. Mortars fling their shells, bazookas roar, machine guns clatter. Klaus and I fire our buckshot as fast as we can reload. The cascades of water from the shells look ridiculously small; and when shots ring out against the metal sides, all that falls off is a bit of rust, which floats away. For more than an hour we keep shooting at the three-legged tower that seems to dwarf the sky.

Then the wind shifts to the north—we can't tell if it's our gunfire or the wind that makes the giant iron stool begin drifting south instead of straight toward us. Slowly, majestically, listing slightly with the wind, the floating temple glides south. The next morning it's still visible to the naked eye.

I notice only now that Roffe's down on the beach with us. His arm is working smoothly; he's even carrying a gun.

CHAPTER 16

WHEN they start to collect the weapons, they discover that Klaus has taken off with an automatic pistol and all the stuff under his bed; someone's also raided Roland's private food supply in the kitchen and walked away with a pair of binoculars and a tent. They order us to search the beaches on the double. No one can figure out how he managed to escape— none of the boats or canoes is missing. Chuck has a theory that Klaus may have found a boat or built a raft out of driftwood he never gave in. No one else has any better ideas, so they report to Roland that Klaus has run off to sea. Whatever's left of his possessions isn't divided up among the rest of us the way it usually is when someone dies; instead it all goes to Roland as the first payment to make up for whatever's been stolen. Of course they cross-examine everybody to find out if we know anything. And give me a thump on the back for healing Roffe.

When I go to bed that night, I find a little piece of aluminum underneath the rolled-up sack I use for a pillow. A message from Klaus. I'm furious. If anyone had found it, I would have been accused of conspiracy and shot! I hide it in my clothes and read it only the next day. In the soft metal he's scratched H-HOUSE. Just as I thought. He didn't go to sea at all; he headed south to Henry's hut. And now the mushy-lipped idiot is sitting down there waiting for me! What he doesn't know is that Petsamo should be arriving there any day.

JUNE and July come and go. I have to work harder than ever. More than half the men are down on the beach. All the daily work—hauling seaweed, cleaning and inspecting weapons, distributing food to the men on watch—the rest of us have to do. Because Klaus is missing I do double duty: I get up at the crack of dawn and work non stop until it's so dark I can't see where I'm going. I sleep only three or four hours. Sometimes they get me up in the middle of the night to stoke the fire. My old cough comes back. And what's Petsamo doing? If he is still at the Convent he could at least send a message—someone goes there three times a week for rapeseed oil and vegetables. I feel completely trapped. And what about Klaus? I suppose he's just sitting around pining away for me. That disgusts me. What disgusts me even more than the thought of his soft mouth is what might happen if they find him. They'd ask him about Henry's hut, how it happened that he ended up there. Should I run away too?

HALF of August goes by. Still no ship in sight. Someone begins to talk about going up to Castle Rock and setting an ambush behind it. Others look for scapegoats. They suddenly remember the time in the spring when we couldn't lure in that ship. Klaus and I were the ones in the little boat. Was Klaus already trying to escape? Was he in cahoots with somebody in the ship? He must have made a deal with them to be picked up, but then for some reason it didn't work out. One guy remembers that Klaus used to wander around at night. Another says that he concealed stuff he found on the beach. Their suspicions always revolve around me. No one's actually said my name out loud. But how long will my success with Roffe's shoulder protect me?

Because we're not getting anything from the sea, we'll have to open up a new supply of rice at the end of the month; only Roland knows how much is left. The talk about Klaus starts up again. Did he find out something about the rice and pass it on to outsiders? In that case, *how* did he find out? It had to come from someone close to Roland, someone who'd been alone with him. Who? Or was Klaus Roland's secret little lover? No one takes that idea very seriously: Roland's only passion is power—and food.

When I get another fever attack, I can't tell anyone: A person my age isn't supposed to get sick. I'm at least twenty years younger than The Boot, the youngest of them. And the punishment for malingering is to be thrown into the water on a cold, windy day and then to sit overnight on a rock in the middle of the breakers. Head throbbing, I drag myself around, seeing things that aren't there: The Tower changes into a huge moon rocket, the blockhouse into a restaurant, the stream into a gushing river of red-hot foundry steel—everything from the Captain's and the library's picture books. Finally the Captain himself steps out of the evening fog, straddles me, opens his fly and salutes crisply.

By nightfall the shakes are over. Sweat pours out; the fever's broken. I sleep like a dead man, but at sunrise two men come to get me. I get up on all fours and shake out the cobwebs, thinking that they want me down on the beach to haul seaweed—but instead they tell me to hustle to Roland's room on the double! What could he want? To find out what's going on with the record player, to listen to the latest gossip among the boys?

But this time the armed guard standing outside the Tower looks nervous; he frisks me thoroughly before letting me in and doesn't give my balls his usual friendly yank. When I get inside, Roland isn't alone; Pretty Boy is standing by the window, his left eye shining an angry pink against his bone-white cheek. Roland's flat on his back in his enormous bed, inhaling and exhaling with long, snorting breaths. His face is blue, and his little eyes bulge out from behind puffy eyelids; his left cheek sags even more than before.

— Take a look at him!

I hesitate a moment before walking over and looking down into his face. The vacant eyes are trembling. His swollen tongue seems to be getting in the way of the heaving, irregular breaths. I pull the cover away; watery shit's run out all over the bed. He's holding his left arm and leg bent, but the limbs on the other side are slack as though they belonged to another body—a drowned man's. No reaction when I pinch his limp arm. But when I try to pry open his bent left arm, at first he tightens like iron, then lets go little by little like a winch locked in place by a cogwheel. His face looks completely changed. I think he's dying; maybe a blood vessel has sprung a leak somewhere inside his purple, fat-padded skull.

Pretty Boy is very jumpy:

— I gotta ask him a few things!

— I think it's too late.

He tries to sit Roland up. The two of us together can't do it. He calls in the nervous guard, and finally we manage to get him into a half-sitting position and prop him up with pillows. Pretty Boy sends out the guard.

— Roland? Can you hear me? *Tell me where the rest of the rice is!* How much is *left*?!

Roland wheezes and begins to slide slowly back down in the bed.

— He's unconscious.

But Pretty Boy ignores me:

— Roland, you're gonna whisper in my ear *everything* I want to know about the rice!

The patient wheezes and drools but doesn't try to turn his mouth toward the ear that Pretty Boy leans toward him.

— It's hopeless.

— Shut your mouth, cunt!

He grabs Roland's head tightly and presses Roland's mouth against his ear. Then he nods a few times and gives me a phony smile. He lets go of the head and gets up, satisfied.

— You didn't hear anything you weren't supposed to hear, did you?

— No.

— But you did hear enough to know that he told me where the rice is?

I don't answer.

— Good. You heard us talking about the rice. But not *where* it is. Now that Roland's dead I'm in charge. And I know where that rice is.

— He's not dead yet.

— Take a good look . . . of course he's dead. You've never seen a dead man before?

— I've seen lots of them.

— Then you can see that he's dead too. As soon as we get more manpower you'll be the one to take care of the sick. But I don't need you anymore right now. Now that you've signed Roland's death certificate.

LATER that day all work stops. We get the order to assemble in front of the Tower. Pretty Boy announces that Roland died that morning. He was clearheaded right to the very end and passed over the reins of power to Pretty Boy according to all the rules and regulations. There's no cause for anyone to worry; everything will remain the way it's always been. There's plenty of rice for the future. And Roland's last wish was that what can't be taken from the sea must be claimed from the land.

Late that evening Roland's big bed is carried out of the blockhouse to a sand hill overlooking the sea and lowered onto a bed of wood chips and dried seaweed. The boys break open some cartridges and sprinkle gunpowder all around. Then Pretty Boy throws a torch toward the bed; it comes to rest at its foot but starts to go out. Just as he's about to throw another, the bed ignites in a white burst of sparks; flames roar, and for the last time we see Roland sit up in bed.

THEY'VE promoted me to weapons carrier. Pretty Boy has changed the pecking order; some have been moved up, others demoted. And I'm not only allowed to carry a weapon; he also likes to come over and talk to me. He seems to trust me more than the others because I'm from the outside. The pecking order isn't the only thing he's changed. Now we're more free to live where we like. I get to move back to the room in the cellar; I furnish it with a cot, table, chair, and an oil lamp with metal reflectors. During the few moments when I'm not on guard duty or doing something else, I keep working on the record player; it seems like years ago since Roland asked me to fix it.

Pretty Boy is the opposite of Roland. He's everywhere, checking over everything, urging us on. But as soon as he leaves the work just about stops. Roland's power came from that strict system of rules where everyone watched everyone else. Because you hardly ever saw him, he took on an almost magical power; his spirit hovered over the whole Prison. Even the size of his body helped; it made him a symbol. But Pretty Boy buzzes around like a fly. He makes on-the-spot decisions but doesn't seem to have thought about the consequences.

The people he's promoted aren't grateful—they just want even more power. And the ones he's demoted walk around giving him dirty looks.

What's going on now is an almost-exact repeat of what I saw happen during the time I was on the Lightship. The Lightship wasn't fast, but she could handle rough seas like no other ship in the archipelago. When the autumn storms came, the rest of the boats had to huddle together in the harbors. But we could lie to among the most dangerous shoals and ride out the rough weather. We'd be the first to take the harvest of the storm in the form of shipwrecks, goods, and people.

During one of our raids, the skipper was killed. The first mate took command without anyone protesting. But he got it into his head to stop the bartering that the crew had regulated by itself for decades. He wanted to make himself popular by showing that everything could be done open and aboveboard. Yet by introducing what he called justice, all he really did was make everybody uncertain about things they used to take for granted. No one liked the new system, not even those who benefited from it. They lost the security of having someone to hate—the rich ones—and started fighting among themselves over piddling differences. The people who ended up running the Lightship cared about only one thing: the letter of the law. We couldn't lie at anchor anymore and wait for wrecks from the storm. Finally we ran aground deep in the inner archipelago. The once-so-proud light tower tipped over. Even though we were in the shallows, many people drowned.

I'm doing sentry duty on top of the Tower. You're supposed to scan the horizon according to a very strict system. The cinderblock wall is divided into sectors keyed to the points of the compass; at certain intervals holes have been bored into the cinder blocks and iron spikes driven in. This way you can check sector after sector without taking a chance of missing anything or going over an area too quickly. It's easy to miss things far out at sea. It's also easy to see things that aren't there, especially at dawn or dusk. And it can even be hard to find the *surface* of the sea. Low-lying fogs can raise it almost imperceptibly; reflections from dark clouds can make it seem lower.

In between each sweep of the binoculars, I also have to check the guards on the beach. One day the one to the south runs up on the embankment and starts waving his arms. When he gets to the top he falls to his knees and fires off a volley. Has he finally seen a ship? But then why is he shooting? I report the news on the pipe telephone down to the block-house. For once Pretty Boy happens to be inside, and he takes off for the beach right away. A few minutes later they relieve me and send me down there too. Two corpses have washed up; Pretty Boy wants to know how long they've been in the water and what they died of. But I can't tell them a thing. They look like beached corpses usually do: unnaturally swollen, all their holes filled with seaweed, sand, and garbage as though they've been down in the depths stuffing themselves. Their white skin is so loose you can pull it off their hands like gloves. It makes us all nervous—is this a bad omen? But at least one good thing comes out of it: For almost a week we don't have the dogs sitting around drooling outside the latrine.

IN September the general mood in the Prison gets worse; when Pretty Boy cuts the rice rations, the tension feels as if it's going to explode into open mutiny. Rumors fly that the rice really is running out, that at the end Roland wouldn't tell Pretty Boy where it was hidden. But then he starts preparations for an expedition. He divides us into new groups and we pack sup-plies, repair tents, oil weapons. Now the suspicions grow even louder. We're talking openly about going out to search for the hidden rice.

But we're wrong. He orders us to march due west. We transport the heavier equipment in boats; when the stream gets too narrow, we roll the boats along on barrels, and that night we camp outside. It's only next morning that Pretty Boy tells us what this is all about. We're on our way to attack and take over the Rabbit-Convent. All because of Roland's last wish that what the sea won't give us, we should take from the land.

The next night the men have trouble sleeping. Why should we take the Rabbit-Convent when there's nothing there but old ladies? Except, of course, for the Finn—but she isn't enough for everyone. Some of the boys think something's fishy; some new power element that only Pretty Boy knows about has entered the picture. Have the lepers suddenly gone on the warpath? Have pirates landed on the west coast? The Boot thinks that there's going to be an invasion from outer space, which Pretty Boy has found out about. At first everyone laughs him down, but then some others start to agree. If it's true, the Convent with its catacombs and underground tunnels is the best natural fortress around against flying saucers. Now no one can get any sleep. They move away from the fire and nervously study the gloomy sky.

In the morning, half the troops line up on the heights north of the Convent; that way we can cut off the Sisters' over-land escape route. The rest of us are going to attack from the ocean side. I don't get it at all. For years the Prison and the Convent got along well; they needed each other and both gained something from being on friendly terms. If only Pet-samo were here to talk some sense into them! I try to persuade Pretty Boy not to make a direct attack. They're not going to put up any resistance. All he has to do is tell them that we're taking over. But he won't listen to anyone:

— We owe it to Roland to carry out his last wish. The Convent has outlived its usefulness. So has the old Prison.

What we're going to do is set up a new one here where we can't be attacked from the sea!

We trot down the hill lackadaisically and fire a few warning shots. The nonsense about an invasion from outer space ended as soon as it got light. Since I'm the last one to have lived here, I have to show them the last stretch of the way to make sure both groups of our men meet at the Chapel. By this time the Sisters have had enough time to gather inside; from far off we can hear their shrill singing. But not even Pretty Boy has the guts to storm a church, so instead we set up a siege camp outside the big doors and prepare to wait them out. There's no direct tunnel from the Chapel to the underground vaults; they have no way to escape.

We pitch the tents, post a guard, then lie down to rest. A whole day passes. Around sunrise the chanting finally starts to wane. But by the time Pretty Boy rouses the boys, the Sisters have started their squeaky psalm singing once again. All day we sit yawning, our rifles across our knees; all we can do is listen to one piercing, caterwauling voice after another—now they're singing in relay fashion to give themselves time to rest. Our supplies are running low; Pretty Boy hadn't planned on a long siege. He sends a couple of men out to shoot a sheep. Later in the evening, we roast it.

AT first Pretty Boy turns down my offer to climb up onto the Chapel roof to see how their supplies are holding out, but when some others say it's a good idea, he gives in. They don't take it for granted anymore that he's their leader. Getting up on the roof turns out to be harder than I thought. We need a rope; hours later we finally come up with a rough cable. We fling it over the roof; then I wrap my hands in rags and shinny up. Lying on my stomach, I look down the old bell-rope hole. While one Sister kneels before the altar singing, the rest sleep or rest huddled together on the floor in a tight cluster. Sister

Signe sits reading the Bible. I count them and try to figure out who is who. The Finn isn't there.

We sleep in our tents a second night. But I stay awake, and in the darkest part of the night I slip outside. It's not very hard; the sand muffles my footsteps, and the sentry's looking over toward the Chapel. Besides, like many older people he has trouble seeing in the dark. In a minute or two I find a hatch and start down into the tunnels. After I find a lantern in the kitchen and light it, I can move more easily. The Finn's where I expect her to be: sitting asleep in the innermost chamber, the one with the crucifix.

CHAPTER 17

I'M rowing the flat-bottomed boat south, straight across the lake. The Finn lies asleep with her head between my feet. By now the fire burning before the Chapel has faded to a flickering spark to the north. The beaches lie wrapped in darkness, and when the boat runs up into the first clump of reeds it takes me completely by surprise. We lurch to a stop so suddenly that I drop one of the oars and fall into the bottom of the boat. The Finn wakes up and starts screaming.

— Be quiet!

I grope for her to calm her down, but she just gets more upset and angry; her high-pitched screams ring out across the lake. I grab hold of her foot and stroke it gently. At first she tries to pull away, then she lets me do it. Her screams change to whimpers and sobs. I kneel in the boat, stroking her foot until she falls asleep. That's when I notice that the oar has floated away. I get into the chest-high water and swim around looking for it. The bottom is soft and muddy. I thought that the south end would be just as rocky and barren as the rest of the lake, but when the light starts to come up I can see endless bunches of tall reeds forming a thick green wall farther to the south.

I give up searching for the oar; we couldn't row here any-way. Instead I stand up on wobbly legs in the stern and paddle with the remaining oar, zigzagging in between the reed is-lands. Several times I almost fall in. The Finn wakes and sits up with a start. But she calms down and crawls into the bow for counterbalance, then a little later stretches over the prow and guides it away from the reeds. Now it's almost completely light; a white sun is rising in the yellow dawn. I turn and look to the north, but the reeds completely hide any view. The biggest ones are over three meters high.

Before long the heat becomes oppressive. We can hear wind rustling the tops of the reeds, but not the slightest gust reaches us in the boat. Pink clouds sail across the sky. Swarms of dragonflies circle around us, moving through the air just as jerkily as we move through the water. The heat is making me dizzy and short of breath, and I have to sit down. The Finn sits facing me. When she pulls off her cap, I see that her hair's begun to grow: thin gray and yellow strands make her look like a dandelion puff or like one of the saints with halos around their heads on the altarpiece in the Chapel. She puts her hand in the brown water and bends toward it.

— Wait . . .

But she's already started slurping. She scoops up water in her cupped hands and stands up swaying, reaching her hands toward me. By the time I manage to bend toward her, al-most all of it's run out. But it's drinkable. So I turn all the way around, kneel in the stern, stick my whole head in

the water and drink, snorting and gurgling. She's laughing
behind me.

WE spend the whole day in the reeds. Dense areas alternate
with small open patches of water. We pole ahead through
winding or occasional arrow-straight canals. Large green leaves
floating on the surface give us the most trouble; their stems are
tough and almost impossible to pull off if you get stuck in
them. I often end up in the water pushing or pulling the boat;
blue, green-blazing or gold-glittering dragonflies sit on the
gunwales, glued together two by two.

We find a rusted-out gasoline barrel and a little farther on
a blackened log sticking out of the mud with an iron-gray rope
wound around it—which quickly crumbles into brown tufts
when I grab it. About a meter down in the snot-green sea grass
is a glittering aluminum can. I get out and pull it up. There's
no lid, and when I empty it black leeches come pouring out.
Behind the next curtain of reeds a wooden platform slopes
halfway under the surface. It's resting on old gasoline barrels—
some still airtight, but most more or less corroded. On the dry
part of the raft is a caved-in hut made of planks and corrugated
sheet metal; it even has a chimney, a red sheet-metal pipe
dangling over one wall. Inside we find some rotting sacks and
a cut-out gasoline barrel with some ashes in it.

She rummages through the hut while I lower myself into
the water and check over the platform; ten meters square, it's
moored with cables and iron rings to a couple of thick poles,
probably old telephone poles, driven into the muddy bottom.
All the wood below the surface is covered with a slimy fuzz.
On the poles green, gray, and brown rings show the changes
in the water level. I don't think anyone's lived here for fifteen
or twenty years.

*   *   *

SHE takes my knife and scratches something into a floorboard: TVLIKKI. I try to say it out loud.

— Tvlllikki . . .

She changes the V to a U. Then squeezes in an extra U and changes the last letter to an E. Maybe she can't spell.

She laughs and puckers her lips, drawing in air with a whistling sound. I copy her:

— Toooolikke!

I take the knife and scratch EDVIN. She reads it with a wrinkled forehead, then says my name without a sound coming from her lips. She looks at me, a question on her face. I nod that she's got it right. Then she shows me with her hands that she's tired and wants to sleep.

— Sleep, Tooolikke.

She nods good-night and lies down on her side. There are still several hours till sunset. I can't sleep. I haven't eaten since yesterday; hunger runs like hot water through my guts. The water doesn't taste as fresh as it did the first time—now there's a strong, muddy aftertaste. Back at the Convent the old men must have noticed a long time ago that not only I but one of the women is missing. Everyone in the Prison knew that Tulikke didn't die and that Petsamo did an abortion on her; a lot of them were only too happy to take credit for making her pregnant. Probably they won't come after me; they didn't give a damn about Klaus. But maybe some of them still want Tulikke? I try to picture last winter's rape. Which men were they? I can't remember even one face. I probably saw only the last part. The really eager ones—and the ones at the top of the rank list—must have done everything they wanted to do before they threw me into the house.

I climb down into the boat to get the submachine gun. Aside from the knife, the loaded gun is the only real equipment we have. What can we find to eat around here? We could probably catch dragonflies—but are there any fish around? There's no life at all in the black part of the lake, but at least here there are leeches. I lie down on my stomach, my face hanging over the edge, and wait for the water to stop moving. But it's almost impossible to make out the bottom. All I can see is my own wobbly brown face with a flat, crooked nose, two small eyes, a bright yellow gum shining through the crack underneath one of my nostrils. I didn't always look like this. I remember a reflection in a shiny aluminum plate from my childhood: an innocent face with a narrow little nose and an undamaged mouth.

IT starts to rain in the evening—round, heavy drops exploding on the surface of the lake. She wakes and looks up, smiling as the drops collect in the folds and creases of her face. Then she opens her mouth to drink.

— Don't do it!

Laughing, she pushes me away. She opens her mouth even wider.

— Stop, you idiot!

I grab her shawl from the deck and put it over her face. Immediately she starts screaming and fighting. We both almost roll off the raft. Finally I have to twist her arm behind her back to make her quiet down. I pull the shawl away from her face with my left hand. She tries to bite me, but I'm too fast:

— Rain! D-a-n-g-e-r!

She shakes her head and slurps the water greedily.

— Listen to me: the rain may *taste* uncontaminated . . . but there still could be white ash in it. Which you can't taste!

She looks like one of Roland's dogs waiting to be kicked.

— I'm not angry at you. Just try to understand: rain, dangerous . . . ash!

I let her go and try to show her with my hands the way the ash is sucked out of the dust clouds and comes down with the rain.

— My Papa died from it even though he was always warning other people.

Silently her mouth forms the word "Pa-pa." Then she takes my hand, strokes it, and puts her hand against my cheek. My eyes burn and sting. I turn my face up toward the driving rain so she won't be able to see me crying. But she can tell from my breathing; she gets up and presses my cheek against her stomach.

I cry and cry. I don't know how long she stays there with my head pressed against her. I get more and more annoyed with myself. When are the tears going to stop? But I can't stop them. Then my teeth start chattering. Soon my whole body is shaking. I pull away from her, curl up on my side, and press my trembling chin against my knees.

When Papa died, when his fingers finally relaxed their death grip, I didn't cry one single tear. I remember getting up and rubbing my ears to get the feeling back. My face was dry and stiff. Just as dry and stiff as Papa's as he lay on his side, his half-open hands level with his nose, whose tip was turning white. I went straight to our food supply and stuffed myself with everything I could find.

WHEN I wake out of a deep sleep, the sun's shining in a clear violet sky. Tulikke sleeps on her stomach, one leg pulled up under her. I get to my knees and sit looking at her face. Her eyes are moving back and forth in slow oar strokes behind her closed eyelids, and the corners of her mouth twitch slightly. I brush away the dry, crackling whir of a persistent dragonfly, then close my eyes so I won't start crying again. I have to press my fingertips against the base of my nose to hold the tears back. As I'm sitting on my knees like an idiot, I feel her hand on one of my feet.

We lie facing each other. She strokes my chest and I hold my breath so she won't stop. My own hands want to touch her but I hold back; I clench my fists till my teeth begin to chatter. She kisses my forehead and it feels like sinking into summer-warm water. For a while I seem to fade out. When I wake up I'm lying on top of her. She helps me in, and the pleasure shoots through me uncontrollably. Sighing, I collapse against her neck. We both giggle.

For a few minutes we both sleep, but then I'm on top of her again, fumbling around. She strokes me and smiles; just like the first time, the smile turns into a laugh. But only for a moment. Suddenly she looks at me, dead serious. The white scar at the base of her nose tightens as she concentrates. It's as though she's trying to read something, to spell her way through a message flickering at the back of my eyes. She puts her hands against my chest as if to push me away—but in the same moment the lower part of my body starts to work. Before I know what's happening, I come—it catches me totally by surprise. We fall asleep. And start again. I don't know how many hours go by. It doesn't matter. Sometimes time moves as slowly as eternity; the next moment it evaporates like breath on a cold day. I rest between her legs, the top of my head pushed up against her crack. My balls are sore, drained dry.

TO swim away the sleepiness in my arms and legs, I lower myself down into the water. Swimming has never felt this wonderful before. But after only a few strokes I'm drawn back to the raft; I hike myself up on my elbows and rest like that, my legs dangling into the water.

— Come in with me!

I pull at her sleeve to get her in; she's sitting wrapped in her shawl and clothes. I try to pull them off, but she gets annoyed and tries to slap my hand. Thinking that she's just playing, I pull harder. Then she takes my hand and bites it hard across the knuckles. My feelings are hurt now. I pull back. She turns her back to me.

Swimming away from the raft, I come upon a flower floating among the flat, deep-green leaves. It's perhaps ten times
bigger than any other flower I've ever seen—as big as an open
hand, white in the center and rose pink around the edges. And
it's not just beautiful; it looks edible too. I want to feed the
pink petals and the white bud to Tulikke. But I can't tear it
loose; the slippery stalk is as tough as wire.

I leave it and dive for an aluminum can shining at the
bottom with a yellow sheen. It's as big as a bucket and open at
one end. I empty out the muck and the little animals, then
swim back with it to the raft. She's still sitting with her back
turned. To get her attention, I slap the surface of the water,
then dive down with the can in my arms. Carefully I hold it
straight up, the opening face down to trap the air inside. I've
done so much diving that I can easily manage a couple of
minutes on just the air in my lungs. When my head begins to
throb too hard I exhale, push my head up into the can, and
breathe in—then pull my head back out again, never breaking
the surface. But she doesn't pay the slightest attention to me,
doesn't even try to look for me! Finally I have to come up.
She's standing on the raft with her legs apart, hands pressed
against her forehead, howling. She doesn't even seem to notice me. I heave myself up and throw my arms around her
legs. I start crying and shaking so much that we both have to
lie down to keep from rolling into the water.

LATER I try to make a fire in the blotched, rusty gasoline barrel. But we don't have anything to make a fire with: no magnifying glass, no pieces of metal or rocks to strike sparks against.
I hit the magazine of the rifle against its barrel, but all I get are
nicks. I've collected some dry powder from the rotten rope and
mixed it with the dry brown innards of a decayed plank. If I
shoot into the mixture it might catch fire—but the sound
would carry all the way to the Convent. Finally I squeeze a

bullet out of the magazine with my thumbs and try to pull the slug out of the cartridge with my teeth to get at the gunpowder. But I realize that my teeth are going to give long before the slug does. So we spend our third night on the raft without fire or anything to eat; I can feel the muddy water sloshing around in my guts.

The next day I cut reeds, which we gather into large sheaves and bind up with some brittle pieces of wire and rope from the boat. If we get heavier rains, we'll need some shelter. We also try to lift the skiff onto the raft and turn it upside down for a roof. We manage to get it up but can't turn it over—every time we brace our feet against it, the raft almost tips over. Instead we leave it on deck and put double layers of reeds across the gunwales, leaving an opening in the prow; in this way we end up with a cross between a bed and a cave we can crawl into. It's very uncomfortable and cramped, the air quickly goes stale, and chaff and itchy little bugs fall out of the reeds. But at least we have a shelter from the rain.

We lie with each other most of the next morning on deck in the sunshine. Now Tulikke's willing to go swimming too, but only if I sit with my back turned and her shawl over my head. But afterward we have to find something to eat, so we take the bales of reeds out of the boat and paddle out among the reed islands. I find the huge pink flower floating on the water; we each take a petal and chew on it a little. But it tastes harsh and bitter. Then I take off my shirt and drag it by the sleeves behind us like a seine; we catch plants and tiny animals—and a white leech neither of us will eat.

We come to a bog with stretches of fern forests. I try to take a few steps in, but my feet sink through right away and Tulikke has to get me unstuck. On the way back she catches a fireblue dragonfly and holds it, whirring, in her cupped hands. Neither of us can make himself eat it.

Where are we?! I've lost my bearings! Wherever we turn

we're surrounded by the same clumps of reeds. I haven't done such a stupid thing since I was a kid! I never even once looked at the sun to keep track of the compass points, much less left behind any markers. It would have been so easy to cut off reeds here and there to blaze a trail back. Now we're in the shit for real! I don't want her to find out what an idiot I've been, so I pole along with powerful strokes. But after an hour or so I can barely get the oar out of the muddy bottom. I have to rest. Tulikke gestures a question: Are we lost?

— Yes.

I sit down and put my arm around her:

— We couldn't have stayed on the raft. We couldn't live there.

But she cries anyway. So do I. You can miss even a half-rotted-out raft!

IN the early morning hours, while we're still sleeping in the skiff, the wind comes up. At first the water's calm, but when the waves pick up speed out on the lake they roll in and churn up the reeds. The boat rocks, the reeds crackle; I haven't been this seasick since my first trawler! I retch over the stern, but nothing but water and threads of slime come up. Tulikke tries to steady the boat with the oar to keep it from overturning against the reed islands. For thirty-six hours the storm shrieks, the water roars. By noon the next day we're so exhausted that the long, rolling aftershocks of the waves rock us to sleep. When we wake up that evening, the skiff's run up into the fern-covered bog.

The next morning we lie together. Afterward my lower parts are smeared with blood. Does she have a knife hidden in there somewhere? But when I wash it off I can't find the slightest scratch. Then I see that she's bleeding too. What have I done? Is this what the sailors were talking about? I try to ask her, examine her, but she pushes me away roughly. I don't understand how I could have hurt her! But she punishes me by not letting me get near her.

CHAPTER 18

THE water's rising. Twenty-four hours later the boat has floated farther in among the ferns, whose leaves lie spread out over the surface. It's not raining, so the water must be coming from a burst dam somewhere. The weather is still, hot, humid; pale as the white of an eye, the sun shines down out of a light-brown sky. All day the water keeps rising; the current streams noisily through the reeds. It's also beginning to look muddy; there's not only a lot of foam and bubbles but also ripped-off leaves, algae, and whole clumps of grass. When I taste the water it's saltier than before. To judge by the sun the flood tide is pushing the boat southwest.

While Tulikke lies in the prow looking for something to eat, I try to steer us a little with the oar. Hunger doesn't bother me anymore. But I recognize only too well the lightheadedness and excited feeling that always come at the beginning of a period of starvation—in a few days they'll be followed by faintness and nausea. But at least the heat is a big advantage. Lack of food makes your body freeze from the inside. Ice crystals form inside your long bones, and then the death chill seeps out through the muscles and flesh—it finally comes out as goose bumps. The reason it's so terrible to starve in the winter is because of this inner chill. But spring is even worse; then the light dazzles your eyes but doesn't keep you warm.

Five long-necked geese fly so close to the foamy surface that their wings leave tracks. They disappear to the southwest. Tulikke's not interested in them. Why can't she talk? Even if we speak different languages I'd like to talk to her. We could teach each other the most important words in our languages. Petsamo said that her muteness would go away. But she doesn't say a single word, not even when we lie with each other. She can scream, but her tongue doesn't make words. I've met mute people before. They could groan but not scream anything like she can. On the Lightship we once took a prisoner who was supposed to know the whereabouts of a barge loaded with oil barrels. Of course, at first no one noticed he was mute. Captives aren't usually very talkative; almost every one I've seen sits with his head bowed and his mouth clamped shut. This prisoner had been knocked around quite a bit before we figured out that he wanted paper and pen. Everyone gathered around him, anxious to see the map he was going to draw showing us the way to the barge. But instead he wrote: I AM MUTE. There was surprise, scattered laughter, then the skipper's "You're just gonna have to beat that out of him, boys." He didn't even scream when they stuck his feet in boiling water; he just rolled his eyes and groaned. When they stuck his ass down into the basin he passed out, and then he died after the whole lower half of his body blew up like a baboon's ass. During the nights I try to stay awake to hear if she's saying anything in her sleep. Sometimes I pinch and poke her too—but I never hear a real word.

We see a little tree or bush ahead, and Tulikke manages to grab a branch and hold us there for a while. The leaves are small and heart-shaped, the branches dark brown, but the trunk, if you can call it that, is white and crisscrossed with brownish-black stripes. I think it's called birk or birch. We see several more. That means there's solid ground under us now.

We pass a low rocky ridge but don't try to go ashore; if the water keeps rising, being on land might not be a good idea. We also see big, round boulders at the water's edge but manage to steer around them.

Then we run aground. This time not on rock—the bump's much too soft and quiet. I climb out and see that we're stuck in sand. By swinging the whole skiff around so that the stern is pointing into the current, I get the boat to slide itself off the sandbar. We see more and more land: stone ridges, sand dunes, half-drowned birch and juniper bushes. Finally we get stuck in the mud for good. From here we can't see any large areas of dry land; air and water just run together in a clay-brown haze.

WE'VE been sloshing through chalk-gray loam. You can't see any water, but as soon as you pick up your foot, gray-white water fills your imprint. Ahead of us are barren moors. Gradually the clay becomes firmer, and soon we're plodding along with dust on our feet. Thousands of flat round rocks, exactly large enough to sit on with your feet pulled up, are sticking out of the cracked earth. In among the rocks are patches of moss and occasional black, straggly, bare bushes with thorns as sharp as barbed wire. Just as I start scouting around for a good place to spend the night, Tulikke cries out:

— Lakka!

I swear that's what she cried!

— What did you say?

She doesn't seem to know that she shouted something that sounds like a word. Instead she's pointing excitedly at the ground, at low thickets with yellow-brown berries! She picks one and holds it up. It's as big as a fingertip, and its surface is knobby as though several tiny berries have grown together. She puts it into her mouth and begins to jump up and down. I pick one too. It has a sweet, strong flavor. Then she falls to her

knees and starts picking. There are lots of them. I don't know
if I should stop her. Does she really know what they are? I've
never seen anything like them before. Could they be as dangerous as mushrooms? I'm so afraid of plants I've never seen
that I can't make myself eat more. But Tulikke does; she goes
on picking and eating until it's so dark she has to grope around
for the berries. Finally we sleep in among the rocks, she making contented little sighing sounds, I with my stomach churn-
ing from the one berry I swallowed.

THE next day Tulikke continues picking and eating. I eat a few
fistfuls too. What have I got to lose? If they're poisonous, they
might as well kill both of us. Afterward, I go exploring.
Beyond the moors begins the tableland I've seen so many
times before: cracked, flat-topped rock cliffs, here and there
pools of sand, occasional gravel ridges. One of the ridges is
scooped out, making a good windbreak. We could camp here
for a while. I search for fuel but all I can find are a few twigs
and some grass. If we drag the skiff up here we could put it
across some rocks to make a roof. Tulikke comes to find me,
her shawl heavy with berries; and we eat till our faces and
hands are dripping with sweet juice. Later, when I crawl up to
her and try to get on top of her, she holds me away—her belly
is filled to bursting.

WE'VE pulled the skiff up, turned it over, and put it on top of
a low wall we've made out of rocks and clay. The last few
nights have been cold, but I managed to make a fire. First I
tapped the gunpowder out of a cartridge with a sharp rock,
then poured it over dry moss on a flat surface and made little
blue flames dance by hitting it with another rock. We have
nothing to cook, nothing to cook in, no way of taking the fire
inside under the skiff-roof. Filled with wonder, we sit huddled

together by our crackling little fire as though it's a new being; the fire is even more precious to us than the sweet yellow berries.

In the flames thousands of old memories flare up. I wasn't just my protectors' lover; I had other duties too. When the old guys sat around the evening fire drinking and playing poker, I was allowed to sit with them too, but only for short periods, just long enough to get warm. Then I had to scamper away and warm the bed for the man whose turn it was. After he crawled in, I'd slip out quickly and hurry back to soak up a little more heat for the next bed warming. The only nights I didn't run in and out of everyone else's bed was when the skipper went to bed early. But the times he fell asleep before he was sure the others were out cold were few and far between.

EVEN though it's fall, the days are still sunny and warm. We sleep, lie together, pick berries. At night we take turns sitting outside and feeding the little fire with moss and twigs. But we've got to find a way to get the fire inside before the frost and rain come, so I start building a fireplace out of flat rocks in one of the walls of the skiff-house. It'd be better to have it more in the middle, but I don't want to make a hole in the boat. Also, dying fires in small spaces can be dangerous; people belowdecks have been poisoned by smoke from a dying fire, those last wisps that are almost invisible but much more potent than ordinary smoke.

The fireplace in the wall doesn't warm very well, but when we put sandstones next to the hearth they manage to store up a little heat. Early one morning as I get ready to take over the fire, I see that she's fallen asleep. The fire's out! I shake her:

— We have only six shots left! And we need them for shooting too!

She pouts and pulls away. But it's her fault! And she's acting as if it's mine! I explode, drag her outside and punch her with my fist. She falls down, taking with her a piece of the wall, and glares up at me furiously. I lift my foot to give her a kick. But then it suddenly dawns on me what I'm about to do and I fall to my knees, try to take her into my arms and comfort her. But she crawls back in underneath the boat. I follow her. She's crouching with her back turned to me. I whisper her name and stroke her back, but she doesn't turn around; she starts shaking and sobbing. I start crying too. After a while I start to feel foolish, crawl back outside, run off across the moors kicking rocks and branches and anything else that's not anchored down. But I can't stop crying.

IT gets hot again; the sun bakes down on us while we're out picking the yellow berries. The soft sandstone warms up the way it did during the summer, and at night we take in flat slabs that have stored up solar heat and lie with each other on the warm, cloth-soft rocks. In the morning we carry them outside and put them against the slope of the ridge where the sun is strongest. I haven't kindled a new fire yet; I'm saving the powder for the real cold.

I'm also beginning to store up firewood. There are plenty of black, dry roots just a little below the surface of the gravel. The easiest way to get at them is to use the boat's thwart to dig in from the side of the ridge just above our house. They're coated with a skin of sand and earth; you have to beat them against the ground to get them fairly clean. While I'm digging I strike a hard object that makes a dull clink. A gasoline barrel? A large can? I drop the board and dig with my hands. It's a large, pale, brick-colored clay jar:

— Tooolikke, Tooolikke. . . !

She comes running from the berry thicket, looking worried that something's happened. But I show her the jar proudly. She knocks on it with her little fists and presses her ear against it to listen. We dig it out. It's about one meter high, almost as

198 P. C. JERSILD

wide, and shaped like an upside-down teardrop. On top is a wide opening filled with a tangle of roots that have grown down to form a knotty plug. It won't come out. We knock on the jar with our hands and rocks, making a hollow ring. Then I hit it a little too hard with a rock, and it cracks. All that runs out is a little sand and dust. I pry a big piece loose. It's filled with black roots, but when we look closer we see something else: Inside a cage of roots a white skeleton sits with its knees drawn up to an unbroken, grinning skull. At the bottom lie small, unattached bones and another skull no bigger than a clenched fist. Eggshell thin, it falls apart when I try to pick it up.

Tulikke starts screaming. I think it's terrible too; all this time we've been sleeping, eating, lying together only a few meters from a grave! The ghosts must have been grinning at us in the darkness! Tulikke won't have anything more to do with it, but I can't resist. Where the baby's skull was lying, I find a piece of chipped stone. It looks like a rough arrowhead. After I drag the jar and its fragile contents across the ridges as far away from her as I dare to go, I smash the whole thing to pieces— and, just to be on the safe side, roll two boulders on top of the crushed skeletons. Finally I cover everything with sand.

We're too scared to sleep. We hear the dead woman singing to her child out in the darkness, the sand screeching under her bony feet. I have no choice: I put two of the six bullets into the gun and fire into the fall night. The echo rolls back and forth among the ridges until it sounds like a full volley. For a moment it's quiet, then the sobbing and screeching begin again. The sounds come and go until dawn. We can't stay here.

Loaded down with wood and a supply of berries for the winter, we break camp later in the day. We've squashed the berries into sticky balls, let them dry and then pressed them between hot stones. The results are black, breadlike cakes with a strong taste of earth and honey.

*   *   *

WE head south, but when the rocky terrain changes to pure sand we turn east. Now and then it seems to me that I recognize where we are. But it couldn't be true. It's been more than a year since I was anywhere near here, and storms and water are sure to have changed the landscape. It takes us four days to get to the sea on the island's east side. We rest there, and I manage to catch some small crabs in my shirt. We can't take a chance on making a fire this close to the sea. The next morning a thin crust of ice covers the puddles in the sand.

I can't be sure if Henry's house is north or south of us. If we go too far north, we'll hit the mouth of the stream and the Tower. If we go south we'll get lost on the island's southern tip. In spite of the danger of being discovered, I decide to head north. If winter sets in suddenly, we'd never manage in the south. Better to move cautiously north and then turn on our heels if we have to. But we get lucky. Just a day later we find the bunker where I spent the night after I left Henry's hut. That same evening after we bed down for the night, the frost sets in.

I start thinking about that winter many years ago when the sea level started lowering *before* the ice had broken up. Frozen fast, many boats dangled high above the water. When we drilled holes in the ice, it was like looking down through the roof of an enormous glass house. Crew after crew abandoned ship and climbed up onto the wind-lashed skerries around the lagoon. The March sun was burning through the thinned-out ozone layer, and when the ice started to split in lightninglike cracks, it sounded as though thunder were rumbling inside the ice itself. One morning a third of the ice in the lagoon broke off and disappeared. From the skerries we could see the bottoms of the boats that were still stuck in what was left of the hanging ice roof.

In the next few days ship after ship went under. Some crews had gone back on board, others had taken as much material as they could from their ships—especially sheet metal and timber to build huts with. The icy night winds took many of us. My crew was among the ones who'd been ordered back aboard. We sat for nights in that dangling ship of ours, listening to the ice crack all around us. By now we couldn't have gone back ashore if we'd wanted to. Only a miracle could save us—and that's exactly what the skipper was waiting for. When the nights were clear, he'd stand out on the ice scanning the sky with his old birding binoculars mounted on a tripod. And then the miracle happened! You didn't even need binoculars to see it. The whole crew stood and cheered when a satellite drifted very slowly across the sky like a small ball of fire far below the white stars.

It was the first satellite anyone had seen for eighteen years. And just as the skipper had predicted, the seawater came right back beneath us, gushing and surging as if a thousand faucets had been turned on. The next day the lagoon was filled to bursting, and the water split the ice from underneath. Out of the five boats that were left, two capsized. We were one of the three who left under our own power. What happened to the people stranded on the skerries? I just don't know.

SOMEONE'S done a poor, hurried job of patching up Henry's house. It looks deserted, but I let Tulikke back me up with the submachine gun while I sneak toward the low door covered with a curtain of sacks.

— Klaus? . . . It's Edvin.

No answer. I tear the sacks away and peer in. When my eyes get used to the dark, I can see that everything's a tangle of tattered blankets, old clothes, piles of roots and a circle of blackened rocks in the middle of the floor. Nothing's left of the beds. In one corner, the table is lying on its side. After a few moments I hear a faint hissing. It doesn't sound as if it's coming from a human being. It takes me a long time to get an idea of where it is. Crawling farther in, I bump into a pile of skin and bones—either asleep or unconscious—which I think must be Klaus.

CHAPTER 19

I manage to get a little water into Klaus. But he doesn't recognize me. He throws the first berry cake back up. When we come we have twenty-two cakes; three days later we're down to half. I comb around for things to eat. Klaus hasn't touched the potato field. In the mornings when the earth warms up, I dig up whatever's left, but all the tubers I find are frozen. That doesn't mean you can't eat them—but I decide to hide them under a loose rock in the hearth. Maybe if we take good care of them, we can get them to grow. Other than the potatoes, I can't find a single thing to eat. But I do come across some useful tools: a fishnet and fishhook, a spit, knives and a spade.

I leave the two of them behind and head for the sea. Tulikke protests, cries, tries to hit me. She knows perfectly well that I have to go, but she doesn't want to stay alone with Klaus even though he can't stand up or see. To avoid any more fuss, I leave while she's asleep, taking a long detour around the graveyard behind the nettle field. But the ghosts can relax. What would we want the gold for now?

I spend that night in the old concrete bunker by the sea. There's nothing to see out in the ocean; it isn't the season. But even in the spring and summer—the peak season—it was empty. Has something happened far away? Has the archipelago been destroyed? Is the autumn rain full of white ash again? I don't want to think about such things, but at least the fear helps keep me awake. The night is so cold it's dangerous to fall asleep. Exhausted, I stagger along the beach the next day. All I manage to get are a watersnake in a tidal pool, a few little crabs and a couple of handfuls of centimeter-long shrimp. The net doesn't produce anything. The next night, bright moonlight guides me home. The minute I get beyond the doorstep, I collapse.

BY the time the first snow flurries come, our food situation has improved a little. Tulikke knows about roots and edible mosses, and I've had a little more success in my trips to the sea. I wonder if we shouldn't move there and live in the bunker; we could probably improvise a sheet-metal stove. But we're not really strong enough to make the move in the wintertime. If we live till spring we'll do it. And if the pirates stay away, we could live pretty well. Besides, it would get us away from the ghosts behind the nettles. I know I should go to the marsh to see what I can find, but I just can't make myself; I might walk over the ice and suddenly see Henry's corpse looking up at me.

By now Klaus is well enough to crawl outside when he needs to empty his bladder or guts. He can tell the difference between light and dark but can't see any details. He recognizes my voice; whenever I get close to him he wants to touch my face—which annoys me *and* Tulikke. He's also beginning to complain about the third person in the hut; whoever it is, he says half deliriously, they ought to go away so that he and I can have the house to ourselves. I don't know how much of his talk Tulikke understands, but I do know she can't stand him. I'm the one who has to feed him and make sure he's warm. She makes me promise that I'll take her along the next time I go down to the sea. But it's too late to go now anyway; strong, bright sunshine can change to pouring rain or snow in half an hour. I can't remember the weather ever being quite *this* unpredictable.

It's harder to gather roots when the ground's frozen. Also, eating just plants isn't good for us. Our stomachs swell up, and we haven't moved our bowels for a long time. All that comes out are stinking farts. Our urine smells strange too. But while Tulikke and I grow weaker and weaker, Klaus seems to be thriving. Yesterday he made a fire in the stove by himself for the first time. He doesn't seem to have made many; it's hard to keep them going when you're alone. When I'm up to it, I poke around for stumps in Henry's wood mine. Thank God we have plenty of fuel.

Klaus gets restless at night; he talks and babbles. At first I thought he was delirious, but now I see that he just wants us to pay attention to him. He usually starts by saying nice things about us, flattering us, but when that doesn't keep us awake he recites his endless pack of horror stories. His favorites are about monsters. He says that after the War, because of genetic mutation, every newborn—people as well as animals—was deformed and strange. On the north coast of Germany he saw people with two faces, one in the usual place at the front of the head, the other in back. His gang—the one he belonged to when he was young—controlled a string of offshore sandbars. In the beginning a constant stream of refugees poured in from farther south in Europe. Of course the gang took their weapons and "taxed" them for all they were worth. They also made the stronger ones join up with them. For many years this was the way it was in the whole southern Baltic.

Hordes of animals also came by the thousands during those first years. Maybe their feeding grounds farther south had been destroyed, or else they were fleeing from radioactivity. Animals seem to have a special warning system that people don't. Many of the animals were mutants. Albinos were the most common—white deer with ruby-red eyes, dirty-yellow hedgehogs with spines as clear as icicles, sky-blue crows and colorless rats with wormy tails. They were followed by equally strange humans: albinos, hermaphrodites, chimpanzeelike giants, and small, pale dwarfs with pointed pixie ears. But the scariest were the double-faced ones. Armed with pistols in both hands, they could shoot equally well backward and forward. Ordinary honest folk who had to whirl all the way around to shoot didn't have a chance. Klaus and his gang had to escape into the sea.

— Enough of that bullshit! I say.

— But it's true!

— Like hell it is! I wasn't born yesterday!

We argue for a while. I've heard thousands of stories like his. When you check them out, *none* turns out to be true—not even the one about the women with the fish tails.

One night he admits it. He starts crying:

— I made it all up . . .

He slips into our bed, wanting to be hugged. I have to jam my knee into his crotch to get him to stop.

— Go to bed! Why do you have to keep us awake with this crap? As if there weren't enough real horror stories to tell!

He stops sniveling and barks:

— Don't you tell me!

— So just stick to what actually happened.

— How can I talk about what can't be talked about?

I've heard that answer before—when I was young and stupid enough to ask them to tell me what really happened. Did the light come before the bang? Or was it the other way around? Is it true that no one can talk about the sound because it made them deaf? Is it true everyone went blind from the flash?

KLAUS's eyesight is so much better now that he's starting to get interested in his automatic weapon again. Even though I know all his ammunition is gone, it still makes me nervous. What did he waste it on? Maybe, just like me, he's been shooting at the ghosts in the graveyard.

Although it's November already, we get a spell of rain and thunderstorms. Tulikke is terrified of the thunder; she clings to me and screams from the moment she sees the lightning to the first clap of thunder. I wish she and Klaus could be friends; they could hold on to each other while I work—that is, when the weather's good enough. At night as I sleep next to Tulikke who lies there exhausted with fear, Klaus creeps over and wants to kiss me. I don't want him to wake Tulikke, so I let him for a while—but when he sticks his disgusting tongue into my mouth, I push him away. For once he gets angry and hisses:
— Pussylips!

I laugh in his face. He slinks back to his corner, insulted. If he had ammunition, maybe he really would consider getting rid of Tulikke—or Tulikke and me. The thought fascinates me. I'd like to be shot in my sleep. With her. I'm more sure than ever that there's something in people, some kind of flame of life; when they die, the flame is set free. I want our flames to be set free together.

WE had to eat the last of our berry cakes, and none of us has enough strength to go out gathering mosses or anything else. Klaus might be able to—he's the strongest—but he won't. He's tried to come to me at night again, whispering love words and slobbering over me with his big tongue. I pushed him away. But I think he noticed that Tulikke and I lay together yesterday right after I turned him down. He'd made me horny; I almost had to force her because she wasn't nearly as interested as he was. Now he's moping in his corner. He won't eat, and when you talk to him he won't answer. It's daytime, but there's nothing to get up for. I try to sleep but it's hard. I already sleep about twenty hours a day.

At dusk Klaus wakes me up. Whispering, he asks me to come to his corner; he doesn't want to wake Tulikke. I do as he asks. He seems different—serious, not sulking anymore.

— This is all I know, he whispers. I can't tell you about what happened above. I was a repairman for the Altona Sanitation Department. I had gone down into one of the sewers to replace a microcomputer that regulated water levels. The safety rules were strict: a thick protective suit with a gas mask and a radio telephone and a battery-powered lamp in the helmet. I had almost finished the job—I had only to put back the cover—when suddenly the earphones went dead. I called several times. No answer. Then I noticed the instruments in the wall: dead too. But that was no problem—I had my head lamp. I followed the special instructions for blackouts: I waited a few minutes, then headed up. The lowest bacteria sluice was working normally except for the lights. But when I started up the ladder over the sluice, the steps were so hot my rubber gloves stuck fast. I wound rags around the hands and kept going to the top hatch. I had to wait there because the hatch was white-hot. When I could finally lift it and stick out my head, there was twilight all around even though it was only lunchtime. At first I thought the town was covered by a very heavy fog, but then I noticed that the clouds were made of dust. The wind was strong—I went back down to wait. The next time I peeked out the dust wasn't so thick anymore; I could see a couple of hundred meters. The street I'd left a few hours before had disappeared. *Everything* was gone. All was a desert of crushed rubble. When I picked up the helmet a little, the roar of the wind and all the fires almost knocked me unconscious. I went down into the sewers again and lay in a niche for the next few days throwing up; what I remember most is the unbearable thirst. My hair stuck to my helmet. For the next ten years I was neither happy nor sad.

*   *   *

HOURS later, in the middle of the night, a volley of shots outside the door. I don't move; Tulikke doesn't either, though I can tell from her breathing she's awake. We lie there without moving until the light starts to rise. Then I crawl up to the window hole and peek out. A lot of snow's fallen, but there aren't any tracks. Was it our imagination? I get Tulikke to come with me to the stove and help me make a fire with the drill. That is when we notice that Klaus is gone. I find him ten meters from the door lying facedown under a pile of glistening new snow. He found our automatic weapon's magazine with our last four shots—and used all of them.

I'VE lost track of time. Maybe it's close to Christmas, maybe a little way into the New Year. We've made long trips down to the sea twice without finding anything. Pack ice was heaped along the beaches, and even if we'd been able to climb over and get to the ocean, we didn't have the tools to drill holes.

Tulikke's found some roots here and there where the snow's blown away. I don't think we'll make it to spring. If we hadn't had the meat, we'd have starved by now. But now that's gone too; yesterday we sucked the marrow out of the last leg bone. We've started eating the frozen seed potatoes I put away for safekeeping. Every morning we have to force ourselves to get up and make the fire in the stove; when the morning comes that we don't make a fire, it'll mean that we've given up. And we pay hardly any attention to each other now— maybe bicker a little over the best place to sleep, but we don't look directly into each other's eyes. I can see my little blue life-flame jumping out of my mouth and rising toward the sky, getting larger and hotter as it goes.

I sit on the threshold with my face turned up toward the hot sun. Where the snow's melted, the ground has already dried out. The Finn won't go outside; she's lying inside huddled against the stove under everything she can find. But I sit here staring at the sun through fire-red eyelids. Among the clumps of gray grass by the wall of the house, tiny light-green shoots are beginning to poke up. The Captain comes sailing toward me from the direction of the nettle field. As usual he's standing in the wheelhouse with his chest bare, barking orders at us in a hoarse voice. The diesel sputters and farts through the rusty exhaust pipe. Heeling, the cutter drifts closer and closer to the bottom of the slope. I get up to grab the hawser as it floats through the air. But my legs won't hold me and I tumble back down on my ass. When I try to get up again, the inside of my skull goes white. Suns and sparks racing around in circles . . .

— What are you doing, having a one-man Christmas party?

The voice isn't coming from the water. There is no water, no cutter. I blink at a violet shadow stepping out from around a corner of the house.

— If you keep sitting there, boy, you're gonna freeze to death!

There are two shadows now. And the sound of crunching snow. They step closer to me and start stomping the snow off their boots. I think I recognize the voice:

— Chuck?

They grab me under the arms, carry me into the house, and lay me on the floor. I raise my hands with my wrists pressed together for them to tie me up. They walk away. The Finn's whimpering by the stove. Then they go outside again. I'm lying flat on my back. I can't get up by myself even though I flounder and strain like an overturned beetle. They come back with a lantern, which they hang from the ceiling. I try to figure out who's with Chuck, but I've never seen him before. He has a wispy red beard and speaks with an accent. Danish?

They get a fire going and heat up some soup. They've also brought potato bread, but all I can get down are a few gulps of the soup. The Finn eats for both of us.

THE next day they tow us by sled across the iced-over rock cliffs. Up until now I haven't thought about what they're going to do with us; I just don't care about anything anymore. I'm not afraid, just surprised they didn't shoot us right away. Or shoot me—and Tulikke after they'd done what they usually do. But I don't ask, and neither Chuck nor the Dane grumbles more than the usual commands: Hold on, lean to the right, get up so we can get the damn sled unstuck.

When we get to the Convent just before dusk, clots of snowflakes are falling and sticking to our eyelashes. They bring us right to the Chapel. The last time I was here it was late summer and a big bonfire was burning before the doors. Now snow has drifted against the north side, and the old doors have been replaced by new ones made of planks and sheet metal; in the big door they've cut a smaller, narrower one, which they have to help us through.

Inside, the room's lit by strong oil lanterns hanging from the vaulted ceiling. Everything's totally changed. The altar and the other ornaments are gone. It's a workshop now—rows of tools hanging on the walls; two outboard motors sitting on wooden crates where the altar used to be; and an almost-complete tractor in the middle of the floor with three old guys standing around fitting it with an iron-plated back wheel. One of them is Petsamo. He comes over and takes me by both hands:

— Edvin! Come down to the kitchen. I have a lot to tell you. . . .

— I don't want to leave Tulikke.

— The Finn?

— I don't want to leave her alone.

— I'll make sure Sister Birgitta takes good care of her. No one's going to touch her now. Things have changed!

We sit at the long table in the kitchen and drink hot herb tea. They bring me a potato bread, which I dip and suck on; all my teeth are gone.

— Let me fill you in on what's been happening. When the two of you took off Pretty Boy was still in charge.

— Where is he? Who are the new ones?

— He's dead. It seems there was a fight the day after you took the skiff, a fight between Pretty Boy and The Boot. Some old grudge. The boys chose sides and started shooting at each other. . . . And the new men: They're Danes who wandered down from up north . . . but that's another story. Pretty Boy got shot. In the middle of it all I arrived at the Prison and figured that something was up because everybody was gone. I followed all of you here, and when I came Pretty Boy was dead and no one knew what to do. The Sisters were still singing away in the Chapel. My first instinct was to leave so I wouldn't get involved. But then a few of them suggested I take Pretty Boy's place. Or rather Roland's place, since they never really took Pretty Boy seriously. They'd got it into their heads that I knew all of Roland's secrets, including where the rice was hidden. I don't, but they wouldn't listen. They'd decided I was their man and got the others to go along with them.

— And The Boot?

— We found him strangled in his tent the next morning. I don't know who did it and I don't want to know.

— And all the Sisters are alive?

— Everyone except Signe. She got pneumonia in October.

— So it's mostly you who's running things?

— Only me, to be precise. If you have to be the one who makes the decisions, you might as well make all of them. It's simpler, and it makes people feel more secure. When I think anybody's got something sensible to say, I listen. Then I decide—alone.

— So you'd make the decisions for me and Tulikke?

— If you want to stay I would. If you don't, I don't intend to force you. . . . You can take as many supplies as you can carry. But from then on you'd have to manage on your own.

— How?

— That's not my concern.

— Where did the Danes come from?

— A boat, where else? It appears that no one can live on the sea anymore. You can't put into port anywhere in the archipelago; if you try you get shot. I don't know what's happened; neither do the Danes. But they had nowhere to go. No fuel. They say they tried to raid a few boats but they didn't have the strength. They took over only one boat all summer, but the whole crew was dead and they decided not to touch it. Finally they ran their own boat aground at the north end.

— Near the lepers?

– Farther north. Where the naval base used to be.

— But no one can live there!

— So they found out, and then they headed south But not soon enough. Some of them got sick. There were eight when thev showed up here; now there are only five One's a chemist

— What's that?

– - Somebody who knows about elements and compounds. How to refine oils, smelt metals He can distill alcohol, too. We're totally self-sufficient now! Can you believe it? *Totally!*

CHAPTER 20

THE winter's so hard that all the passageways down to the Convent are either frozen shut or always covered with snow. Though the volcanic water in the black lake keeps it from freezing over, the ice banks around it grow larger and larger until a wall of ice rings the lake, a glassy ice hill several meters high. The lake water eats into it every time the weather warms up a little—and if you lie at the top and look over the edge, you can see millions of long icicles forming a stockade. On some days the cold and snow are so bad we stop work at the Chapel. But it's warm underground; even though we keep only a couple of fires going, the chamber pots are never frozen over in the morning.

Including the Danes, twenty-three of us live in the Rabbit-Convent. It's not really a Convent any longer. The Sisters wear veils only now and then, and there are only occasional services held in the little vaulted room with the crucifix. But it's not like Roland's Prison either. Things are more relaxed— the pecking order is gone, and there's no strict division between weapons carriers and plain workers. Of course there are some fights from time to time. Roland's boys find it a little hard to get along with the Danes, who still stick together. But if you can believe what people say, almost everyone thinks that Petsamo runs the place in a smarter, more efficient manner than either Signe or Roland. He doesn't like to be contradicted, but as he said, he will listen to you a long time before making his decisions; afterward it's too late. In one way he's like Roland; he's suspicious and always wants to have an idea of what people are saying behind his back.

There's enough food. Not a lot, and it's strictly rationed according to body size and how hard your work is—people who work outdoors get more than indoor workers. Some stealing does go on in the kitchen and storerooms, but Petsamo has an almost eerie ability to find the thieves. No one is ever told who commits the crime; Petsamo keeps everything between himself and the guilty one. The punishments are never made public either, but naturally we can't help noticing that sometimes somebody has extra work. The talk about the rice has died down; Petsamo's said once and for all that he doesn't know any more than anyone else. For the time being, the rest of the rice won't be touched. We live mostly on potatoes: soup, bread, mush, boiled, fried, roasted, hash. During the fall they also did a lot of fishing, and whatever they didn't salt, smoke, or dry was frozen in blocks of ice.

Aside from the daily work, we have two goals: short-term survival . . . and long-term survival. Of course they're connected. Our short-term goals are to farm the land for some years, developing what Petsamo calls a "practical technology," and to make absolutely sure that we're left in peace. This last point doesn't seem to worry Petsamo very much. It was constantly on Roland's mind, but Petsamo says that nowadays things have changed. We don't expect any major raids from the sea, at least not during the winter. Actually there's more danger that people like the Danes may show up and need our help to survive. That's when we might have to do some shooting.

The tractor in the workshop has become a gathering place. It's the only large machine they brought over from the Prison, and sometimes the boys stand around talking about the old days with V-8s and jets; but everything that didn't have any practical use was left to rust. We're rebuilding the tractor to run on rapeseed oil; we hope to have it ready by the spring. Actually we could run several tractors if we wanted to, but one or maybe two are enough. And if we do get the tractor going, Petsamo plans to build a power station driven by propellers when it's windy, diesel when it's not; the Danish chemist thinks he can smelt and rework metal if we can build up enough power. Electricity would also free us from the heavy job of hauling up fresh water by the bucket. Aside from the tractor and a couple of small motors, the activity in the workshop centers around farm tools. We do some weapons maintenance but nowhere nearly as much as in the Prison.

The long-term goals are a little different. Out of the twenty-three of us, only Tulikke and I are under forty. None of the others is under fifty. Half of them are at least sixty, and three are seventy. The big question is how many more we can support. We could take in a few people who could pull their own weight. But Petsamo keeps saying that as long as he's in charge he's not going to let anyone in who weakens the organization. Having to care for five or ten more sick or decrepit people might jeopardize the rest of us if one year the crops fail or the winter's too severe. And he doesn't think there's much chance of younger people coming along.

Barring catastrophes and epidemics, in five years we can expect the group to shrink to fifteen people; in ten years it may be half of that. After that it'll go even more quickly. The last few people won't be able to run the organization the way it's run now. They won't be able to work very hard or even do much to defend themselves. So Petsamo's plan is to build a special, separate "dwelling unit" in a safe place that could be maintained with a minimum of effort. We'll take the vacuum-packed containers of rice along with other staples and store them there. The Danish chemist thinks the place could be heated by ground heat or volcanic water from the lake. We kid around a lot about the "Terminal," which no one but Petsamo seems really to take seriously.

I miss living with Tulikke. Men and women live in separate dorms; only Petsamo has his own room. At first I tried to hide my feelings for her, but everyone knew anyway. I'm mostly embarrassed in front of Petsamo—even though he hasn't said a word about it. Tulikke and I try to meet outside, but it's not easy now in the wintertime; I'm hoping it'll be better in the spring. Since we came here, we've only done it once. At first we were too weak; now I don't even know if she wants to. She likes me to sit next to her and put my arm around her, but when I show her I want her she slaps my hands. I don't understand her. On the raft she couldn't get enough. Maybe women work the way they say animals do: They only want to at certain times of the year. I want to all the time.

Now that I'm stronger, I spend a lot of time with Petsamo. Of course he's the one responsible for the sick, but he lets me do quite a lot. Often Karsten the chemist comes along too. Petsamo wants me to learn as much as possible from him, so they give me an old chemistry book to read. But it's hard to concentrate. Most of the time I sit and dream about Tulikke's crack and breasts. Petsamo has also given me the job of building a model of the Terminal. I have trouble concentrating on that too; the thought of it turns my stomach. Maybe it's childish, but I can't help feeling like throwing up when I picture the last one of us lying sick and lonely surrounded by hot-water pipes, rice, and fresh water.

He also wants me to learn how to farm. It's never interested me very much—if I had my choice, of course, I'd learn about navigation and ships' engines. I wouldn't mind spending more time fishing too. In the wintertime they fish through the ice, but this spring they're going to outfit a little fishing boat. I asked Petsamo to let me be part of the crew, but he thinks I know enough about the sea already. And there's no need for navigation; the fishermen will never be out of sight of land anyway. I'd like to know more about religion and mystical things—how certain people can know beforehand what's going to happen or find lost things or locate water with a divining rod. But they don't need those things either, except maybe the divining rod. Although we already have all the water we need: They're even trying to build a rain-water reservoir with a sand filter.

— I want you to practice your writing, says Petsamo one day.

— What for? Aren't numbers enough? I'm good at them.

— To plan, you have to know how to write, he says, pointing for the millionth time at the pile of drawings and descriptions of the Terminal.

— There are other people here. . . .

— You're the youngest. No matter how much you fight it, sooner or later it's you who's going to be responsible for the others.

While I'm dawdling over the chemistry book or the writing exercises, I think a lot about that word. Responsibility. I think about it almost as much as I think about what Tulikke has between her legs. Of course I know how to take responsibility. Since Papa died, I haven't done anything else. No one took responsibility for me except me. Take care of Number One and fuck everybody else, that's what I was taught. If you take responsibility for others, all you get is trouble. For this place to function, though, we need someone like Petsamo. But I'm not like that. I've got my hands full taking care of myself. And if I hadn't I would have been dead long ago.

SPRING comes. By March all the snow is gone except around the black lake, where a hard ring of ice glitters in the sun. It's so slippery that it's impossible to get to the lake. But that's no great loss—I'm the only one who wants to take a dip in the volcanic water. The ground bubbles and seethes. Green, yellow, rose-colored grass sprouts on the southern slopes. When the gray, spiderweblike grass from last year is dry, we burn off the meadows. Ever since Pretty Boy's attack early in the fall, we haven't needed grazing land for sheep. Except for some rabbits that we keep in cages, we concentrate almost completely on farming and fishing.

On one of the first days in April, we pull the tractor outside. It refuses to start on rapeseed oil. Karsten the chemist suggests warming it up with a mixture of diluted diesel oil and methane oil. We have very little diesel oil, but we can distill methane. So a week later we try again. This time she starts. It's the first time I've ever seen a group of over twenty people standing around a coughing diesel and weeping with joy. Decorated with grass and dandelions, she chugs her way up toward the fields while the rest of us—singing, waving, crying—follow like seagulls behind a boat.

There's a newly repaired plow already up there which we hitch on. But just as we're about to start, Chuck collapses. We have to carry him back down to the Convent. It's something to do with his heart; his pulse is slow and just as irregular as the tractor was before it warmed up. His breathing is also beginning to sound labored. Petsamo calls it a lung edema—liquid and blood collecting in the lungs because the damaged heart can't pump right. He's foaming at the mouth and keeps moving all the time; to calm him down we force a couple of good shots of booze down his throat. Petsamo goes back to the plowing. I have to sit with Chuck all afternoon—he's always just about to roll out of bed or slide down the pillows piled behind his back. At sunset Petsamo finally comes to relieve me.

I go up to take a look at the newly plowed field. I've seen fields that haven't been planted but never one just after it's been turned. The glistening black earth smells strong and sweet, and the roots of last year's grass are as white as potato sprouts. I pick up a lump of soil and squeeze it. It's so strange that all life begins in the soil: The seed grows, the rabbit eats the leaf, the human eats the rabbit.

Tulikke comes running up the hill. I'm so glad to see her; it's been a long time since we could talk to each other alone—

if you can call it talking when I talk and she listens carefully, trying to understand my words, imitating me with silent lips. She runs straight into my outstretched arms. She's crying. I start crying too. As we stand in the middle of the plowed field, halfway up to our knees in earth, I'm flooded with happiness.

But Tulikke isn't crying because she's happy. She's scared. Slowly, in bits and pieces, I find out what happened. A man hurt her—who? She imitates someone cooking and stirring. Karsten the chemist. What exactly did he do? She pretends to unbutton a pair of pants. Then she won't show anything else. But I'm angry now; I shake her till she goes on. So Karsten unbuttoned his pants—then what? Blushing, she sticks a forefinger in front of her belly. Karsten took out his prick—go on! She shakes her head and shows how she ran away from him.

— Didn't he ever grab you?

She shows how he just stood there with his stiff prick. I laugh and lift her into the air. I can't *count* all the old men who waved their pricks in front of me! They're not the dangerous ones—the ones you have to watch out for catch you first and take their pricks out later.

She calms down and finally begins to look happy. I pick her up a few more times, and then she's laughing and hammering her fists against my chest. We both start to get excited. I kiss her neck and press my nose between her breasts. Then I carry her over and lay her down on the tarpaulin that was covering the plow; she takes me in right away. It's the most wonderful feeling. I'm about to burst but I don't come right away; I work and work. Finally I explode; the world turns white as sperm before my eyes.

While we're standing holding hands near one of the hatches leading to the Convent tunnels, Petsamo appears, looking very grave

— How's Chuck doing?

— It's over.

I drop her hand. I feel as if we caused Chuck's death by lying together.

AND then they give me the tractor detail for a few days. Tulikke comes up with me; we lie together time after time on the tarp. One of those times Karsten follows us, and after we're through he comes out and says he's going to tell Petsamo. Go right ahead, I tell him—then Tulikke can act out the little scene with the unbuttoned pants and the stiff finger. Spitting at us, he stumbles off.

But for a while Tulikke and I can't see each other. Petsamo asks me to measure the temperature in different parts of the lake; it's important if we're going to pipe in hot water for heating. They've managed to make a thermometer in the workshop with markings instead of fixed degrees, so even though you can't get exact temperatures you can compare readings. That's all we need. I row around on the black lake and sleep in my one-man tent either on the beaches or in the boat. Covering one little piece at a time, I gradually work my way around the whole lake—including the southern end where it turns into reedy swamp. One of those nights I spend in the reeds thinking about my time with Tulikke on the raft. I wish we could live here and go to the Convent only once in a while. I'd also much rather live here than in the underground Terminal. But of course we'd freeze to death.

THE minute I get back, Petsamo wants to see me. On my way to his room I'm in a good mood; my papers are full of scribbled calculations. The lake's heat seems to come from a hidden spring on the east side next to a canyon that runs between the Prison and the Convent. It's a perfect location for the Terminal, which could be chopped into the high hill where the canyon meets the lake. From up there you can see the entire lake and the Convent, and on a clear day there is even a glimpse of the sea to the east. But Petsamo's not interested in my readings. He pushes them aside:

— Is Tulikke pregnant?

— Tulikke?

I sit down on the bench. If anybody around here's pregnant, of course it's Tulikke—everyone else is too old. And if Tulikke is pregnant, there's really no one but me to suspect.

— Not that I know of.

— But *I* know. Haven't you noticed how much bigger her breasts have gotten? And how she moves in a different way?

I haven't noticed anything. She's just gotten more beautiful. I thought it's because we love each other. I feel more beautiful too.

— She hasn't said anything to me.

— Not to me either. And it's not because she's mute; she knows how to make herself understood. She avoids me; she won't let me get near her. I have to examine her. Or else you're going to have to do it yourself. Evidently she doesn't push *you* away.

I find her in the kitchen and get her to go with me to the fields. As usual, we lie with each other. At first I look at and squeeze her breasts and stomach. I feel like a traitor. But soon I forget about it and we make love with a passion that blots out everything else. We come together again and again; as soon as one climax dies down, we go to work on another.

That night I have to report to Petsamo:

— I don't know. Maybe.

— It's an easy examination. If she starts to feel sick in the mornings, we'll know for sure.

I want to leave. But he keeps me there, tries to get me to look him straight in the eye. And I do try, but my eyes keep wandering away. Then I can't help laughing.

— All you can do is laugh?

— I'm not laughing at you. At myself: I feel silly.

— Silly?

We stand staring at each other. Then he says:

— She can't have the child.

I know he's against babies. Once I promised him to look at it the same way. There's no point in starting a new generation; it's all meaningless. Before now I didn't really have any feelings about it. But now it's Tulikke's baby. And mine. She's already been through one abortion. This time, even more people would have to hold her down. But I'm not going to let that happen.

We talk all through the night. That is, Petsamo talks—about having to look rationally, realistically, at the situation. He calls Tulikke and me romantics.

— What's that?

— When you let yourself be fooled by life.

He starts reeling off his collection of stories about other pregnancies and abortions he's done here. About how radiation destroys our genes so that our children are born deformed—and their children in turn, and so on for generations to come.

— But not *everyone*, I protest. There must be some who'll be born normal.

— I haven't seen any yet. Besides, there's no guarantee that the mutation won't show up in succeeding generations. Edvin, you *are* a romantic. Sometimes I lie at night marveling that in spite of everything you still are! And that it's a great misfortune for the people here you're going to be responsible for when I'm gone.

So finally he's said it straight out: I'm going to be his successor. Naturally the others have hinted at it. Some of them kid me by calling me the Crown Prince. Up till now I haven't paid any attention; it seemed too far away. And I don't pay any attention now. I'm still thinking about his talk of mutation. I know he's wrong.

— *I* was born normal. And that was after the War!

— And your harelip? You can't deny that.

— I wasn't born with it. It was . . . an injury.

I walk away without explaining. If he doesn't want to take my word for it, he doesn't have to. I'm not going to tell him about something so painful I can't even tell it to myself. I wasn't born with a harelip! When Papa died, a big fat man took me. He didn't just crush my ribs. I got mixed up in a jealous fight between him and my next protector, a ship's engineer. I was only a kid. The engineer lured me to him by offering me a seagull's egg, a delicacy I'd heard many mouth-watering stories about. The egg turned out to be an empty shell. But the engineer took what he wanted anyway. Later, I had to apologize to the fat man. He stood in front of me, legs apart, and said that he was going to teach me a lesson. He didn't have to say anything more. I fell on my knees before his crotch; I'd learned that lesson a long time before. But it wasn't his prick that was sticking out; he'd hid a knife in his pocket.

CHAPTER 21

WHEN we decided to leave, Petsamo refused to talk to me, but he made up a list of what we're allowed to take. Now we're standing in the storeroom before Karsten (he's in charge of the supplies) as he piles up a tent, blankets, army boots, a tinder box, fishhook, animal traps, and assorted clothes. We get a sealed one-gallon container of rice and all the seed potatoes we can carry, but we're overloaded already. Petsamo wrote that we should each get an automatic weapon with six full clips; I'd rather have a shotgun and a revolver. We argue back and forth.

Karsten says he's not at liberty to change anything on the list on his own initiative—and at the moment Petsamo's in the middle of the lake getting a more exact fix on the hot spring.

I ask Karsten what he wants. He shuts his eyes, pretending not to understand.

— I don't have gold. . . . But I could draw you a map where you can find it by the kilo.

He polishes his nails with a rag dipped in weapon oil. I pull my crucifix out of my shirt and lay it on the table.

— Metal. Let me see hers.

Tulikke hands it to him. He must have seen right away that they're identical, but he studies hers, rubs it with the rag, bites it. He spits and whispers:

— Her.

— You want her?

She's understood—and she's already backing toward the door. I grab her arm and hold her there.

— How do you want her?

But neither one of them wants to discuss it. They just stand with their hands in front of their privates, glaring at the dirt floor.

— Is it enough if you show it to her?

— She has to hold it too.

I turn toward Tulikke, put my finger in front of my fly and wiggle it. Then I laugh just like I laughed when she showed me what Karsten had done. But she doesn't think it's funny; she tears her arm loose and heads toward the door.

— You can't hunt rabbits with a submachine gun!

Maybe she doesn't understand what I'm saying or maybe she's too upset. I wrap my arms around her thick waist and haul her over to the counter. She squeezes her eyes shut and shakes her head but doesn't resist.

— I'm going to be standing right in the doorway. If you try anything dumb, I'll come back one night and kill you!

He just snorts and tosses his head as if he doesn't take the

threat seriously for a minute. I leave them alone and stand in
the doorway with my back turned. I pick up some rocks and
smash them into the ground as hard as I can. About five minutes later, I look in again. They're standing on either side of
the counter: Tulikke looks exactly the same, but Karsten's
breathing heavily, as though he's been running. I pick out the
best shotgun in the collection and then choose a small, light
revolver, which I test for a long time to make sure there isn't
the slightest flaw in the mechanism. I stuff six bullets in the
magazine and take a whole carton of buckshot.

— Petsamo also left a package for you, says Karsten only
after I'm standing with my legs spread, my back bent under the
weight of the overloaded backpack.

I find a worn old book, *Pregnancy and Birth*, wrapped in
a piece of fabric. When I open it a piece of paper falls out—a
rough map of the southern end of the island. He's drawn a
thorny borderline starting from the spot where we left the boat
north of Castle Rock before we went into the Coke Desert.
Then the line runs due east across the Land of the Lepers and
meets the coastline about three days north of the Prison. No
writing is on the map; there's no need for it. It's clear that
south of the borderline we'll be considered outlaws. What's it
like up in the north? During all my trips around the island I
may never have been north of that borderline. But I already
have a plan. We'll stay there for the first few months and then
work our way down cautiously. There's no way in the world
they can guard such a large area for any length of time; even
by next year a few more of Petsamo's group will have died off.
And in three or four years we'll probably be able to walk
around openly down here without their being quick enough to
find us and chase us away.

WE take our time leaving. The first night we put our tent up so
close to the Convent we can still see the lights. I go back in

the dark and steal whatever I can lay my hands on: some extra knives, a jar of honey, a blanket hanging out to dry, and a bucket full of fingertip-sized new potatoes. We boil the potatoes in the middle of the night and feast on potatoes and honey. Afterward, I'm so stuffed I can't even lie with her; I sleep like a log.

Since it's raining the next morning, we just lie with each other in the tent. But it feels a little dead, as if neither of us is really interested. If I get her pregnant again, would she have twins? Her breasts are bigger and harder now, and her nipples have changed too; they seem like buds opening up into flowers. Later that day the rain stops but a strong wind rips at the tent, so we stay where we are, eat some dried fish and go to sleep. A volley of shots. When I catch my breath, I crawl out with my shotgun cocked. One of the Danes is standing a little way off with a submachine gun pointed in the air; when he sees me, he fires another short burst of shots. We start pulling down the tent. Tulikke helps me get the pack on my back, and we plod off to the north.

AFTER a few days we reach the cliffs in the center of the island. A hot, sunny day—only the breeze makes it bearable. No matter how much care I take with my feet, the heat gives me blisters. I try to make a sled out of ropes and long roots, but it falls apart almost immediately due to the rocky terrain. We load everything on our backs again. This time I don't walk more than a few steps before I stumble forward and cut the back of my neck on the corner of the rice container. Discouraged, we sit down and open it—even though it's our most valuable provision.

That morning Tulikke won't come out of the tent. Her stomach hurts. I lie down and press my ear against her taut belly. All I can hear are her intestines gurgling; she's probably just constipated. The best thing would be for her to move around; but she won't, so we stay in the tent. Soon I hear a volley of shots to the south. Now one of Roland's boys is standing on a boulder. So they're going to keep an eye on us all the way to the border.

WHEN we reach the sandy region southeast of the Coke Desert, the walking gets easier, and we can also put some of our gear on the tent and drag it behind us. I press ahead. Tulikke gets tired and starts to stagger; I put her on the tent and pull both her and the baggage. Anger gives me strength. I'll show that cold son of a bitch that we don't need him to survive. I've been on my own at sea since I was six! No fucking landlubber is going to break me!

At night a huge, low moon makes things a little easier. I push on and she gets her second wind. She gets off the tent and helps me pull, but after a few hours I have to tell her to stop; it could hurt the baby. If I myself don't come out of this alive, you can be damn sure that one day my son will come sweeping out of the north and drive all of you into the sea! Finally, in the brown dawn, I collapse. We don't even have the strength to put up the tent; we just lie there and sleep till the sun starts to bake down on our heads as though it's shining through a magnifying glass covering the whole sky. We march ahead. Now Tulikke's the strong one—walking behind me, pushing *me* on.

By nightfall I have a feeling we're very close to the border, maybe even over it. After we put up the tent and make a fire, someone shouts to us—one of the Danes, the one who's been guarding us the last few days. He asks if he can come sit by our fire; now that we're over the border, he no longer considers us outlaws. We're feeling good—proud of what we've done—so we say, Sure, join us. This may be my last chance for years to talk to someone who can answer. He offers us corncakes and after we've eaten asks if he can tell some jokes. Of course he can—even if Tulikke won't be able to understand everything. He's got an endless supply, and before long I'm rolling in the sand while Tulikke sits giggling, slightly confused. I ask him where he got them all:

— It's my profession, he says. I'm originally from Jutland, but like everyone else I spent a long time at sea. I wasn't handsome and I had nothing else to sell. I was never very strong either; they always gave me the shittiest jobs just to break me. On landing parties they sent me ahead as a guinea pig. But then I learned that there's some value—you might even say power—in making other people laugh. I taught myself to mimic people. But you had to be careful whom you mimicked. I did impressions of skippers behind their backs and got paid for it by their secret enemies. I mimicked anything that paid; it was always a safe bet making fun of the sick, dying, blind, deaf, lame, lispers, 'leptics, and stuh-stuh-stuh-stutterers. People who'd got ants in their pants or their clothes caught on fire. More than once when I mimicked the wrong person I got the shit kicked out of me, so I began to collect stories instead: clean jokes, dirty jokes, scary stories or stories about crimes, anything supernatural, and even true stories. I also put on little one-man skits and taught myself to play a wooden flute. I can dance on one leg while people clap. I can dance like a bear. I can fart through my mouth and ass at the same time and wiggle my ears. I can sound like different kinds of guns and then have the audience guess what they are. I can hang myself without a rope and fuck without a partner. I can do an impression of the Creation and Destruction of the World, acting the whole thing out in pantomime.

We sit openmouthed, staring at him, hardly daring to laugh for fear that he'll stop. He acts out what he calls our expulsion from Paradise, mimics the way we dragged ourselves across the sand, shows us starving to death in the desert and throwing ourselves on the ground, dying of thirst. We laugh so hard we almost piss in our pants.

— Whenever you get an audience, you gotta make use of it, he says as he winds up.

I want to give him a present, but I don't know what. I offer my ski boots and the neat little revolver. Tulikke wants to give him her crucifix and a kiss. But he turns everything down; he says we've already paid him. We try to make him stay but he slips smoothly away and lumbers into the night like a bear on two legs. Then he stops, waves his paw, and licks the honey off his claws in great, greedy strokes.

BECAUSE we know the next morning that we're not going to be awakened by shots, we sleep late. I try to act out some of the Dane's simpler routines. At first she thinks it's funny but then quickly gets tired of my clumsiness. I wish I could be the world's greatest clown. I'd make everyone, friends as well as enemies, laugh uncontrollably—laugh so hard in fact that they'd suffocate themselves if I didn't set them free.

As I lie smiling at my imaginary successes, I hear a scraping sound outside the tent. A rabbit gnawing at something? The dry rustle of a lizard? Very carefully I click the safety off the shotgun and start to pull up the zipper in the tent. About thirty dark-skinned people are squatting in a wide circle around us. They're wearing torn sacks pulled over the tops of their heads and their shoulders. Their arms and legs are as thin as boathooks, and their skin is dirt-gray as though they've been rolling in ashes. Some are missing the tips of their noses. Some have sunken eyes behind dead, shriveled eyelids. Some are missing the last joints of fingers. One's ear dangles down like a curled-up leaf on a thin stalk.

When they see me, they smile. Most of them still seem to have their teeth, but on a few the front ones have been filed down to triangular shark's teeth. Very carefully I slip back in, pull down the zipper, and press close against Tulikke, falling into the rhythm of her heavy breathing. I'm trying to imagine how the Dane would mimic the lepers, but that only scares me more.

A few hours later she has to go out to pee. I try to talk her into doing it inside, in the empty rice tin. Of course that just gets her angry and she tries to fight her way outside. When I hold her back, she bites my knuckles. I rush past her and stand between her and the lepers. But there's no one there, nothing but a jug of water and some fried potatoes wrapped in a cloth in front of the tent. Tulikke's happy and scared.

— A good-bye present from the Dane, I say.

WHO'S my daughter going to marry? A prince who'll come sailing across the water in a dreadnought with raised cannons. He'll step from the captain's bridge onto the ladder alongside the ship, climb down and walk toward us on the water, wreathed in red flowers and sheaves of golden grain. He'll be wearing a suit of aluminum armor, the breastplate shining with a faint yellow glow. He'll step onto the beach with pale-blue velvet boots and walk toward my daughter with his arms outstretched, the white plumes on his helmet billowing behind him like smoke.

I flip the dream backward like the pages of a book. The second time it goes faster; now he's speeding across the water with all the ship's flags snapping in the background. He jumps up the embankment in one neat leap and immediately asks for my daughter, who's standing waiting with her head hidden by a partly transparent lace veil; a belt of dandelions is around her waist. He lifts the veil to kiss her forehead. There she stands, my deformed daughter, her skin green and warty as a toad's. The cleft in her palate runs from her forehead to her crotch. The prince throws himself on her and breaks her apart like a peapod.

WE head farther north toward what I hope is uninhabited territory. I never let Tulikke out of my sight for a moment. At first she thinks I can't do without her, but when I won't even let her empty her bowels in peace she gets angry. I still don't leave her alone.

We arrive at one of the many arms of the Coke Desert. The going gets so rough we have to stop dragging our baggage and start carrying everything. But by now it's gotten a lot lighter; I have an easier time than Tulikke walking in the slippery coke. Her belly's growing fast now. Every day she has to cut open the seams of her pants a few more centimeters. How far along could she be? She must have got pregnant in Henry's hut; if it happened on the raft in the marshes, she'd have had the baby a long time ago.

Something is glittering in front of us in the gray coke. She sees it too. I don't say a word, just kneel down and have her help me off with the backpack. I pick up the shotgun and walk forward, throwing pieces of coke. I think about blasting it, but it might be an unexploded grenade or mine. It could also be something valuable. Finally I get so close I can touch it with the barrel. An empty beer can. With the writing completely rubbed off, it's not worth much, even to collectors. But we take it with us anyway. We can use it as a mug.

That evening, since we can't put up the tent in the coke, we lie under the open sky, using the tent as a sleeping bag. I tell Tulikke all about the constellations, the hidden pattern up there that not only controls our destiny but can also guide anyone who knows how to read it safely across the Seven Seas. She falls asleep and I start thinking about the *Diana*. Has the Captain managed to keep her off the rocks and out of the shallows, away from floating mines and shipwrecks? Do you still sleep with your precious treasures—your sextant, plumbline, watch—stuffed into your pants?

It's a quiet night but I can't help listening for snapping or rustling in the coke. I probably couldn't see them. Even in daylight they dart, wriggle away quick as worms, then stop for a moment, heads cocked, checking, checking. I don't hear a

sound. But in the milky dawn chill I find an armful of potatoes and a jug of water not five meters away. I drink the
water and stuff the potatoes into our provisions sack. The clay
jug I fling out of sight by slipping it over the gun barrel and
swinging around with all my might.

FOR nine days we search for the library by zigzagging back and
forth along the edges of the Coke Desert. Things are going
O.K.; the nights are dry and warm. I fill up on the nightly
offerings and feed Tulikke from the food sack. She worries a
little about my bad appetite, but I tell her the most important
thing is for her to eat for two. I'm sure that the library is
nearby. I'm not even very worried when she stumbles and her
ankle swells up; I just make her comfortable on the tent and
give her the loaded shotgun. Then I take the revolver and go
out searching in all directions, always keeping her in sight
even though she's only a small speck on the horizon. I know
you can see both coke and sand from the library, as well as low
gravel ridges. On the last day I drag her behind me on the
tent—I've spotted some low ridges that fit the picture in my
head. Sure enough, before nightfall I've found the ruin.

Hardly anything's changed. Another piece of the ridge behind the building has collapsed, and the winter rains washed
out one of the gables. The old entrance can't be used, but we
can get in through a window. I'm not absolutely sure if we're
north of Petsamo's border, but it doesn't really bother me. Petsamo and Halvar are the only ones who'd dare come here, and
I can't imagine either one coming all this way just to check
on us.

Tulikke's amazed. In spite of her bad foot she goes inside
and digs around among the books. When she finds a little
book written in a foreign language—it must be Finnish—she's
overjoyed. She sits right down to read—and reads for hours
and hours, leaving all the practical work with the tent and

unpacking to me. I ask her about the book, what it's about, but she waves me away. On the cover is a young girl with blond braids sitting on a fence eating something that I don't think is a potato but might be an apple; it pretty well fits the descriptions I've heard in the past. We had a hand on board the *Diana* who couldn't stop babbling about fruit whenever he got drunk.

While Tulikke's reading, I explore the place. There's a chimney I didn't notice the first time, and oddly enough it isn't caved in or filled with sand and gravel. But there's no fireplace; the chimney seems to go down without a break all the way to the sand-filled basement below. With one of the stolen knives I start chipping into the chimney wall. The brick is porous; I can probably build a little fireplace. And we've got plenty of fuel; even though I'd rather burn roots than books, there's probably enough for two winters. Coke would be even better, but the coke in the desert is totally burned out. Or maybe it isn't even coke, just some kind of volcanic rock. I make a real feast for us. But when she'd rather stay with her book than eat with me, we almost get into a fight. Finally I have to tear it out of her hands. She gets her revenge after supper; when we're going to lie with each other, she refuses to let me kiss her.

EARLY the next morning a terrible scream wakes me up. Tulikke comes tumbling in and throws herself into my arms, trembling and sobbing. I know what's going on, but I look out anyway through the broken window. The lepers are sitting on their haunches in a semicircle around the library. I step over the windowsill and walk toward them. They don't move, just turn up their faces and smile. It's only when I'm about to step right on them that they drag themselves out of my way, still on their haunches. I start talking to them. They hang on my every word as if it's a revelation. But they don't understand a thing. So I start waving my arms to shoo them away; they nod happily. A few of the bravest imitate my wild gestures and grin as though to tell me to keep doing it. Then they just wait there—pleading, expectant.

But I march straight through the crowd. When I turn around, I see that they've turned around to face me. One of them smacks his lips, imitating my marching steps. I dart to one side and run forty, fifty meters. Out of the corner of my eye I see them spring to their feet lightning quick and follow me. But the minute I stop and turn around, they sink slavishly back onto their haunches, nodding and smiling as though I'd done something wonderful. I walk back to the library with my eyes glued to the ground.

They've put new gifts right under the window: water, potatoes, and a dozen sticky black balls. They look like the gummy cakes we made out of the yellow berries last fall, but these aren't the least bit sweet; dripping with fat, they have a bitter aftertaste. It's not the first time I've had cakes made out of squashed insects. Papa and I lived a long time on crushed cockroaches. They tasted all right; the worst thing about them was the shells that you had to pick out of your teeth for a long time afterward.

WE lock ourselves into the Library. No one tries to break in, but we do get a few glimpses of a grinning face above the windowsill. I keep repeating to Tulikke what Petsamo told me: They mean us no harm; they worship us. Days can go by without our seeing them; then suddenly one morning they're back again. Whether we see them or not, new gifts keep appearing by the window. Our own supplies are practically gone.

It's so hot now that in the middle of the day the boiling air shimmers above the coke and sand. We can't go outside. Slowly the midsummer heat penetrates inside too. The first few nights we were cold; now we can't even stand to be in the tent. I build a bed out of books. Unlike the floor of the tent, which gets sticky, the books stay at a comfortable temperature—but if you make a sudden move they slide apart. Tulikke's suffering from the heat. Her taut belly itches constantly, and now her belly button sticks out like an extra nipple. I bathe her belly with water, then blow on the skin. Sometimes it relieves the itching, but other times it tickles her so much she can't sit still. I also put my ear to her belly and tell her about the strange burping sounds and sudden kicks. She wants to hear too, but she can't reach her belly even though it's become a shining, majestic mountain.

What's worst is having nothing to do! Tulikke reads the Finnish book again while I try to keep myself busy by building the fireplace in the chimney. It gets done much too fast. She wants me to read but I can't sit still. I want to go hunting for rabbit or hedgehog but she won't let me; I can't leave the ruin except when she or I has to go to our latrine among the rocks by the collapsed part of the ridge. Sometimes horniness hits me like lightning. I can't get on top, so I try to get into her from the side. But it hurts her. Then I get jealous of the baby inside her.

When I think I'm going crazy from having nothing to do, I sit in the windowsill and look at picture books. But they bother me. The worlds of the past don't interest me anymore. I want to know about the future—and the books have nothing to say about that. I've even lost my interest in animals, ships, famous buildings. Every day I read a little of *Pregnancy and Birth*, the book Petsamo gave me, because I know I have to; but it just makes me feel inadequate.

I do what I've done many times before: try to get her to talk. She has everything she needs: tongue, voice box, normal lips. While I say the words slowly, she makes faces along with me, aping whatever I do perfectly—but she doesn't make a sound. We write words in the sand to each other, but that goes too slowly. Finally, just like all the other times, I give up. She doesn't have to talk; it's enough if I talk and she accepts or rejects what I say. Anyhow, we don't have that much to say to each other.

Weeks pass without seeing a leper. I don't lie awake at night listening for the one who sneaks up with the gifts. And Tulikke gets a little braver too; now she'll let go of my hand when we go out to the latrine. Before long she feels safe if I just sit in the window. Our quiet life hasn't helped her constipation any; she can spend hours out there. Usually she's careful to go at dawn when there's enough light but the sun hasn't started to beat down yet.

Early one morning she goes out without waking me—or else she woke me and I fell asleep again. Still groggy, I jump to my feet when I hear her loud screams. They snuck up on her after she'd sat down on the latrine, and now she's sitting like a mad queen, the lepers looking from behind like a lot of sacks piled on the ground around her. There are more than ever before—probably more than forty. I swing myself over the sill and start screaming at them to go away. But as usual they just nod cheerfully and mimic my flailing arms. They look like bottom-heavy birds trying to take off on skinny wings. I race through the crowd and station myself right next to Tulikke.

The empty path behind me starts to fill with creatures from the back rows who drag themselves in on one knee and one foot. The one in front carries a knife that glitters in the morning light. He looms amazingly tall when he stands up and stretches himself on long stork legs with swollen knees. With one whoosh of the knife, he cuts off one of his earlobes and throws it at our feet. Then he staggers backward, the hood of his sack pressed against the wound.

Quickly someone else takes his place. With a lightning-quick upward motion, this one chops off the tip of his nose and flicks it toward us. A third comes up from behind, an old lady with flat, sagging breasts swinging from side to side. I turn away so I won't have to watch her push a stick into one of her eyes.

I peek through my fingers at them. No one else comes forward, but one points proudly at the bloodspots in the sand. I bellow as loud as I can—Go away! And they jump to their feet as though they'd just been waiting for the signal. Bowing and kneeling, they begin to pull back. It's only when they get a hundred meters away that they stand up and turn around; then, shuffling away in a half run, their backs bent, they disappear into the distance.

CHAPTER 22

WHEN we reach the west coast three days later, the boat is just where Petsamo and I left it: a little north of the large stretches of rock pillars. Its sail, mast, and oars are missing, but the aluminum hull is practically undamaged even though the waves must have battered away at it. We rig up the tent's center pole for a mast, use a loose thwart as rudder, and raise the tent itself as a sail. The boat can hardly sail; tacking is out of the question—all it can really do is drift downwind. But the first day we get lucky and catch a northerly wind, which holds until the afternoon, then drops almost completely off. I paddle with the thwart, but it's almost impossible to keep her on course. So we head for the shallows where I can wade and tow her behind me.

For almost two days a stiff southwesterly keeps us pressed against the rocks. We wait it out, then I start towing again. On the fifth day Castle Rock rises before us like a low-floating thundercloud etched sharply above the sea.

At this point I carefully follow the procedure Petsamo taught me. Before we land on the narrow reef, I fire three of the six shots in the revolver. We drift for a long time without getting any answer. Has the old man died up there on his Rock? Have other people taken over the fortress? But then the answering volley finally comes.

Before I start the climb I put up the tent for Tulikke in a shady crevice. I unload and organize the supplies so she can get to the most important ones easily. I bring back fresh water from a spring and gather a pile of dead bushes for fuel.

— If I'm not back tomorrow before noon, you're absolutely forbidden to go up by yourself.

She knows exactly what I mean. She begins to cry. I don't touch her. I can't comfort her now; I feel just as bad as she does. We eat some potatoes but I don't have much of an appetite. When I think about what's going to happen, my whole body ightens. I load the shotgun and stick the revolver in my back pocket. The last thing I do is pull off my good army boots; I feel stronger when I'm wearing them but I can move faster without them. Behind me Tulikke's crept into the tent; I'm glad I don't have to look at her now.

It takes a good half hour to find the foot of the steep path; it's really well hidden. The climb itself goes faster than the first time. I'm not wearing a pack and don't have to worry about an elderly protector. When I reach the place where the plants begin to grow thickly, I pull off a revolver shot. The answer comes immediately—so fast in fact that the two echoes blend together. Halvar's on his guard. The echoes frighten a couple of birds from a rock shelf—I think they're doves.

Now comes the hard part. I have to try to remember the exact series of numbers that tells me which steps are mined and which aren't. I can't walk too slowly; that would make him suspicious. But I've stayed awake many times in bed burning those numbers into my skull, as if I knew that someday they'd mean the difference between life and death. At first it goes well, then it gets harder; rain and storms have changed the cliff face, and it's not always clear where one step ends and another begins. But the wear and tear also have their good side; they've exposed a lot of the mines. Apparently Halvar hasn't had the energy—or felt the need—to keep the steps in better shape.

He catches me by surprise. Instead of waiting at the top of the steps the way he did the first time, he's hiding behind a sharp bend on the next-to-last plateau. When he sees me, he lowers his weapon and brightens. Then he raises it again and says:

— Petsamo?

— He's coming. He's just out of shape.

He puts the automatic weapon over his shoulder and hugs me. Then he walks the last few steps ahead of me. I let him have a ten-meter head start while I pause and look at his bent back and the fat, sunburned roll of flesh on his neck sticking out from under his hat. Suddenly he turns around:

— How tall is the Eiffel Tower?

But he doesn't expect an answer; he just bounds happily up the steps. He stands at the top gazing out at the reef:

— I didn't see the boat.

— We came from the north.

I walk up next to him and try to breathe slowly and deeply so I won't get dizzy or black out if I have to make a sudden move.

— And you found the library?

— The directions were perfect. But we stayed too long and had to hike back home.

— Did you find any books for me?

— Petsamo has them.

He walks ahead of me toward the house and the gravel path, where he stops and starts laughing. Then he picks a flower, comes back with it, and sticks it in my sweater:

— Bet no one's ever given you a *boutonniere* before! What kind is it? The Latin name please?

— Petsamo said you should make up a fire in the stove. And start heating water for your ears.

He takes my arm and begins to walk toward the house. I can't think of an excuse to slip behind him. At the foot of the steps he stops and punches me in the belly:

— Go and help him if he's gotten so goddamn old!

I turn around and trot away from the house. Over my shoulder I can see him standing there taking the carbine from his shoulder. Instinctively I hunch over, but he never points it at me; he just pulls it off and leans it against the banister. I swing around quickly. Now his back is to me as he walks up the steps. I aim at his kidneys and empty both barrels into his back. He lurches forward against the steps as though he's been hit in the gut with a swinging boom.

THERE'S plenty of food: potatoes, rice, even flour. Vegetables overflow the garden; carrots burst out of the ground, spinach grows like trees. A barrel of salted mackerel has survived the heat, but the dried meat we find a week later is riddled with yellow, black-headed maggots.

For a while I try to keep watch over the long gravel reef between Castle Rock and the main island, and I even scan the ocean horizon morning and evening sector by sector. But I never see anything interesting except the doves nesting in the cliff face below. So I start working on Halvar's gauges and instruments; I read them and record the readings on his old charts. But I don't know how he sent his reports out on the air; I just listen instead. I hear crackles and screeches from time to time but never any clear signals or voices. I keep listening anyway; when there's nothing else to do, I sit with my earphones on and my chin in my hands, and sometimes I fall

asleep that way. I only wake up when I hear the sound of
Tulikke's heavy, creaking steps in the gravel.

Every evening after we eat and Tulikke curls up in the big
bed, I do a round of inspections. I watch the sun slip down
into its slot at the edge of the horizon. Before I head back, I
take Halvar's automatic weapon and shoot off a volley into the
foaming ocean among the shattered boulders where I threw
him before I went to get her. So far, no ghost has appeared.
But one morning, in a thick fog, I saw Henry and Halvar tottering up the gravel path together, supporting each other.

I haven't been asleep two minutes before Tulikke wakes me.
The bed's soaked; her water must have broken, but she has no
labor pains. I get the book. All night we wait for them to start,
but she doesn't feel anything unusual; she just keeps falling
asleep, and I keep waking her up so she'll be ready.

It takes a full day for the first pains to begin. I boil water
and lay out clean rags. I pile pillows behind her back so she
can lean against them with her feet braced against the foot of
the bed. The pains go on all night, but they're not very strong.
Sometimes a half hour passes between each one. I push my
ear in her belly; I think I can hear a little heart beating deep
inside. Then the pains stop. We both fall asleep. They start up
again when the afternoon heat is at its worst—real labor pains
now, and she screams every time. In the evening they die
down. But the little heart's still ticking.

The next morning they begin again. Now even stronger;
they shake her body from her chin to her calves, and her
screams are so loud they take her breath away. I try to make
her push instead of screaming. But she acts confused and I'm
not sure she knows who I am; she keeps trying to push me
away. I keep kneading her belly. New waves of contractions
come so fast they turn into convulsions where one seems to
merge into another. Her whole body is arched and quivering.

Then there's a calm period. I try to feel inside from below. The hard skull is pressing against her pelvis as though it tried to come out too high, and the heart doesn't beat the way it did before; now it's an uneven buzz.

The childbirth book is full of good advice: medicine to be shot into her veins; an intravenous drip to be inserted; suction or forceps to be used with great dexterity. If it should become necessary, says the book, a quick cesarian section is recommended. A new wave of contractions rips through her body.

A few hours later she relaxes and falls asleep with a contented expression on her face. I can't hear the baby anymore. I shake her and slap her face to get her going again, but she's too weak even to put up her hands. I let her rest for a while. Then she seems to feel better and begins to hum a strange tune. I crawl in next to her and try to hum along. Sometimes words slip out among the notes—I've never heard them before, but they sound like words, pieces of words. I'm afraid to disturb her; I just lie silently behind her, my arms around her quiet belly. Suddenly she raises herself onto her elbows and laughs a high-pitched laugh, then lies on her side with both hands clenched underneath her chin. I stay completely still, trying to breathe in smooth, calm waves against her back; I'm trying to think my own breathing into her body. I fall asleep. When I wake up she's already begun to stiffen; I leap up, chilled with disgust.

I'M kneeling next to her as she lies on the porch partially wrapped in rugs. The hunting knife is in my right hand while with my left I feel her stomach to figure out the baby's position. Is Petsamo right? Is my child a deformed monster with a dog's head and seal's tail, a monster shaped so grotesquely that it could never have fit through the birth canal? I stand up and fling the knife as far as I can into the lilac bushes. Then I go into the kitchen and eat. I eat for hours and hours, but I don't taste anything and I'm just as hungry afterward as I was when I began. But I'm cold, shaking with cold, even though the temperature is close to 30°C.

When my teeth stop chattering, I get a spade and start digging in the soft earth under the berry bushes. I dig all night until I hit bedrock. Then I bury not only Tulikke but all her clothes, her crucifix, the sheets she slept on, the rags we never used, and the kitchen stool she used to sit on in front of the stove whenever it was too hard for her to stand up.

I throw some provisions—potatoes, flour, dried fish—over the cliff in the direction of the boat. I chuck the sail and net over too. But I have to drag the mast, oars, and weapons all the way down the path. By the time I get everything together it's evening. All that's left to do is to load the boat, secure everything down, and get it into the water. When I'm about to push off I change my mind. I jump out and pull the boat back onto the reef, cut the ropes and toss out the cargo. All I keep are the oars and the weapons.

The sun's evil eye glares metal-hard above the horizon. After I row past Castle Rock I shoot both barrels of the shotgun up toward the summit. Then I shove the still-smoking barrels into the water and let go of the butt. As I race down the diminishing path of sunlight all I have with me is the little revolver.

SCENARIO II

In late winter of the following year, new people came to the island. The cold had been so severe that the island was surrounded by a band of pack ice two nautical miles wide. Originally from arctic regions, these newcomers arrived in long boats with bone frames and skin hulls. After having abandoned the shantytowns forced on them by "civilization," they'd returned to a nomadic way of life. At first a few thousand had made their way around the Polar Cap, but as time passed they'd split up into smaller groups. The group that arrived in fourteen long skinboats numbered about eighty: twenty men, thirty women, and thirty children and adolescents. They also brought along a large number of dogs, several brown pygmy reindeer, quilted tents, sleds, harpoons, nets, axes, knives, cooking utensils, and as their main weapon crossbows made of bone, steel pipe and twisted sinews; they depended more on these crossbows than on rusted, ice-locked automatic weapons. They pulled their light boats in across the pack ice at the northern tip of the island.

After staying only a few days, however, they paddled south, this time landing about halfway down the island's east coast. The restlessness of their domestic animals had told them that the northern end was dangerous. Due to the instincts of these animals, the skin-boat people had managed to avoid the heavily contaminated waters around the North Cape of Norway, the Straits of Denmark, the mouths of the Swedish rivers and the Gulf of Finland. Of course, by this time the worst of the radioactivity had diminished, but there were still cesium, plutonium, strontium, and widespread leakage from refineries, nuclear power plants, chemical plants, arsenals, and nerve-gas storage depots. Like sleepwalkers, the nomads from the north had threaded their way between dangerous land and contaminated water, surviving a month here, a year there, at the edge of the white areas of the map. Due to the ice there were no pirates in the Baltic to attack them. The mainstay of their diet was fish, which they always let their dogs sample before they themselves ate anything. Their few reindeer had never had the kind of peaceful environment they needed to propagate into a herd—but they were considered too holy to eat.

In early spring the skin-boat people left their winter quarters on the east coast and made their way across the island's central plateau. Before long they encountered the lepers, whom they considered animals; they considered *all* living creatures except themselves animals. Some, like the reindeer, they thought of as holy; others, like the lepers, were regarded as inedible and therefore were left in peace as long as they did no harm to human beings or domestic animals.

Shortly after their arrival, rumors spread through the Convent that an alien people had landed in the north. No one, however, had seen them as yet—and at this point, the Convent had troubles enough of its own. Around Christmastime, one of the older women, Sister Rachel, had seen a blaze of radiant light over the black lake, and a voice had spoken to her out of the light. Every time the event was retold, this light came more and more to be regarded as a sort of airborne Burning Bush. God's voice had told Rachel that another group of people was threatening them from the sea and that another Flood would come to engulf all who didn't repent of their sinful ways.

At first Sister Rachel's admonitions were met with embarrassment and scorn; Petsamo told her to keep her visions to herself. But she continued her Doomsday preaching. In March, the ice and snowbanks from the unusually hard winter began to melt rapidly, causing the level of the lake to rise. The fields around it were inundated. The same thing occurred every spring, but this time the water rose higher than usual. The level of the ocean rose as well, and brackish water crept up the estuaries and poured in over the lowlands. The flooding wasn't particularly dramatic, but it was enough to give more credence to Rachel's predictions. More and more people rallied around her. She and her followers spent half the night praying to God and speaking in tongues. God said that the nonbelievers were to be cast out from among them—but before long there weren't any. Only one person steadfastly maintained his neutrality: Petsamo. Disappointed, but also relieved to be free of responsibility—and perhaps even gloating a bit—he left the Convent for Henry's hut.

IN the beginning of the summer, the skin-boat people followed their reindeer inland toward better grazing in the south, and established summer quarters at the edge of the Coke Desert. The lepers were driven from their caves and away from the land where they cultivated potatoes. Since they no longer kept boats, they had no choice but to flee overland toward the southern end of the island. Since they preferred to move at night and hide in caves and among the reeds during the day, it took some time before they reached the Convent.

Around the same time the first lepers were spotted near the Convent, Sister Rachel had another message from her Heavenly Light: Everyone who came from the north had been sent by the fallen angel Lucifer to tempt and deceive the faithful in the Convent. The evil ones could be identified by the dark color of their skin; they were to be driven off like vermin. Consequently, all lepers who showed their faces in the vicinity of the Convent and its arable land were shot on sight. Over the course of the summer the moderate flooding had subsided, and the people in the Convent realized that this could not have been the Great Flood that God had warned them about, but only a prelude. They therefore directed all their efforts to the lepers, who were hunted and driven out onto the thin fall ice, where they either fell through and drowned or were picked off by snipers on the sand dunes.

In October, the skin-boat people pulled back from the territory originally inhabited by the lepers and reestablished their winter quarters on the east coast. It was a winter of great privation for the people in the Convent. Because they had been promised that the Great Flood would deliver the faithful from earthly labors, they'd neglected their farming. They starved and prayed and had new visions. Exhaustion and malnutrition undermined their physical health. Some withdrew into private meditation, others flagellated themselves in the Chapel—which had been cleared of all tools and implements. After Christmas, several died.

In March the skin-boat people broke camp again to find new grazing land for their reindeer. Now there were no longer any lepers between them and the Convent. They thought of the Convent people as animals who could be allowed to stay in their subterranean tunnels as long as they didn't become a nuisance or attack the holy reindeer. But the people in the Convent, who now numbered only about ten, saw the newcomers as savages from the north. Unlike the lepers, they were not humble or self-effacing—but they did have dark skin. These new faces were more reddish brown than mud-brown, but there was no doubt about what they were: emissaries of the Devil. In spite of the Convent people's automatic weapons, the battle was brief. They were trapped in their tunnels by smoke and fire. Those who managed to escape were hunted down by the dogs. Later the same spring, the nomads reached Henry's hut. They considered it an animal dwelling place, and for the time being gave it a wide berth. But by then Petsamo had taken his own life.

NOW the skin-boat people were the only humans on the island. Their numbers increased slowly, but their dogs and reindeer increased quite rapidly. The brown pygmy reindeer flourished among the mosses, heather, and lichen of the chalky soil. Their dogs encountered the remaining dogs of Roland's pack, and after some preliminary territorial battles, the original dogs were absorbed into the new pack.

The flooding had brought about certain mineral changes in the soil, which improved the island's plant life; other animals began to thrive too. Rabbits bred quickly and became food for humans and dogs. More and more birds came to the island, although only a few nested. In the middle of one hard winter a pair of foxes came trotting over the ice and settled on Castle Rock, which had been left untouched by the skin-boat people because they couldn't get their reindeer up there. The foxes multiplied, feeding on frogs, voles, and rabbits. But they rarely managed to get at the doves on the ledges of the inaccessible cliff face. More than a thousand pairs of doves were now nesting in Castle Rock's cliffs.

The winters grew colder and colder, and it became more and more rare to see the ocean free of ice. One year contaminated rain clouds drifted in over the island; but the reindeer reacted immediately, and the people stayed in their quilted tents until the rains ended. They had also learned to wash or throw away anything that had been left out in the rain. But they didn't escape completely unharmed; some of the smallest children died of internal bleeding.

AFTER the skin-boat people had been living on the island for exactly ten years, the final catastrophe occurred. By now the doves were nesting not only on Castle Rock's ledges but also in the cliffs of the main island. But not all of them were descended from the first pair that had built their nest on Castle Rock; many had come in flocks from the mainland around the Baltic. Some of these newly arrived doves brought diseases other than the usual parasites and fungi. The skin-boat people, who not only worshiped reindeer but also enjoyed decorating themselves with feathers, welcomed the doves happily. Of course eagles and white falcons were the birds who dominated their myths and legends—but in their absence, they made do with dove feathers. It was because of this that the skin-boat people quickly caught the virus the new doves brought with them.

Four decades earlier, when the entire biological system had been shaken to its foundations, a host of new variations and mutations had arisen from the chaos. Though the doves themselves exhibited no symptoms, this new virus was one against which the skin-boat people had never had the opportunity to build defenses. It penetrated and spread through the rich neural tissue of the human body, especially the lobes of the brain, causing a new strain of encephalitis whose victims grew apathetic and uninterested in human relations. Everyone became totally self-absorbed. They had no physical symptoms, but ultimately their altered emotional state was incompatible with the hard living conditions on the island. The men stopped hunting, the women stopped nursing, the elders stopped telling stories around the campfire. No one took care of the dogs and the reindeer. From the moment the first person was infected, it took only four months before everyone succumbed—to apathy, starvation, or other complications.

THE doves multiplied. At first the pygmy reindeer grew into a real herd but were later destroyed by the dogs and the foxes, who'd grown more bold over the years. When the reindeer

were gone, there was an invasion of black rats. Adept at climbing, the rats soon managed nearly to eradicate the doves by
taking their eggs and their young. Then came the gulls who
drove the last doves from the cliffs and hunted the rats with
great success. Animal life passed through various phases and
plateaus, at times seeming to achieve temporary stasis; but
soon the balance would be upset again. Changes of climate
and new diseases rolled in over the island like thunderclouds,
and soon the flora become subject to the same struggles for
survival as the fauna. Seeds from the trees and lilac bushes on
Castle Rock showered down over the main island, where they
began to take root. But none survived. Though there were no
longer any unfortunate humans to pull up the tender shoots,
those plants that weren't suffocated by the shifting sands were
eaten by rodents.

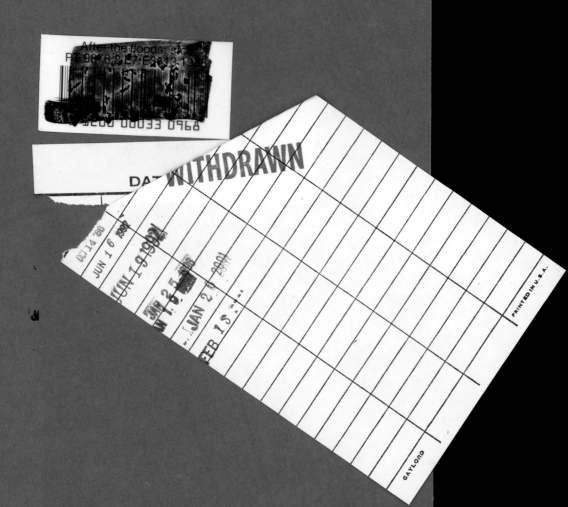